This Is How We Talk

A Novel of Tel-Aviv

This Is How We Talk

A Novel of Tel-Aviv

Julian Furman

**FREIGHT
BOOKS**

First published 2017

Freight Books
49–53 Virginia Street
Glasgow, G1 1TS
www.freightbooks.co.uk

ISBN 978-1-911332-27-5
eISBN 978-1-911332-28-2

Typeset by Freight in Plantin
Printed and bound by Bell and Bain, Glasgow

the publisher acknowledges investment from
Creative Scotland toward the publication of this book

Julian Furman was born and educated in London to an Argentine father and a Japanese-German mother. He spent much of his childhood in recently-opened China, and in Israel. Julian holds a Masters in International Studies and Diplomacy, and worked with the Knesset's Constitution Law and Justice Committee. He is married and lives between London and Tel-Aviv with his wife, two daughters, and two (female) dogs.

For Ruby, Charlie and Penelope.
Thank you.

Yonatan

She said 'get out', so what could I do? I got out.

Perhaps she didn't mean it, but she'd said it so many times.

I don't want to turn the TV down: Get out.

Why should I change the baby? Get out.

I had to take it at face value once.

The sunset is spewing streaks of pinks and oranges over the White City, but night isn't here yet. I haven't seen Tel-Aviv at this hour since baby Ben was born and the nice, comfortable, lazy life we built was exploded like a mortar in Sderot. When did out here become a threat? When our existence became reduced to those three tiny rooms.

I raise my hand to check the time, but my wrist is naked. The fight broke out as we were about to wash the baby so it must be around eight, and my watch is still in one of the little pink plastic grooves of his bath. The one that has occupied our shower.

Five minutes after, and I can't recall the cause of the fight. Lia says I'm good at filtering out noise, but it's memories too. Of babies crying, the mechanics of defence and attack. Forgotten too: the warmth and love and affection that brought baby Ben to us.

Today was progressing just like any other day. I arrived home from the photography school, and we were washing the baby in a bitter silence. The beginning of the rest of the night, when she would feed him and I would withdraw as she put him to bed. In the kitchen the vegetables were already laid out beside the knife, waiting for me. As I chopped the salad, she'd slope up the stairs. The night would pass silently, lost to our computers, to the news on *Mako* and *Ynet*, the stories of summer 2011. An endless silent loop of Hizballah and Assad, and the protests spurred on by the rising cost of cottage cheese.

Just like yesterday. Just like tomorrow.

Not tonight. Tonight the pattern is broken.

A cyclist's elbow narrowly misses my head, and he turns and yells as I cross by the petrol station towards the little roundabout that leads nowhere. Haphazardly and illicitly parked cars block the eastern curve.

The torturous midsummer heat burns me from the inside. I need a drink and so I cut to Allenby Street, to our local *pitzutziah*, where I scan the shelves. Everything anyone would want right now, whenever now is. The guy behind the counter follows me with his eyes, all trimmed goatee and piercings and identikit inconspicuousness. He may have worked here for years, or tonight may be his first night. I want something high proof, and I check my pockets, realise I don't have my phone or my wallet, only a single, solitary hundred shekel note, forgotten there who-knows-when. I could head back, collect a few necessities, the most basic at least, but I can't bring myself to turn around. If Lia were asleep, perhaps, but she no longer really sleeps. Nor is she ever truly awake.

With a knot forming in my stomach, I realise what I'll have to do, but some crazy sense of loyalty holds me back. I can't steal from my own *pitzutziah*. The store where we buy milk at 2 am, where I picked up the extra bottle of cava on Lia's birthday, where we rush for nappies when we run out too soon for the next two-for-one deal at Super Pharm.

So I leave and cross Allenby, narrowly dodge the front wing of a bus. As I dart out of its way, a *monit sherut* – part taxi, part bus, entirely neither – honks wildly and skids to a halt. I give a pacifying wave and as its engine grumbles and picks up speed once more, both near misses cover me in a thick, undulating cloud of black diesel that floats off towards the strip club on the next block.

This *pitzutziah* may seem like a functionally identical kiosk, but it is the competition, too far by a few paces to fit into our lives. Above the neon and the dusty overstuffed shelves, its ancient building is graffitied red by Hapoel Tel-Aviv Ultras, hollowed out and empty above the ground floor like the remnant of a long-forgotten war.

The guy behind the counter has the same goatee, and I can see the clip of his nose stud from the inside of his nostril because his head is craned up towards a television. A football game is playing. He's grinding his teeth and these next few minutes will make or break his night.

I've never been one for sports, not since the endless summers in my parents' moshav up north, whiling away the long hot days, always picked last.

The liquor cabinet is over at the back and I make my way over to it, leisurely, so it seems I'm browsing. My back is to the attendant and I can tell by his grunting that the game is going from bad to worse. Adrenaline and fear pool in my fingertips. It's the most alive I've felt in months.

He breathes in sharply and pounds a fist upon the counter. I seize my moment in one short, swift movement, and before his anguished groan is complete, a half-litre of vodka rubs against my thigh. My hand spreads through my pocket to conceal its weight, and I turn to leave. Our eyes meet. My steely gaze holds. This is not our *pitzutziah*, my *pitzutziah*, so I feel no guilt. More, even, that I feel as if I'm scoring points for my side of Allenby, the worse side. Some small subjective, redistributive justice.

'*Bassa*,' I say, and I motion to the TV screen. He nods and grunts and picks something from around the stud in his nose. Then I am free and out on Allenby once more, and all the excitement has nowhere to go and nothing to do, and I want to scream or to punch something, but instead I jog back across the junction to Kerem Hateymanim, my neighbourhood, and wonder what the hell now.

There is a queue outside the Minzar. I watch as a crackhead slopes up the little pedestrianised alley to harass all the good people in line for the bar. I recognise him behind the signs of prolonged addiction: the skin like leather, the raw scabs dotted across his face, and the rancid swelling of his leg. He used to live on a bench in the tiny park behind our building, barely more than a tiled patch of empty ground surrounded by untended shrubs. That was, until the municipality grew frustrated with him and his kind, tore out the benches. Now they claim bare ground, squat and move by the motions of the sun. Every season he looks closer to death.

I took a photo of him once. When I still took photos. Then he was sitting cross-legged in the middle of the pedestrianised part of Nachalat Binyamin Street watching a television that wasn't plugged in, the screen black and cracked all across in a toxic rainbow. It was raining that day – one of those biblical storms that arrive once or twice a year when the roads flood and the air is like the sea but sandy – and his face and hands were thrust skywards. He seemed both damned and saved. It was a popular photo, but not a good one, badly framed and overexposed, but still the gallery sold out of the run and I even sold a few extra as artist's proofs. Its success has always troubled me.

He sidles up to the queue with that sloping, jagged limp and takes all the poor, healthy people by surprise. They are horrified by the spittle and the facial ooze, his calloused and cracked, outstretched hand, and they scatter like crabs. The line crumbles as he lurches through. The security guard pushes himself up from his chair and I seize my chance and good luck, dart past the barrier into the bar.

The night is searing and wet, just like every night in August, the month when even the cold water from the tap is hot. The cigarette smoke hangs in a static cloud. I used to smoke.

Fifty a day to zero overnight; torment and sweats for months afterwards. A socially countenanced addict in withdrawal. I've only succumbed once since: at the opening of the exhibition I attended alone, when Lia was waiting at home, in a jacket and nothing else. It tasted like metallic ash on my tongue. I really want one now, but I only have one hundred shekels to last me the uncertain length of this night, and I don't want to waste my money even on the singles they sell at the *pitzutziot*.

Instead I breathe the smoke in the heavy air, take in Tel-Aviv at the bar. A smattering of men sit alone, nursing whiskys; they share the assembled stools with couples attentive only to each other, and small groups in fierce conversation just the right side of friendly.

'I love dogs!' says the man next to me as I pull up a seat. His hand is just close enough to his date's that they don't touch and I think of all the pugs and pekingeses sold from cardboard boxes on Shenkin Street every Friday morning, of how many must end up back in boxes, by the side of the road.

The bartender asks me what I want and I ask for water. 'Tap water,' I clarify. She scowls. I don't hold it against her. I ask the guy on the date – the one who likes dogs – to hold my seat and I head to the toilet with my glass in my hand. I have to fight my way down the stairs as there are some people watching the game and it's cramped and hot as hell. I squeeze into the bathroom. The blue tablet bubbles as I pour the contents of the glass into the urinal and refill from the bottle of vodka in my pocket. It sloshes and settles; looks just like water if you're not paying attention.

When I return to the bar my seat is gone. The shift change between the day-drinkers and the night-drinkers is imminent, and I don't have to wait long for the stool beside the guy's date to free up. I wince as the girl's doughy eyes gorge on him, feasting on every mannerism, every word. I assume he's a musician of some sort, but his bravado seems thin-set. He'll trade dreams for accounting before choice becomes necessity.

I sip the vodka. It smarts going down, but I try not to betray my distaste as the bartender's eyeing me. I prefer whisky, but whisky doesn't look like anything but scotch. Groans rise and a cluster of guys enter, nearly crying into their Goldstars. The game is done.

I drain my glass and wait for that blessed light-headedness, but it doesn't come. I'm no lightweight when I want to be drunk. The faux-musician who didn't save my seat shifts on his stool, and as he leaves the girl catches me watching her. Her green eyes flit away and she fiddles with her phone, building an imaginary wall between herself, the world and me.

'What do you see in him?' I say. I lean in. 'Is it that he likes dogs?' I touch her finger and she snaps it away. 'Really. What do you see in him?'

I figure I have two, maybe three more minutes to extract some form of acknowledgement, so I decide to change tack. 'He's an *efes*. A nothing. So what's the attraction?'

She's pretty: light tan, with soft brown freckles on her face and her hair tied in a scraggy knot above her head. The delicacy of the muscles in her arm promise a slender frame somewhere under the ill-fitting synthetic pink and yellow. One hand leans upon her glass, the other traces the crack of her lips.

She is flushed red now, looks straight ahead. 'It's because he's a musician, right? An artist.' She straightens. 'But this is Tel-Aviv. Everybody's an artist here. Talented and brilliant and loved because they can play Hotel California on the guitar during long army nights in the Negev.' She turns her head slightly, looks at me from the corner of her eye. There is the shadow of a grin. 'He'll be a musician while he's at university and then he'll play a few chords at get-togethers while he collects his pay cheque and plays with his kids and doesn't fuck his wife.'

I go for the vodka, forget it's already drained.

'Or maybe not. Maybe it'll be worse. Maybe your future husband will be him.'

I jerk my finger towards the dishevelled, bearded man in my old seat. He's making out heavily with a tumbler of whisky, far from his first, and in a sudden wave of nausea it strikes me that I may as well be pointing to myself.

I need to leave. I'm already on my feet and pushing my stool back under the bar.

'Hey,' says the girl. She has swivelled around on her seat, is blocking my exit. Her hands fall on my hips. 'Where are you going?'

'Good luck on your date,' I mumble, push past.

She grabs my forearm.

'That's it?' she says. 'I was sure you'd try harder.' She fumbles in her bag and pulls out a pen and paper. Holding the cap between her teeth, she jots something down. 'Call me,' she says, and pushes the note into my hand.

I nod and make my way through the bodies and the chairs and the tables and the cigarette smoke. As I pass the stairs, the girl's date is coming up. I shove him hard and he trips backwards, tumbles into a heap in the room below. The ensuing commotion makes it easier to slip out into the darkening night.

Two guys with flutes play to the waiting line, and everyone is pretending to not keep a wary eye on the crackhead who now leans against the slowly decomposing carcass of the late Allenby 58 nightclub. I look down at the paper, at the name 'Mayan' written in an elegant feminine hand. Beside it, a phone number.

'Shekel?' moans the addict. 'For food?'

I forget I have no change, so I pull out the hundred shekels and curse my stupidity. His dead eyes maybe glint for an instant, so I give him Mayan's card instead. He looks at it blankly.

I turn and head south down Allenby, and for a moment by Burger Ranch, where the ancient men sit on wrought iron chairs soldered to the ground, watching the city but not each other, I wonder if he'll call her.

It is Yonatan's twenty-fourth birthday: June 6th, 2005. The chilled breeze from the air-conditioner assaults the little party as they push open the door, climb the few stairs that rise at a right angle, parallel to the window, into the restaurant. The oppressive heat of the summer has yet to arrive and the nights are still comfortable, if no longer chilly. The laconic fans slicing and mixing the air above their heads only cool them further, and they shiver, each in order, front to back.

At the forefront: a man slipping easily past middle age. He grips a large bag. Garish wrapping paper pokes from the top. Once, he may have been attractive, but now his hair has been pulled from his head, teased out through his ears and his nostrils. His belly has been allowed to grow, to sag perilously over his jeans, to wage war with his shirt, worn thin and bleached by years of laundry. Despite his unkempt appearance, he still commands the easy authority of a man of significant physical stature. The hostess gives him all her attention.

She leads them to a table by the window: white tablecloth, white walls, white ceiling, white floor. There are four seats; she pushes the extraneous white chair up and under, tucking it away. They finger their menus in a gruff silence and the woman tuts and arghs and raises her eyes to her son opposite.

'Yonatan, what do you recommend?' she says. She opens her

mouth wide as if to utter a follow-up that does not arrive.

'The fish cakes are good,' the boy says. 'The sweet potato *levivot* too.'

His beard is growing in nicely. Overcoming the patchy thinness of its start, it now enjoys a deep rich lustre. His grey hairs are years away.

'I don't much like fish,' she says. 'You know that. And I don't like all these fancy Tel-Aviv restaurants.'

'This is hardly fancy, Mum.'

'What's it called?' His father turns the menu over and over in his hand, still searching for a dish that isn't there.

'Orna and Ella.'

'That's right,' he nods. 'They say it's good. Though I don't see why we had to come all the way down here. This city's too expensive. Too *posa*.'

'I wanted to show you where I live, Dad.'

A sliver of dribble settles in the stony cleft of his father's chin.

'I know Tel-Aviv, boy,' he says. 'I knew Tel-Aviv before you were shitting in diapers.'

'Avraham,' his wife scolds, pinches his elbow. 'We're supposed to be celebrating.' She turns to her son. 'Don't antagonise your father.' After a while: 'So how does it feel to be out of the army?'

The boy shrugs. He doesn't want to be difficult, knows that this is not a sufficient answer, that it is not what either his father or his mother want or expect. Yet it is the blunt truth. He's been free for a while now, but the euphoria – expected, deserved – proved fleeting. It has been replaced by a listless impatience in the hours and days behind the counter at Disc Center in Dizengoff Center, talking music, saving his money, studying for his Psychometric Entrance Tests, feeling time pass. His hair has grown out, his beard is untrimmed. His nights, unremembered, often last for days.

'I don't understand why you don't just come home.' His mother is waving at a waiter behind his shoulder as she speaks. They order, and when they are left alone again, she begins in the same breath, as if she had not interrupted. 'Come home. At least until you find a place of your own. Maybe we'll even help you with that.'

The boy smiles wanly. He will not go home. Lior, a friend of a friend of a friend, has shacked up with a girl Lior won't call his girlfriend. Their non-relationship has freed up his studio, and though it lacks a proper door to the bathroom and black mould creeps upwards towards the ceiling, it is cheap and offers a plane of removal from home, from the community of his youth, from the army, from everything that came before.

'He can pay for his own apartment,' snaps the father. 'We are not a bank.'

'It's OK, Mum,' he says. His smile does not slip. He has come to love Tel-Aviv, wandering the streets one by one, learning the city's secrets. Every day, his affection grows. Once gleaming white, it is now left to its own devices: ugly, weathered, yet moulded to its inhabitants like a well-worn pair of shoes.

He lives among the cluster of streets named not after biblical scholar rabbis or the Jewish poets taught in school, but rather the British patrons of Jewish nationalism. King George himself; Arthur Balfour who declared Britain's support for Jewish statehood; Viscount Allenby who captured Jerusalem from the Ottoman hordes. The crumbling facades of its buildings lend his part of the city a dignified, refined exoticism.

He wants to explain this to his parents.

'But Tel-Aviv isn't safe.' His mum speaks through a mouthful of sweet potato. 'I'm sure we can find a way to give you some more privacy at home.'

'It's not dangerous. You're exaggerating,' he says, though his daily routine sometimes seems little more than a parade of memorialised atrocities: to the bombings in the market (as he buys vegetables), the bombing outside the bar (as he jogs along the beach), by Dizengoff Center itself (as he sits behind the till). 'The Intifada's over,' he says, but his words have no weight.

'It's not the Arabs we have to be worried about any more,' says his father. He picks at his wife's plate, at his son's plate, scoops forkfuls of their food to supplement his own.

'Do we really have to talk about this now?' says his mother. 'It's been so nice.'

Yonatan has been waiting for the subject to arrive; he is surprised it has taken so long.

They have been inundated with the news all day, and there is not a soul in the state who hasn't internalised Prime Minister Ariel "Arik" Sharon's timetable for the evacuation of all Jewish settlers from Gaza. The cars that drive up Shenkin Street flutter ribbons in the evening air: blue and white for pro-disengagement, orange for anti.

'They've got to be moved,' Yonatan says. He immediately regrets speaking.

'It's a disgrace,' says the old man. His voice is gruff and steely. His eyes flicker. 'No Jew should move another Jew from their home. Other people have been doing it to us for millennia. Now we're doing it to ourselves.'

'Those Jews' homes happen to be slap bang in the middle of over a million Palestinians. And soldiers like me have to protect them.'

'You're not a soldier any more,' his father says.

'Well I was.'

'In Judea and Samaria.'

'That's not the point.'

'Isn't it?'

His father leans back, crosses his arms. Yonatan sighs.

'Hitler would have approved,' his father says.

Yonatan's mother pokes at his father's leathery hand.

'Avi, we haven't seen Yonatan for far too long.' She glances at him across the table. 'He's so busy. Let's not talk about this nastiness. How about you give him the present now?'

His father places the oversize bag on the table. It fills the free space between the reds and oranges and whites of the food, the plates, the tablecloth. The letters BUG are clearly visible on the bag, and Yonatan likes to imagine his father in Dizengoff Center, entering from the western entrance of King George

Street and becoming lost in the maze of gently ascending alleyways and surprising spiral stairways. Maybe he'd catch a glimpse of him from his job, lost between the major chains and tattoo studios, the empty storage lots and the tunnel and skybridges that course over and under the street to link both sides of the mall, the polished west and the eclectic, ramshackle east.

'Go on. Open it.'

He does as he is told.

'They said it was a good camera,' his father says. 'Not the best, but we shouldn't exaggerate.'

'Nikon,' his mother says. 'That's Japanese.'

He is surprised, touched even.

'It's great, Mum. Dad. Thank you.'

'Well we had to get you something,' his mother says, 'and you never tell us anything about your life. Or the army. Just that you were a photographer.'

'I took photos, Mum. That doesn't make me a photographer.' He does not want to talk about the midnight knocks on doors.

His mother pokes her husband's hand once more. 'See that Avi? Our son. Always so humble.'

'Good he says he's not a photographer,' his father says. 'Means he might actually get a proper job. None of this arty bullshit for Tel-Aviv fags.'

'Avi, remember. The gays are nice people.' His mother has gone red. Her eyes zip around the restaurant's tables and at the effeminate waiters.

'I never said they weren't.' His father leans back, stretches his arms over his head.

Yonatan watches him, notes the lines around his face, the blotches where the sun has curdled the pink of his skin. There is no venom in his father's prejudice. He's a musket at a modern arms fair.

As he thanks his parents once more, packs the camera back under the table, he knows he has finally left them behind.

I make it as far down Allenby as the great synagogue and Har Sinai before I double back. Beats slam and cool young things fall out of Port Said, replacement for the Teder pop-up. So many infamous nights in this city have Allenby as their locus. Once this artery of sleaze was Tel-Aviv's most prestigious shopping street; before that, an enterprise of unalloyed hope, rolling sand dunes on all sides. We live here now, Lia and Ben and I, in the little Yemenite enclave tucked at the road's northern edge. The *Teymanim*, the Yemenites, the only people to walk to the Promised Land in a fever of religious destiny. Once here, they created their ethnic ghetto, an ignored warren of narrow streets close to the sea where the roads were only recently paved.

But then the Second Intifada burnt itself out, and the bombs stopped spreading pictures of bone and flesh daily into people's living rooms, and now even Kerem Hateymanim is expensive. We and they live side by side in a dense urban soup of mutual resentment. But they've owned their houses since they were built; we only rent from those few who bought from families that sold out and moved to the suburbs. In two years our lease will be up for renewal, and the rent will have surged again, and then we will be gone; they will have won.

Two years is a long time. Two years ago I wasn't married, I

didn't have a child. In two years there could be war. The Arabs or the Iranians could fulfil their promise and the country could cease to exist. Better to focus on tonight.

Yosef Halper, New Jersey's finest export, is sitting on a chair between the pavement and his shop in one of Allenby's once-grand eclectics. Central European pomposity peppered with Arabic curves. He guards the rows and rows of thumbed, warm English tomes, the air thick with the scent of paper that's been wetted and dried, wetted and dried. I'm tempted, but I skirt his gaze, cut through away from Allenby's bustle into Montefiore Street and walk up towards Kikar Albert. Another crackhead occupies the single bench so I hang a right and traverse Bezalel Yafe Street onto Rothschild Boulevard, crossing the road by the drawing school to avoid anyone from the scene I may know. A group of people mill on the corner and I try to make my way past. None of them speaks Hebrew and the louche singsong of French follows me. *Tzarfatim*, French. A less considerate individual would call them *Tzafrokaim*. Marrakesh for generations, then Paris for an instant, yet to call them Moroccan is to acknowledge their past, to label them Arabs, and nobody's an Arab here, not any more. They are cultured European Jews, holidaying in the Holy Land.

'Trop de monde,' says a girl in a floaty skirt. She clutches a designer handbag, all quilted leather and gold. Before us, the city's most prestigious boulevard is now little more than two thin strips of grass framing a row of tents that spears off in both directions, smothering the walking paths and bike lanes.

They shuffle slowly, blocking my path, and I wish them all away though I know they won't leave until the temperature drops once more and the city can breathe again. For now they're here: in Daddy's apartment on Ben Yehuda Street, parallel to the beach. Bought as an investment, so that his family can connect with 'their state' and 'their people'. They will never realise that all this – the tents, the protest, the anger that they find such an obstruction to their enjoyment – is aimed at them.

I take a swig of my vodka and wait for the little party to be lost in the crowd. A woman walks by pushing a stroller, and I peer in, see if it's a boy or a girl. Blue eyes gaze out at me, and I feel a sudden unexpected pang for Ben, sleeping as I know he must be in the cot squeezed into the corner by the window of our room.

I lean against a tent supported on a wooden frame at head-height and imagine the touch of his skin. A sign beside the tent reads 'My duplex on Rothschild', and someone has crossed it out and written instead: 'If I was a Rothschild Boulevard'. You don't have to be the country's greatest patron to afford to live here, but it helps.

July 14th, that's what this movement is called. Named for the date that Daphni Leef, to protest the high cost of living, planted the first tent on the corner of Marmorek Street and Rothschild. Before it multiplied and thousands flocked here and to the satellite camps inaugurated throughout the country under the banner of *Tzedek Hevrati*, social justice.

The scale and organisation is dizzying. The atmosphere is charged. Blue numbers like those on every building in the city have been stuck on the tents. There are portaloos and kitchens and compost heaps, and tarpaulins slung out to provide shade from the brutal summer sun. Televisions hang in impromptu bars and a few stoners drink beer, share spliffs, as music television plays overhead. It's all so genial, so structured, so un-Israeli; the atmosphere of a party, one winding up or winding down, where everyone is good friends. I should have visited earlier. Had I been coping.

I step over a girl in her underwear. She sits cross-legged on the tarmac drawing a garden in chalk on the ground. Below it, in large pink letters, she's written 'People's Paradise' and, as I pass, she looks up and flashes a welcoming smile. I notice the belly, round and inflated, the protruding belly button with the two holes that once housed a ring. I smile back. This baby is not mine.

Feedback crackles from a microphone and people groan in concert. The noise comes from amidst a collection of La-

Z-Boys, ripped and stained and splayed out in a half-circle around an unsteady stage. A hand-drawn sign welcomes me to 'The School', and I sink into one of the chairs towards the back and take a few more leisurely swigs of the vodka.

A man brandishes the microphone like a sword, paces in a small circuit as he speaks in a voice that dips and rises balletically. A man well versed in holding a crowd. He looks what my mother would call "respectable". Slick in his blue suit, white shirt open at the collar. Respectable like our esteemed ex-President Moshe Katsav, the convicted sex offender, was respectable. He is so incongruous to Tel-Aviv, where clean clothes can make one feel overdressed.

The pitch of his voice is slightly too high for his muscular body; I know him. As he launches into a familiar tirade against the tycoons and their families, I wonder if I can leave before he sees me. He's pointing a hairy finger at a board arranged with a collage of the usual suspects: Ofer, Dankner, Tchuva, Ben-Dov, Strauss. 'Public Enemies' the board reads. Each time he speaks, he jabs his finger into one of the faces with such violence that I fear he will break a knuckle.

A procession of talking points: Netanyahu's economic liberalisation, the inequality, the starving holocaust survivors, the privatised monopolies, a powerful few – borrowers and lenders from the same public pot – rigging the system with impunity. Now and then his eyes fall on me, quickly move away, part of the public speaker's book of tricks.

A *monit sherut* drives past. On its side: two pretty young things kissing as they show off their passports. One is Israeli blue, the other Iranian green. Above them: 'Israel Loves Iran'. No doubt Bibi, the magician, the politician with a dozen political lives, will use Iran to stoke the ever-present fear of annihilation, to cool this emergent insurrection, to continue business as usual. Or his wife, Sara, will tell him to. Everyone knows she's the master and he's the puppet, though nobody is bold enough to say so. Not openly, not in the press. The Prime Minister's Office sees to that.

A finger is stabbed hard into the smiling septuagenarian face of Isaac Hoffman, the original tycoon, and I know he's seen me now as I've let out a laugh that turns a row of heads. I try to bring it under control but I can't, because this very man used to fuck this very tycoon's granddaughter, soon after he died, when the family fell apart and very publicly scrambled for the scraps of his empire.

Maoz. That is so fucking Maoz.

Never the smartest, but the boy had huge, steel, unembarrassable, inhumanly arrogant balls. He had dreams and aspirations, not of working in London, New York or Hong Kong, but of owning London, New York and Hong Kong. No, ambition was never his failing. It was easy to suspect that he didn't believe anything, didn't believe *in* anything, had no moral compass or red lines. He doesn't believe what he is saying now; he'd just as soon be one of those people whose eyes he's gouging with a fingernail than one of the angry horde.

He sees me grinning, and he grins right back. I take another *shluk* of my vodka. The bottle's half empty and I'm starting to notice some effect. There's a pleasant lightness to the night which accompanies the swig. My chair's lever has broken off and I can feel the mechanism disassembled beneath my back. A spring digs into my thigh and so I shift and the back slides backwards, luxuriantly reclined.

I take in my compatriots-in-polite-fury. Most are clearly not here for the learning. There are Tel-Aviv's ubiquitous alcoholics, trading soiled cardboard for plump pleather; a few ageing hippies in dreadlocks and colourful bracelets, relishing it all. Two girls sit in the front row and take notes after each of Maoz's breathless sentences. During breaks in his monologue, they nod to each other. They could be mouthing "amen".

He doesn't believe any of this, and neither should they.

'And if we stopped giving these *dossim* money for every religious baby they spit out, and made them work instead of study Torah day in, day out, forced them to go to the army like you and I and our children, then maybe there'd be more money for us and our families!'

Frantic applause mixes with derisory laughter and not a few cheers. A *doss* in the black suit, white shirt uniform of the ultra-religious, a black hat upon his head and *tzitziot* down by his waist, wanders by. He is leading a gaggle of children by the hand, probably from one of the schools with the barricaded entrances on Ahad Haam Street nearby. He looks at us all, catches fragments of the rebuke, speeds up. Nobody but me sees, and I notice how the few religious out tonight are giving the protest a wide berth, traversing the pavement either side of the boulevard, separated by cars, far away from the activity of the central strip.

The girls are on their feet and clapping. Their pens are gripped between their unstained teenage teeth. They look so fresh. Maoz takes a bow and then kneels between them for a moment, just close enough that he inhales both their breaths, and the sexual energy coursing between all three in a tiny triangle makes ripples in the night.

Before I can break away, he is beside me.

'*Maniak*,' he says, and I take his clammy, outstretched hand and shake it hard.

'Long time,' I say. My leg has gone to sleep so I hop a little like a pelican as I wait for the sparkling to stop, and we just stand there like two old acquaintances with little to say as the girls watch us.

'What are you doing here?' he says.

'I could ask you the same,' I say. I run a hand over my shaved head.

He slaps me on the back, a bit harder than is strictly friendly.

'Come with me to my tent,' he says. 'I need to change my shirt.'

He slips off his blazer and there are pools of dark sweat all over his torso, his pits, his back. It would be disgusting if it didn't make him seem to glow supernaturally in the yellow light. He always had this otherworldly attractiveness, even fresh from the army, new to the lowest rungs of academia.

Always so good looking, so value-free, so dangerous.

His tent is very near the junction with Hahashmonaim Street, close enough to the shadow of Habima Theatre to be among the second circle of tent city royalty. A tent with a single number, perhaps; maybe just a teen. The girls follow a few paces behind. They are whispering and laughing but just far enough away that I can't hear why.

He unzips the entrance and I'm not entirely surprised to see the interior almost completely bare. There's a sleeping bag and a neat little pile of deodorant, wet-wipes, condoms and lube. Beside them, folded and placed on a plastic sheet: a change of clothes. He pulls off his shirt fully in public, and the girls swoon and I swoon a bit too, at the rippling muscles which tense and relax and refer back to his days in *Sayeret Matkal* and the rumours of special operations he always loved alluding to, but never commented on. He pulls on the clean tee-shirt, flexes his biceps, sniffs his underarms and smiles.

'All good,' he says. '*Yalla.*' This time I'm ready when he slaps me on the back. 'Pizza. Let's get pizza.'

Tony Vespa is bursting at the seams. Men, women, kids, alcoholics, drug addicts; they all spill out onto the little balcony and onto Rothschild. The whole country is here, from the hardcore professional protestors to urban urchins on a night out. The media huddles around with their mobile phones and their cameras while the satellite trucks ride the pavement and fight with a compost heap for the last of the black tarmac where the boulevard becomes Habima Square. Local tourists stare bemused, here to say they were part of "it".

I ask Maoz what "it" is.

'Who gives a shit?' he whispers. His smile, so pearly and seductive, sends me to the vodka. 'Give me some of that,' he says and I watch him down what must be a quarter of the bottle. He has paid for the pizza, stale and cold, so I can't complain, despite the bottle's cost. More than money.

'Look,' he continues, mouth wide as he oxidises his food, 'it's just something that's gone national. That everyone's caught up in. Call it viral moral outrage. There's no meaning to it; it's just an excuse for a party on Rothschild that never ends.'

'But you have a tent,' I say. I've seen it.

'Sure.' He shrugs. 'Think of it as a fuck-pad. Everybody's gotta have somewhere to fuck. I recognised early that this would be big, and so I'm really close to all the founders' tents. I'm only a handful away from Daphni Leef herself. That gets the girls wet. Gives me… authenticity.'

'So you don't live here?'

I've left most of my pizza. I'm not hungry, rather the thirst is burning me, and I'm nearly out of vodka. He leans over, doesn't ask, takes the rest of my slice and shovels it into his mouth.

'Fuck no. Why would I want to stay in a fucking tent? I've got a great apartment in the Akirov Towers. Fuck here, go home to sleep. What about you, big guy? When was the last time I saw you?'

I have no intention of reminding him. Anyway, he's moved on and his grubby mitt, all slick and shiny from the pizza cheese, is pawing at my hand, rotating my wedding ring. It burns on my finger so I fumble with it, slide it off and into my pocket.

He leans towards me and I smell my vodka on his breath. 'Don't worry,' he says, 'I won't tell anyone that you're married. When was the wedding?'

'A while ago,' I say, and I recall the hundred or so people crowded into the hastily-arranged wedding venue by Kibbutz Ga'ash. A race against time so she wouldn't show in the photos.

'You?'

'No,' he says, puffs out his cheeks. 'No way. One is not enough.' His hand pumps like a piston and I'm embarrassed for him.

He winks and I turn to see the two girls standing behind us. I try to continue what amounted to our conversation, but Maoz is already up and on his feet and bounding from the pizzeria with his arm around one of the girls' waists. I am no longer a desirable fixture of his night.

The bottle feels light in my pocket so I take it out and drain whatever dregs remain. I toss it in the bin, overflowing rubbish onto someone's tent and only then realise that Maoz has left the second girl to trot by my side.

'Hi,' she says, 'I'm Milli.'

'Yonatan.'

Our footsteps fall into sync and I can't decide if I want her to stay, or go my own way.

Perhaps better to not be alone.

After his birthday, Yonatan does not stay long in Tel-Aviv.

Lior's non-relationship quickly collapses and the room on Balfour Street is reoccupied. For a token sum he is allowed to sleep on the couch, but Lior is a tiresome roommate, and the lack of privacy is soon unbearable. Yonatan takes the *Psychometri* tests, receives a 680 score, and fills out a university application. Then he checks his balance at the bank, withdraws dollars, quits his job, and follows some army acquaintances to Ben Gurion Airport where they board the sleepless red-eye into the sweltering ripeness of Bangkok. He has never travelled outside Europe, and the brash chaos of South East Asia intimidates and excites him in equal measures. All his belongings reside on his back; all except the cash strapped to a pouch that remains on his chest even when he sleeps.

After a week wandering the streets, sleeping in "traveller" hostels whose comfort and sanitary conditions put even the worst days of the military to shame, he gravitates towards an area of the city populated exclusively by young Israelis, all post-army, and settles into the little enclave with unrestrained abandon. His life is easy, familiar, and cheap; a limitless procession of short-lease friendships and overnight girlfriends, bars full of drinks and drugs and ethical elasticity. He eats noodles from street vendors and baits the go-go girls in the bars for sport. There is no need to pay with his constant stream of companions *behinam*.

One day he follows a particularly attractive girl from a kibbutz in the Negev down to Phuket. They row within hours over something entirely inconsequential and part ways beneath a flurry of half-felt insults.

For months he drifts between the islands – Kho Phi Phi, Kho Phan Ghan and others – renting small rooms for next to nothing, oftentimes with an outside hammock that he can either sublet or retreat to after the seemingly endless parties that demarcate the days, the weeks, the months that all the while drift by.

The seasons boil together in a tropical sludge, so he cannot state with any accuracy the date that he logs into his email, only to find an urgent notice from Tel-Aviv University. He has been accepted to the BA in Economics, but the message threatens to reallocate his place to another deserving applicant as they have yet to receive his confirmation of attendance despite numerous reminders. He clicks through his inbox and finds an index of thousands unread. A full dozen are from the university, and he is gripped by a mortal panic as he realises it is already September – September 2006 – and that Thailand has consumed over a year of his life. Time has stood still in the airless heat of the tropics. He came here to remove himself from Israel, from his real life; it is a shock that Tel-Aviv carried on regardless.

In the moment he can vividly sense the motion of time upon his body, of his ageing.

He composes an email to the university, reads it once, twice, three times. The words on the screen seem unreal. After it is sent, he trundles through the roads of the island. He doesn't remember where he is, how long he's been here, even where he has been staying. It is something primordial that guides him through the traffic-clogged streets, trudging between the colourful little concrete shrines that celebrate a Thai religion in which he takes no interest. The dense vegetation claws out over the buildings, the sidewalks. It all seems suddenly so strange.

He gazes at his room as if for the first time. It has a wooden door to the street and a single window that cannot be closed. Only a mosquito net separates the interior from the elements. There is a mattress on the floor and he notes with some revulsion the stains upon the sheets. He has not changed them since his arrival weeks before. His clothes lie sprawled across the brown tile floor, a few surviving Castro and Golf items from Israel mingling with replacements purchased as their ancestors became too worn. Everything is faded from wash and wear. Here and there lie discarded remnants of past lovers, forgotten friends, totemic like the burned out hulks of tanks and armoured cars that decorate the road to Jerusalem. The air is thick and heavy, and he feels intense revulsion at its state; at his state.

In the bathroom he fondles his long beard. What was once a symbol of his freedom is now absurd. He hacks at it with toenail clippers until in places he can see the pale pink skin beneath. Such a contrast to the leathery brown of his nose, around his eyes. He runs his hand through his hair, notices how patchy it is in places – his crown, around his temples, random spots atop his head.

He begins packing his things into his bag, but they won't all fit and so he pours the contents out onto the mattress, intends to begin again. Right at the bottom he finds the Nikon camera, the parental gift, forgotten and unused. There is some life to the battery still, and the few pictures he finds stored in the memory are from Tel-Aviv: of Lior, of old men playing chess on Rothschild, a sunset from the Honey Beach in Jaffa. A short story in a loop beneath his finger.

A whole year of his life does not exist.

'*Maspik*,' he mutters to himself. 'Enough,' and he slings the camera over his shoulder and retraces his steps back to the internet cafe.

By nightfall, he has already arranged his journey back home.

'So you're friends with Maoz,' says Milli from somewhere behind my left shoulder. 'How do you know him?'

'We went to university together,' I say.

'Cool. That's cool.' She is dragging her feet and smudging the chalk pictures on the ground. 'He's an amazing guy. With the start-up and all. A real inspiration. It's great that he's protesting with us here. That he wants a fairer country.'

I've seen his face in the paper, *The Marker* or maybe it was *Globes*, tossed out by the neighbour the day after. One of the twenty new high-tech princes, or some such accolade. Code. Grow. Sell. Be rich. That was the long and short of it.

'What was it he made?' I ask.

'Cloud social integration,' she says, but each word is less certain than the last. Then all that remains is her dragging her feet. 'He sold it for a hundred million dollars. Or something.'

He did what everyone in his position does: sold it to the US so that they could grow, employ, bring others along for the ride. Israeli princelings don't create a court.

My sobriety is taking sandpaper to my throat.

'Where can I get a drink?'

'I know a place,' she says. Her feet no longer drag.

There is so much noise, so much chatter and music and activity in the tent city, framed by the crawling traffic either side. The residents are up in arms, but nobody buys an apartment on Rothschild for peace and quiet. The constituent sounds of the protest are the molecular ingredients of any other day's soup.

I suspect I know where Milli is leading me. We're already running out of road: first Allenby, then Nachalat Binyamin and the next junction is Herzl Street and the hoardings which abruptly sever Rothschild from its last block. 1 Rothschild towers dark above us, no lights lit in its empty floors. One day this will be a small paved plaza, but the barrier is a more eloquent separation: us here, the five million dollar apartments there.

She slows down, waves to a boy half in, half out of a tent with a three-figure number. A latecomer.

'Just a friend from the army,' she says. I didn't ask.

'You're at the Kiriya,' I say, the giant military base on Kaplan Street. She'll be released before it is relocated to middle-of-nowhere desert. She thinks it's a question and nods.

We duck off the street by the neat tables and chairs and carefully cultivated Paris-in-the-Levant vibe towards the courtyard in the back. The building wears its decrepitude like a medal of valour, the pre-state structure held up by steel beams rotting in the wet heat. My heart sinks. The doorman doesn't recognise me, doesn't wave me through with a knowing smile and a welcoming nod. I don't recognise him either, and as we make our way towards the tiled bar I search for a single familiar face.

All the stools are occupied so we hover by the till and the service side, waiting to steal the attention of someone as they come or go or do their jobs. The top shelf holds the whisky and so I scan it for my favourites. I don't know where the next alcohol will come from, so I want to maximise both the pleasure and the effects.

Milli waves at the barman and he slides down to us.

'Bowmore,' I say. 'Make it a double. And for the girl—'

She orders something embarrassing and pink. The drink of

someone old enough to drink, young enough to not know why. Suddenly I know that she signs her name with a heart or a star.

'It's nice, isn't it?' she says.

Yes.

'Have you been here before?'

Yes.

'Do you come here often?'

Yes. No. Not any more.

I turn slowly, take in the tables, the booths, the stage. I try to identify each chair I've sat in, each spot in which I've danced, we've danced, Lia and I, so tight that no air escaped between us. Lost in each other's heat.

The reminiscence feels both vivid and ghostly. The place is just the same as I left it last, but all the human furniture has changed. Déjà-vu punctuated by misgiving.

Milli scratches at her collarbone, and I can see the tattoo there, the mathematical equation for the Greek letter "phi". The numbers are obstructed by the black lace of her bra, the straps of her top.

The whisky arrives.

'Can I try some of that?' she says. They've given me the double divided into two shots, so I give her one because there's no danger of her actually drinking it. Or so I think. Instead of gagging and handing it back in disgust, she downs it in one. There is an instant of calm and then she splutters and coughs and I'm afraid her eyes will pop out.

'*Kol ha-kavod*,' I say. Well done.

'What was that?' she manages between gasps.

'Like I said,' I say, finishing the other shot and motioning for another while her drink is still being chilled or mixed or shaken or stirred. 'Scotch.'

Her glass finally arrives accompanied by a little green umbrella and I'm touched by the innocent joy she radiates as she opens and collapses it. It makes me feel guilty for what I need to do, but I remind myself that circumstances are extraordinary, and that perfect morality is a sucker's game, for *frayerim*. It's not as if I have a choice. When the bill arrives I use the drink as an excuse to look away.

I didn't have to order such an expensive drink. J+B or Ballantine's would have demanded a fraction of the coin, but I'm getting older and the ends no longer justify the means. I still want to be drunk, I just don't want to suffer getting there.

Still, I want to apologise, but instead I say:

'Aren't you going to get that?'

'Maybe we should just split it,' she says and takes one of those long, thin purses from the deep rectangular bag slung over her shoulder.

'I'd love to,' I say with a smile full of sadness and regret and deceit, 'but I have no money.'

She thinks I'm joking, looks at me quizically, her mouth an uncertain smile. As the realisation of my sincerity creeps visibly across her face, she removes a two-hundred shekel note as if extracting her own tooth.

'That's a real dick move,' she says.

I try to hide behind a petulant gaze, but my face feels contorted and vulgar.

'I'm sorry,' I say. She turns, shakes her head, tuts silently. 'Really, I am.'

'You owe me sixty-eight shekels.'

'Fine.'

I wonder if we will know each other long enough for me to pay her back.

A song I love comes on, and a rush of adrenaline pushes me to my feet. I am about to pull Milli to the dance floor when I see she isn't equally enthused, doesn't even seem to have noticed our good luck.

'Don't you like them?' I say.

'Who?'

'The band.'

She turns her head slightly, listens. Her vacant stare tells me that she doesn't care about the music, yet I still want to tell her the band's name, to roll off a list of their hits I've danced to here and in Thailand, but all she says is, 'I don't really like vintage stuff.'

'Get me another drink,' I say. 'Please.'

She doesn't even dignify my request with an answer.

'Fine,' I say and I knock over a glass or two, unintentionally grab a shoulder, a breast, a buttock as I feel my way outside. I expect Milli to desert me, to be on my own once more, but as I stand on the corner of Lillenblum Street and Rothschild, I sense her by my side.

'I thought you'd've left me,' I say. I find I'm glad she didn't.

'Not until I get my money,' she says. 'Now how about we go somewhere else? I know where there'll be free drinks.'

When Yonatan lands in Bangkok in mid-September 2006, he avoids the scrum of tuk-tuks, counts and double-counts his remaining money in a locked toilet cubicle, and then takes a taxi to a proper hotel with crisp white sheets and doormen guarding the entrance. He gets his clothes washed, his hair cut at the hotel barber. He even splurges on a wet shave.

His El-Al flight is not for a few days and if he is careful, his money will stretch, even in this relative luxury. He wakes early and walks the city with new eyes, watches its natural rhythms, and eats noodles and meat on sticks from vendors in small stalls. He is mindful to avoid the Israeli areas.

His camera lends his meandering a purpose, and he photographs the colours of life around him: the workers in their yellow polo shirts; the green tuk-tuk drivers on their breaks, smoking and dangling their legs from their vehicles; the office workers dressed neatly in black; the night workers in skimpy neon. He does not drink, does not go in search of adventure. He feels clear-headed and focused, and as the images mushroom, he toys with sending some of the prettier pictures to Yaeli, a girl who works at the *Maariv* newspaper.

When one morning he turns a corner to find the road blocked by a tank, he is not scared. Weapons of war, free of intent, are still mundane to one so recently released from the army.

Curious, he walks closer. Instinctively, he slides the camera from his shoulder, checks that it is switched on, that all the dials are set correctly. As he is about to document the scene, the tank's hatch swings upwards and open, and a disembodied torso in olive camouflage emerges into the grey air. The two lock eyes. Yonatan lowers his camera, turns, walks away.

No sooner is his back to the tank than he is already reprimanding himself for his cowardice. He reminds himself that he is a soldier too. He snaps a few bland, frustrated pictures of the gutter and then dissolves into the crowd. He is adamant: if he sees something unusual again, he will not be cowed.

He does not have to wait long. Soldiers are stationed throughout the municipal centre; some are in tanks, others stand around at intersections. All are heavily armed. Throngs of people mill at a respectful distance, chatting, watching, waiting. Yonatan flits through the assemblage, his finger seldom off the shutter. He climbs lamp posts, squats in ditches, always on the move, always searching for a better view.

He comes across a group of foreigners, stands a little apart and listens to their excited, hushed gossip. They confirm what he has already intuited: they are in the midst of a military coup. How odd he finds the very idea of an army overthrowing the people. At home, in Israel, it would be inconceivable, the state's army its fathers, its mothers, its daughters and sons. The army *is* the people, the defensive fist of *Am Israel*, composed of its individual fingers, its myriad of bones.

But Thailand is not Israel.

Here is a place where people can take up arms against their own country-folk without muddying the boundary between civilian and soldier. This, he thinks, is the luxury of a nation without enemies.

The foreigners keep talking, but he is no longer listening. The coup fascinates only as an idea that stirs the first pangs of true homesickness. Emotional and exhausted, he sits on a kerb.

An old woman in yellow breaks free from the crowd and rushes towards a tank. Yonatan watches a soldier raise his weapon and, in a rush of anticipation, expects him to fire. But he has misinterpreted the situation, and he watches as the soldier slings his machine gun across his shoulder and accepts the flower from the woman's hand with a delicate nod.

In a single motion, the camera is raised to Yonatan's eye; the shutter has been pulled.

The soldier tucks the flower into the yellow band around his arm; Yonatan hasn't noticed how the Thai flag on a nearby building has perfectly framed the scene, or how the sun breaking through the grey clouds has lit the soldier with an angelic halo and painted the old woman's features soft and welcoming like the supplication of the saved. The moment is already lost and exists only in his camera.

That night, he sends Yaeli a selection of images. He does not check his email again before his flight home, so it is not until he passes the newsagent at Ben Gurion International Airport's arrivals hall that he finds the image has been published on *Maariv*'s front page.

The cab to Florentin only takes a few minutes. We cross Harakevet Street into Gan Hachashmal and as the stores selling hipster fixed-gear bikes disappear, the road becomes more pockmarked and there's masonry and graffiti everywhere. The meter is rising and Milli is staring at it as if she's trying to think it into stopping. May as well try for peace in the Middle East.

The driver is old skool. His cab smells of stale cigarette smoke and he sits on one of those seat covers made of rotating wooden baubles that clack as his weight moves and the car turns. They're a dying breed, guys like him; nowadays taxi drivers sit on over-plump aftermarket velour with *Turbo* printed on top.

He's convinced we're married and it's getting boring telling him we're not. 'You make a lovely couple,' he's saying, again and again and again. 'My wife, she would love you. So nice to see young people in love. You should make children, *be-ezrat hashem*. God willing. Life is nothing without children. No joy.' I wait for what I know is coming.

'And if we don't have children, the Arabs will win. They breed like rats, so yes. Have children. Lots of children.'

There it is, the complete sales pitch, the carrot and the stick. Immortality and bliss; destruction and subjugation. I no longer feel any obligation to speak. In the descended quiet there's a constant click-click-click as he opens sunflower seeds with his teeth. He picks the meat from within with his tongue, then tosses the husks out of the open window: old skool. He never stops, even when he's speaking, and little globules of seed and husk and spit spray across the steering wheel. A fine layer of salty dust has settled on every surface.

Milli tells him to stop and he pulls up, bumping against the kerb so hard that I'm certain he's done his car some damage. He collects the change with one hand, the other just keeps working in that perpetual cycle: bag, mouth, window.

As we leave, he says a prayer for us, our never-to-exist children, our perpetual war.

Florentin's grimness upsets me. It's been up-and-coming since before the city had a state. It's not dirty – not by south Tel-Aviv standards at least – but neither is it clean and pleasant. It's just stuck in this fug of *stam*-ness. The gallery is slotted among warehouses and showrooms touting cheap industrial wares, the roll-down storefront blinds rusted and loose on their runners. I've never heard its name and can only assume it holds a few no-name artists on its books, all of whom will sink without a trace before they've had a chance to even briefly tread water. Eventually the gallery itself will shut up shop and another will open in its place, the same but with a different name, and then... and then... and then... So it is in Florentin.

I was lucky, even if it doesn't feel that way now. That photograph from the Thai coup vaulted me over this stage and I progressed directly to Gordon Street, with the champagne openings and the pedigree to ask for inflated sums. Enough to keep the gallery rich.

There is a table out front replete with wine bottles with twist-off caps, and bowls full of Bamba and grill-flavoured Bisli. I am tempted to hide a bottle down my trousers, but I restrain myself. Instead, I slam down two glasses.

'Why are you so desperate to get drunk?' Milli says.

I pour another glass and turn away to carry it into the too-bright lights of the gallery. Nobody past thirty should have to talk to a teenager about life.

The lights are blinding and the pictures are badly printed, mounted worse, and hung haphazardly on the walls. They are nauseatingly predictable: shot in a dark club and then edited to death in Photoshop with a few pre-set combos.

I check the price on stickers beside the work and sigh; I know how much it costs to print in this city and there is no way he will make any money even if it is sold. He? She? The work is so androgynous that I cannot locate any markers. It has no personality, let alone gender.

'It's great, isn't it?' says Milli, suddenly behind me. I restrain the urge to shout, to rebuke her, even a sudden fleeting impulse to violence. I wish I didn't have any moral red lines. Like those settlers in the *shtachim* who shoot kids.

'Yeah, it is,' I say. My teeth grind and the grating reverberates in my ears like fingernails on a blackboard. 'What do you like about it?'

'Well.' Her tongue pokes out, is clamped between her lips. 'It's that one I really like.'

She begins to lead me by the arm but I incorporate a giant detour into our short journey to refill my cup. The photo is huge, each pixel the size of a fingernail. Grain is passable, its randomness adds an earthy character. Pixels are too pure and organised; here the blown-out highlights are a sea of empty nothingness.

'You're looking at it too close,' says Milli. 'You need to step back.'

I do as she instructs and realise as I shuffle back that I am finally drunk, that I have to squint and concentrate to steady the image. Two girls stare into each other's eyes with the tell-tale signs of infatuation. One has a hand in the other's lap, the fingers curled around her crotch.

No, the girl's partner is not playing along. Her eyes are slightly askew, preoccupied with something enigmatic in the crowd. The light is acute but narrow – a source must be suspended above – and leaves a multitude of questions in the inky green of the blacks behind.

I concede to Milli that she is right, that I like it. She does not gloat.

There's one more unopened bottle of wine and I decide to discard any pretence towards politeness and claim it as my own. As I screw off the top, I look around and take in all the attendees. Most are friends and family, fawning all over the artist's lucky break.

People are looking at me funny and I realise I am slugging directly from the bottle. Lia would be horrified, and so I smile an embarrassed smile but here, without her, it proves more of a leer. I block everyone out and watch Milli who is shadowing a particular guest's movements a little too closely. He takes a step, she takes one too, always two paces behind. I try to understand what it is about him that's of interest: black tee-shirt, khaki shorts, those ubiquitous white flip-flops with the Brazilian flags, but all I can find is the small innocuous camera slung over his shoulder. I know what it is and I know that with the lens attached, it costs more than I made last year.

I stumble forward to get a better look, but I must have finished most of the bottle too quickly because I fall onto someone small and pale and standing in my way. I can't tell whether they're male or female, but I try to push past again, and again they block me in.

'Are you OK?' they say. He says. I've decided he's a he.

'I'm fine,' I say; I slur. 'Can I just get through?'

I try to pass him once more, but I find myself being supported by the doorframe instead. The room is swirling and my stomach desperately wishes to relieve itself of everything churning away inside. I check I am still standing and, to quiet it, take another swig from the bottle.

'You should probably go easy on that,' he says.

I look for Milli. It's tough for my eyes to focus and I have to concentrate hard to stop my head bobbing around the fulcrum of my neck. I think I see her, but I'm not sure because too many people are wearing the same god-awful mismatched clothes. If it is her, she's very close to the man with the camera, too close for anyone not intimately acquainted.

'Milli!' I call, but perhaps it's not her because she doesn't turn, doesn't look at me, doesn't react. As I yell, I stumble forwards and the boy reaches for my bottle. I pull it away just in time. 'Mine,' I say. 'Who do you think you are?'

'Actually, I'm the artist.' He hurls his status at me.

I grin crookedly and he mistakes my disdain for deference.

'What do you think of my work?' he says.

I taste reflux, sharp and acrid.

'I think,' I begin. I lean in just close enough to smell the oddly feminine scent on his neck. I want to tell him that he has some talent, that his work shows potential, but that despite all that, not to bother. That this is not for him, that everything is rigged against him. That it's not his fault.

But instead I say, 'It's shit.'

It draws itself out, confused, unintended. When it settles to silence, he looks at me blankly. 'Shit,' I repeat. The words surprise me still.

I barely finish before I am looking the other way, and fire is radiating through my nervous system. He's hit me all right – right in the teeth and one of the molars must have pierced my cheek because I can taste blood. It swirls and I swill it around my mouth and spit a globule of red at his feet.

'Why the hell did you do that?' I say, and manage to block another punch as it aims to load itself into my jaw.

I stumble backwards half a step and, just to avoid another blow, I throw my entire weight onto him, and everyone is looking at me as I straddle him and try to pin his arms to the floor.

'Look, you've got it wrong,' I say as he flails against me. 'Stop it. Let me explain.'

Nails dig into my shoulders and pull me up to my feet. I've been kneeling on the boy with all my weight on my knees, digging into his arms to incapacitate them. I stand up and brush non-existent dust from my legs – isn't this what you're supposed to do in situations like this? – and take in all the staring rows of open mouths, at the boy breathing heavily on the floor.

'I just wanted to give him advice,' I say to the assembled gaping mouths. 'And then he punched me.'

'What the hell did you do?' a woman yells and the momentary paralysis of the crowd is broken.

'Run,' orders Milli, and I know her instinct is right, and so we barrel from the gallery as fast as our feet will take us. We are already out into the street before I notice I am missing one flip-flop. We're being followed and it is amazing that we make it to Shalma Street without being caught. A line of cabs are stopped at the lights and as they turn green Milli swings open a door just as the driver lurches forwards. She shuffles along the bench as the wheels are still turning and I fall in hard and pull the door closed.

'Where to?' the driver says in a thick Arab accent.

'Just drive!' I yell and when we start to move I wind down the window and stick my head out to watch as the crowd vanishes behind. The driver eyes us in the rear-view mirror as the obnoxious wailing of a Middle Eastern singer assaults my ringing ears. He looks suspicious and nervous, but he's an Arab so what will he do?

I rub my face and taste the blood from my jaw. My hand drops to the side, exhausted, and it hits something hard. I look down to see a familiar, twenty-thousand dollar camera between the seats.

'Milli,' I say, and I hope that, between the alcohol and adrenaline, the words are distinct and clear. 'What the fuck is that?'

Yonatan drops out of university after barely two semesters. The term 'dropping out' makes the whole process seem dramatic, though he simply stops attending class one day, doesn't reply to emails, doesn't answer unrecognised numbers on his phone. If the act itself is uneventful, the shrapnel of the decision ricochets through his life. His father refuses to speak to him, and after a while his mother's approaches dwindle too.

The removal of routine leaves him with vast swathes of time. To stave off boredom he prowls the city with his camera, day in, day out, stalking strangers and documenting little moments that pique his interest. He meets Yaeli, the girl who placed his photo in *Maariv*, for a coffee at Pua in Jaffa's flea market. The unmatched chairs in the overstuffed room mean that she towers over him on her plump chaise longue despite her minuscule frame. Over coffee and alfajores, he tells her about his work, feigns an approximation of artistic integrity. He invites her back to the one-bedroom apartment he rents on Fireberg Street and, after quick sex, he walks her through the thousands of images that overflow from his hard drive.

Patiently, delicately, she progresses through the morass.

'Some of these are strong,' she says, 'but they don't quite hold together. They're lacking in focus; some overarching theme to tie them all together.' She rubs the back of his hand with an outstretched finger. 'I could help you, if you like.'

He nuzzles her neck.

That weekend, they aggressively arrange and cull, cull and arrange. They pause only to screw and to venture into the stormy night in search of pizza, shawarma or beer. No matter the hour, they are never alone; Tel-Aviv never seems to slow. Finally, the torrent is a taut, elegant series of a dozen images, fragments of life. Each is dramatic, intimate and compelling, beautifully framed and meticulously processed.

Two weeks later, the series is published in the *Maariv* weekly magazine; a few days later a gallery on Gordon Street invites him in to discuss representation over Italian espresso in fine porcelain cups. Yonatan and Yaeli toast his success at a Cava bar on Nachalat Binyamin.

'I'm really happy for you, but I think our fun is coming to an end,' she says with a smile. 'I've met someone.'

She doesn't call him again.

June 2007 arrives, and the heat starts to build once more. Pressure grows from his gallery to provide work, something they can use to sell him to collectors, to build up a profile before the deluge of international prospectors arrive for the Fresh Paint contemporary art fair in November. He does what he has become accustomed to doing; prowling the streets with his camera, stalking the unusual and unexpected. But this time, something fails to connect, and without Yaeli's guidance, he feels rudderless. The ground beneath his feet seems too familiar, and the sights and smells at ground level no longer hold any allure. Each night he empties his files into his computer and retreats in disgust. Tel-Aviv is a hive of activity, but he senses all the excitement is occurring above his head. Giant cranes swing lazily through the day and night, towers growing, teasing of bountiful heavens just beyond his reach.

Still his gallery calls, keeps urging him to produce, to provide. He runs out of excuses, and so it is with relief that the brown letter arrives, alerts him of his looming call-up for military reserve duty. As he is preparing to leave, packing his bags and planning his journey to the base, his father calls his flat.

'When's your *milluim?*' he says.

'A few days.'

'You better turn on the TV, then.'

The screen flickers quietly in the corner, blurry footage of fighting, playing on a loop. It could be anywhere.

'They're killing each other this time.' His father laughs gruffly. It collapses into a cough. 'Makes a change. At least they're not killing us for once. Crazy Arabs.' He pauses, and Yonatan hears the breath rasping in his chest. 'Stay safe, son.'

He listens to the commentary, learns of the brewing Palestinian civil war that will pit Fatah against Hamas, will replace one with the other in Gaza. Good bad usurped by bad bad.

In the bus, he worries he will be sent in, somehow embroiled in someone else's struggle, terrorised in that strip notorious for urban warfare and cramped death. Even after the evacuation, the disengagement, he could still have to risk his life for that cursed territory.

He needn't worry, though, for the closest he comes to Gaza is on that bus travelling to the base in the Judaean desert, where he spends the next weeks, days, lost to the uniform.

'We should just push them all into the sea,' says Noam, a tall, baby-faced boy from a city in the south who served in the border police. Word has arrived that troops are evacuating *Fatahniks* from Gaza to the West Bank. 'The only good Arab is a dead Arab.'

He offers Yonatan a cigarette, which he gratefully accepts.

We enter the central bus station from Levinsky Street. There are crowds of brown and black and yellow people milling around outside and I wonder whether any of them are pushing one of my series of stolen bikes. The world's largest bus station when it opened in the 90s, it left its predecessor to drug dependency and squalor. And periodic explosions. The floor rises and falls like small hillocks beneath our feet. Ram Karmi, the architect of this nightmare place and of Dizengoff Center too – one despised, the other loved – wanted it to be like the city inverted, to have the outside brought in. Somebody at the planning stages should have pointed out that Tel-Aviv's flat as roadkill.

Signs hang low over our heads but I know better than to follow them. They're just an inside joke, dissembling to the uninitiated that there is some organising logic to this hell. Milli supports me while I hop. The floor is filthy and I am reluctant to let my bare foot touch the ground despite it already being black after running through the streets of the city. We turn left and stalls line both sides of the corridor, "Kalvin Klein" tee-shirts and "Channell" bags spilling towards us and forcing us to weave between them. Each shop is barely two paces wide and every one has placed speakers at the entrance, bombarding us and the few others that loiter with a different music. *Mizrachi*, trance, techno, rock; my aching head is in a blender.

Milli stops abruptly and I nearly fall, but she catches me mid-lurch and pulls me into a store. A fat woman sits behind a makeshift counter smoking a cigarette. The doughy rolls of her stomach erupt over, under and through a tiny sparkly top which may once, long ago, have been the right size. She eyes us suspiciously and I want to yell at her, to tell her that Milli's camera costs twenty thousand dollars so we don't need to steal, but I am steered over to fake versions of those flip-flops with the damn Brazilian flag in not so neat rows along the wall.

'You shouldn't walk barefoot,' the woman yells. 'You'll get worms.'

'What size are you?' says Milli and she picks off a nasty pair in mismatched pink and green.

'Really?' I say. 'I'd prefer the white ones.'

She doesn't listen, just carries them over to the till.

'You're really going to make me wear those?'

'I'm paying. You'll wear what I buy you.'

The indignity of it all smarts, but then I stub my naked toe on a pile of mops and curse the night, the woman by the till, the flip-flops, this place.

I feel as if everyone is staring at my feet as I lead Milli through the alleys for what seems like an age. I'm looking for the little plaza with the McDonald's – the only icon in this landmarkless place – and though I find it, we've inexplicably managed to rise two floors and the escalator is out of order, so we keep going until we reach a dead end. The tables of the schwarma joint are ringed by abandoned businesses, dust settled around their doorways and ripped posters advertising long-past gigs covering their windows. It looks half-way to sanitary and I offer to treat Milli.

'To begin paying you back,' I say.

'You have money?' she says, surprised.

'A little. I just didn't know when I'd need it.'

We order pittas but the man doesn't listen and I try not to look at his fingers and the filth encrusted under his nails as he spreads the greasy lamb and turkey mix and rolls the *laffot* like papyrus. I tell him to load mine up with *harif* and hummus and salad and even chips, anything to soak up the booze. Milli has hers plain with *tchina*.

'That's only a quarter of what you owe me,' Milli says. As we wait, she picks *hamutzim* and eggplant from the cesspool trays into little plastic dishes. I will not be touching them. 'And that's not including the flip-flops.'

Even if not tonight, I will pay her back entirely.

I gulp the bites down in silence. The grease drips down my wrist and onto my shorts. I know better than to try and wipe it off so I just accept it, leave it there. A rubbish truck passes next to our table. The driver jumps out, hauls litter into the flatbed, climbs in, drives off. The yellow light whirs and skims off the walls. No building should be large enough to accomodate its own ecosystem of internal, motorised vehicles.

'How do you turn on the focus?' Milli says.

She is fiddling with the few buttons on the top and the back of the camera and I can see that none of it is making any sense to her.

'It doesn't have autofocus,' I say, and I take it off her to save it from the grease on her shiny fingers.

'So why is it so expensive, then?'

I walk her around all the details; explain the company and the camera's history, give her a crash course in photographic basics. Shutter speed. Aperture. ISO. Tell her how the lack of a mirror helps steady the image, and how the 0.95 on the lens means it can see better than either of our eyes.

Hers glaze over.

'How'd you know so much about this stuff? You a photographer?'

'Something like that,' I say. There's a long pause; I'm grateful she doesn't dig.

'So how do you focus?'

I steal a metal tin of napkins from a neighbouring table and hand her a bunch. She wipes her hands and I inspect them before I hand over the camera. I hold up the box napkin-side to her and tell her to twist the focus ring till the two *b'tei-avon*s overlap. She's having trouble so I lean over with my free hand, place my fingers lightly on hers and guide them slowly.

A click. She hunches over the camera like a penguin over its chick and then yells in frustration. I have to grab the camera to save it from catapulting to the floor.

'What's wrong?'

'It's not in focus. Who would buy this piece of shit?'

Her words smart.

'Who would *steal* this piece of shit?' I say.

She thinks for a second and her tongue peeks out again from between her lips. She opens her mouth but then just shrugs.

'I just saw it was a Leita.'

'Leica,' I correct her.

'Whatever. I knew the name and that it was a big deal and I knew it was expensive and I figured that if he could afford to buy it once, he could afford to buy it again. And anyone stupid enough to pay so much for a camera deserves to have it stolen.' She shrugs again. 'You can have it if you want.'

Instinctively I say no, but everything in my body is screaming for me to take it. I nearly bought one once, in London. An almost attainable dream.

A cloth wipes down the table and I follow the hand and look up into a dark, scarred face, skin thick and black and pitted like liquid oil. He picks up the stray pickles Milli has been poking around and collects the shards of lamb and lamb fat into his bare hands. His eyes are bright red around the jet-black corneas that bleed into their surroundings.

Is he Ethiopian, or an Eritrean or Sudanese refugee? It's so difficult to tell. Laughs rise from below and I lean over to look down at the giant Ms of the McDonald's below, where a group of black men are noisily owning the plaza while sharing a beer. This place is a sanctuary of sorts, for all those not kosher enough for the Jewish state. This is their world within ours, just as it was the world of the South East Asians before them. To meet, to play, to talk, without fear of apprehension.

There must be thousands of these Africans in Tel-Aviv now. Their flight *to* the Jewish state seems absurd. They plaster our walls and clean our dishes, set up their places of worship, their restaurants, their shops, their illicit economy. The latest in a long line of outsiders occupying the lowest rungs of society: Arabs till Oslo, then Filipinos; now the fleeing African. In a few years they'll be kicked out too and someone else will take their place, to battle with the illegal Palestinians for work.

The man finishes our table. I can't guess his age, anywhere from not-quite young to nearly old and I wonder about his story, watch his beaten manner, all hunched and thin, long-limbed and obviously abused. He is different from the Arabs and the Asians before him, those who could go home, did go home. Or maybe he's an Ethiopian Jew and I'm a bigoted Haaretz-reading Ashkenazi, seeing black as black without distinction.

As he heads off towards the stand, Milli asks him to wait, digs into her purse to pull out a gold and silver coin. She presses the ten shekels into his hand.

'No,' he says, crossing his arms across his chest and cocking his head to the side.

She insists and he smiles white teeth, so bright against the tar-dark skin.

'*Toda*,' he mouths. Thank you.

'Why did you do that?' I say.

'He obviously needs it more than I do. Don't worry, you don't have to pay *that* back.'

'That's not fair.'

She shrugs.

'Isn't it?'

Somehow I manage a smile through my shame.

'Let's go,' I say. 'Let me take you somewhere fun.'

When Yonatan returns to Tel-Aviv from his reserve duty, he begins scouting the more affordable parts of the city for studio space. He finds a giant empty room in a labyrinthine building, surrounded by ramshackle mechanics' shacks on one side and the city's north-south Ayalon highway on the other, and signs a rolling monthly lease. That first evening, he watches from the window as the sunset splatters pastels over the smeared brown-grey of the city's inner industrial wasteland, makes it beautiful for an instant before spluttering into darkness. The night is cut by the red and white lights of the highway, the annotated drum of a million lives.

The fleeting sense of beauty, of connectedness, so moves him that he works till dawn removing thousands of photographs from the boxes that litter the floor. He spreads them across the raw concrete, searches each and every one for that spiritual stillness and serenity momentarily glimpsed.

He can find none.

The next day he seals off a corner of the studio, spends the afternoon trawling the second-hand photographic stores of the city for discarded dark room equipment. By nightfall he has started work on a new project, combining voyeuristic snapshots with carefully choreographed still lives of colourful discarded objects he collects off the street. To these he adds paint, prints, intricate lighting; creates grand, magnificent, complex landscapes. He invites the other tenants to sit for him – other artists, micro-factory workers, prostitutes and designers – and works in a flurry of inspiration. By the time the winter smothers the city in a wet chill, he has a body of work to present to his increasingly frustrated backers.

'This'll make you famous,' says the gallery owner. For once, he means it.

An air of unease pools outside the Central Bus Station. There are refugee men loitering in groups and eyeing us as we pass, and I shiver in the pungent heat. It feels like they're stripping me and tallying up the value of my clothing, extrapolating the value of my wallet, its contents.

They're wrong.

It must be a tricky game for them, working out a metric to weigh risk and potential return. If indeed they're planning to rob me at all. As a police car slips noiselessly by, the lights on but the siren off, the group looks away, kicks dust at its feet. These *mistanenim*, these infiltrators.

It would be quicker for us to turn, to head up through the pedestrianised alleys of Neve Shaanan, but we would no longer be in Israel then, so I choose to stay on Levinsky. I do not relish being the only white man in Africa. Milli would be easy prey. It's she who now commands their attention, and the looks seem grounded in a different type of economics. I look at her for the first time as an object; to get a clearer view, I pull off her loose-fitting top with my eyes – over one slender arm and then another, follow with her belt and skirt, making sure not to damage the fabric as I tease it over her knees, her toes. Now she's in black lace underwear, no bulge in her panties; she is recently waxed and all is smooth and soft.

I see her.

She isn't the type I usually go for. The soft down that litters her arms is faintly repulsive, but now I want to stroke it delicately with my fingertips. Not my type at all.

The pounding music that spills from one of the African bars echoes in my heart and a predatory tingle spreads. My hand rests upon her shoulder. My mouth is dripping with the rusty taste of anticipation and I slurp in the sticky saliva. I lick my teeth and they tingle too, just like my fingers running themselves over her tanned skin.

Milli turns and smiles at me. The illusion vanishes and my hand is suddenly heavy and conspicuous.

'What?' she says, and she points the camera. We both know the photo is out of focus.

'Nothing.' I shift my hand so it rests lightly. 'I just wanted to check you know the way.'

I let her lead me through the brothels and drug dens, cross by the abandoned British customs house, down Begin Road and up Carlebach Street at Maariv Bridge. It's still early but an untidy queue snakes from the door under the gallery. A few people are licking ice cream cones bought from the machines nearby. There's a barrier emblazoned with the club's emblem, a half-cat half-dog, its two heads pulling in opposite directions, that presses back against the most eager of the crowd.

Lior's familiar face glares down at a clipboard. He's perched on a stool, his throne of power, that pulls people towards him, each vying for attention. He looks tired, bloated, worn; a mildly eroded version of my impromptu landlord years ago. His energy, though, is undiminished. Time moves slower in Tel-Aviv's clubs.

He greets me with fabricated insults, as if the long gap between last time and this time were a product of more than just life. He waves us over and leans over the barrier to pull me to him in a bear hug. He smells of cigarettes and cheap cologne and something else that smoulders in my nose like light decay.

'*Achi*,' he growls, and then he pushes me backwards so that all I can do is grin ridiculously as he looks me up and down and down and up, like a carcass at the butcher. 'Where have you been?' Milli stands with her knee bent demurely. She smiles broadly. Lior grins and searches for a diplomatic way to ask the undiplomatic question. 'She's new, no?'

I introduce them and state without stating that upon Milli, I have no claim.

'You know,' he says, turning to her, 'I have known him forever. He used to live in my home.' He curls my arm in his and puts too much pressure on it so that I must almost kneel beneath him. 'And then he met this girl and fell in love and he said nothing would change, that he would still come to the club, to the parties I throw. Did he keep his promise?'

'Did you?' says Milli. I don't begrudge her playing along.

'No,' says Lior. He tut-tut-tuts and shakes his head. 'He lied. But we are *hevre*. I can't be angry at him. Now what is your name, *motek*?'

I have done my service to our shared history, so as he flirts with Milli, still twirling her leg and pulling at stray hairs, my wrist is stamped and I descend the stairs into the netherworld of pounding bass. It feels as if my ears will liquefy and my eyes will bleed.

God I've missed it.

A cloud of smoke hovers above the hundreds of heads, cut by lasers. There are bodies everywhere, all thrusting spasmodically. The girls shake their hair as if they're beating off a swarm of angry bees; the guys punch and kick in pugnacious rage at invisible foes. On the walls, rows of little multi-coloured LEDs paint towers of light that peak and fall to the music, hundreds of dots whirring and shining red and yellow and bathing us all in a hypnotic glow. There is no dance floor; just dance where you are. Just dance. Everybody is ageless here; I will exist, eternal.

My feet skip towards the bar, endorphins rampaging. The bartender seems familiar, but everything seems familiar here. I'm sure we've slept together at least once, but nothing of such insignificance matters. She pulls out a shot glass, pours from a bottle. I don't see the label but from the colour it is either absinthe or chartreuse. The burn going down. No sooner have I returned the glass to the bar than it is refilled again and again. I know better than to accept the fifth. These drinks have a delayed punch and it is a poor newbie who doesn't anticipate the future, blow from by the liquor still to come. She shrugs and pours herself one instead, and when it's done motions to me to lay my hand palm up on the bar. With a we-used-to-know-each-other-once wink, she fills it with two tiny pills and balls my hand into a fist. Bringing it to her mouth she bites down hard on my knuckles. I feel her puncture the skin and draw blood.

I wander, light-headed, lost amongst the throng. Eyes closed, I feel the bodies surrounding me. I let the tide of motion guide me, bring my hand to my face. I am about to pop those two little pills onto my tongue but as I loosen my grip my hand is thrown violently away and my mouth is filled by something soft and mobile and warm and aquatic. My arms are wrapping themselves around a slim waist as it grinds against me and something gropes at my penis.

The kiss lasts an eternal instant, and then she is dragging me through the crowd towards the bathroom. If I had wanted to scramble on my hands and knees for the pills, the opportunity's gone, and in the pit of my belly I feel a sadness for them: they are a ticket to somewhere I desperately wish to go.

There is no mystery or magic to sex in a cubicle. This one locks, not that anyone pays us any attention as we slide inside. I graze my elbow against the wall but even the blood feels warm. It doesn't hurt. My vision's all blurry again, the walls are falling in and the ceiling and the floor are swapping places in a constant circular motion, so I sit on the toilet seat and attempt to gaze at the girl I am about to fuck.

Who is she?

She's hitching her ugly skirt around her waist and moving her panties to the side. It takes a moment to move from the bare slit up to her face, and another for some shards to emerge and merge in the haze.

'You!' I scream. It's a strange relief.

'You didn't call or text me,' she says and pivots at the waist as she unbuckles my belt and pulls my shorts down. My penis is struggling to reach horizontal.

'It's only been a few hours,' I say weakly. 'And I don't have a phone.'

Her face is all business, without any expression, and I watch her glazed eyes, pupils wide, as she slips me into her mouth and begins sucking and slurping as if consuming an over-ripe peach.

The music sounds distant now, fainter somehow, and the noise she is making is lurid and grotesque against the vibrating walls. I got this girl wrong; so very wrong. Sitting there at the Minzar with her 'I like dogs' boyfriend, she seemed so pure. Yet now she's spitting saliva on a stranger's penis and teasing his balls with her teeth just centimetres from a toilet bowl.

Perhaps I wasn't wrong, though. Perhaps she wasn't like that then, but she is like that now.

The thought hits a soft, wet wall. She's slid me into her without a condom and the sensory overload leaves no space for anything at all. It's all happening too fast and I look down at her waist and see the smooth brown skin against the fine pink lace panties bunched up in the valley where her pelvic bone begins.

My view of her face is blocked by the hair streaming down over her eyes, and I smell alcohol and something else – maybe me – on her breath which is hot and heavy as she pumps up and down and side to side like a rotary piston.

Everything goes white and my eyes are clamped shut and I can't hold it any longer. I explode deep into her and it feels like a sink being drained of every last drop. I groan and open my eyes and she's looking down with eyes and a mouth that are all contorted and saying 'is that it?' I try to catch my breath, but it is not easy because she presses on my chest as she climbs jaggedly off of me. She reaches down and severs some sheets of toilet paper to mop up the frothy cream dribbling down the inside of her leg.

Should I say something? What; thank you? It's such a pathetic scene, and before any words form, she is already adjusting her clothes and unlocking the door.

'I'll call you, Maya,' I yell after her. 'Really, I will.' She stops half-way through the open door and she turns to me, silences me with all the fury pooled in her features.

'It's Mayan, asshole,' she says. She's terrifying. 'Fuck you.'

I want to point out the irony of the statement, laugh a little even, to lighten the here and now, but a shaft of light blinds me through the doorway, and in its glare I see Lia, Ben, our apartment. My life.

What am I doing here?

'Hey,' says a head stuck through the doorway. 'It's our turn. Get out.'

The head is joined by another, loose with stimulants. His eyes grow wide at the sight of me in all my glory: my dick still wet and gleaming in the focused glow from the single spotlight directly above, my trousers down by my ankles. 'No,' he says with a smile as he pushes his partner in. 'He can stay.'

His hand is on my leg before I can fasten the button of my pants. My blood is pulsing wildly behind my eyes and the panic gripping me is relentless. I throw the thinner one against the wall and he breaks into a twisted laugh, his eyes and teeth ultraviolet. The music grows louder as if it is following me out, pushing me on. I grope through the queue to the toilet and faces turn to stare and laugh and fingers point. The dance floor seems so changed in the space of a few minutes – that veneer of seductive promise violently stripped to reveal something darker, more threatening. My chest refuses to draw in any more air. The music continues, but everyone seems to be frozen. Mayan is staring at me and so is her guy from the bar, the one I shoved down the stairs in a fit of misplaced bitterness. I feel like a lamb, seconds before its throat is slit.

'That's him! The guy that pushed me.'

When the blow arrives, it is so loud that even the music is cowed. My wrist pops as it hits the ground. There's no pain, and my brain switches to smaller things: the wet stickiness of the floor, the cigarette butts half-smoked, the scent of alcohol and human fluids. I roll onto my back as feet stomp away from me, clear a hole, and above me too many faces look down. For a moment I think they will help, but then a shoe connects with my temple and another knocks my head to the side, landing just above my eye.

Limbs move and the music fades back in through the momentary respite, now with two beats. One thumps with the lights flickering on the wall and the other flows with the blows, pounding at my face, my arms, my torso, my still-wet balls. There are too many for one person; he must have brought some friends.

I don't feel them and yet they keep coming as I scramble to my feet and haul myself towards the stairs, grasping wildly and scrambling at the furniture, flesh, walls, anything at all. A perfectly judged punch sends me sprawling onto the floor once more, but I don't let it completely halt my progress and I manage to get a hand up to the railing and climb, one foot after another, towards the sickly glow of the electric street lamp overhead.

Lior is surprised to see me. Deftly, he pulls aside the barrier as I barrel past and I can just about tell from the angry shrieks chasing me that he has bolstered my buffer. I wish to thank him, for his help, for his friendship, but I just keep moving, keep stumbling on and on to get as far away as my busted body will take me.

I don't get far. In the plaza of the Cinematech my feet give way and I collapse on a bench. My head is curved down by one side and I find I don't have the strength to lift it. A soft hand cups my forehead, helps me ease down against the wooden slats.

A familiar voice says, 'What did you do?'

'Milli,' I mumble, but I can't manage any more. There

are shouts behind us. She is standing over me, struggling against my pathetic movements with a confused concern. The adrenaline is already breaking down in my muscles and my bones, and I can feel an overwhelming stiffness spreading through my body. It seems to radiate outwards from my wrist. 'Help me.' I want to say more, but all the strength and dignity have deserted me.

All I am still capable of, is to cry.

The February rain is lashing down upon Tel-Aviv like retribution. Yonatan's is the gallery's first major exhibition of 2008, and the opening is at eight. He is late. He has already finished most of a bottle of cheap Cava, bought by the crate for a steep discount at a stall in Carmel Market. A few friends dropped by earlier, but they have tickets to the Balkan Beat Box at the Barbie, and though they have promised to swing by later, he knows only a few will.

He totters slightly in the short walk up Shenkin to the corner of Rothschild, crosses to the central strip and waves at the procession of passing cabs. There seem to be more than usual and three nearly pile into each other as they fight for his fare. He climbs into the back of a white Volkswagen, and settles in as he gives the driver his gallery's address on Gordon Street. It takes a few minutes to register they are heading the wrong way, south, into the gridlock where Tel-Aviv becomes Jaffa.

He protests a little too loud, smacks a seat back in frustration, swears at the driver and swivels in his seat, points through the window behind his head.

'It's my own opening,' he says, surprised by the pitch of his voice.

'*Al ti'dag*,' mumbles the driver. He can't seem to find anywhere to turn the car.

'What's wrong with you?' says Yonatan. 'It's Gordon. Not like I gave you a road name in Ajami.'

'I'm not from Tel-Aviv,' he says.

'Well what the hell are you doing picking people up here then?'

As he walks the driver through the one-way system, the radio is on, tuned to *Kol Israel*. Calm voices tell of rockets fired from Gaza to rain down on the communities of Israel's south. Finally, they are pointing north.

The alcohol churns in Yonatan's stomach.

'So you're from the south then?' His voice is overly soft, forgiving.

The back of the driver's head doesn't move.

'Bad down there?'

A pause. A nod.

'Life has stopped. All the time there are sirens, then a few seconds to get to a shelter. There's no work. Nobody goes out.' His shoulders shrug. 'But I need money. That's why I came up here.'

The city drifts by. It starts to drizzle and then rain. They pull up outside the gallery and Yonatan can see the owners, his parents, a smattering of friends and acquaintances, art critics and buyers all swirling behind the drop-smeared glass.

The meter reads nearly fifty shekels. It is far too high a sum for a short hop from the centre to the centre, but still he holds out a hundred and opens the door before the driver can count out change.

'I don't want your charity,' he says as Yonatan's door slams. 'You Tel-Avivis, you think you're better than us. You live in your own world.'

'You could just have said thank you,' Yonatan says.

'Fuck you,' yells the cab driver as Yonatan walks away, crosses the pavement. As he enters the gallery he is greeted with polite applause and a smattering of drunken cheers. The cab ride, the superfluous hundred, the south, the rockets, Gaza; it all fades, safely barricaded beyond the gallery doors.

My eyes are burning and everything is blurry as Milli helps me into the little security cubicle that blocks the entrance to Ichilov Hospital like a fallen tree. There's nothing interesting in my pockets – no keys, no wallet, no phone – so I don't even pause for the guard before lumbering forward through the metal detector. He doesn't try to stop me, doesn't pat me down, doesn't ask if I have a weapon, and I can't help thinking that's all it would take for a terrorist to blow this place up. A little self-immolation and a determined gait.

I limp my way towards Emergency. Giant letters, filthy with dust, tower over the hospital's buildings, spell out the names of dead, forgotten tycoons. A loose flagstone sends me messily to the side, and Milli has difficulty supporting my weight. I'm leaning heavily on her, and my leg and hand are throbbing. I try not to tally up the individual pains, prefer to let the constituent parts merge into a single smothering agony. The doors slide open and a commotion forces us to flatten ourselves against the reception desk with its bulletproof glass and its smudged fingerprints. Paramedics rush in from the ambulance bay, and an old man is wheeled in on a stretcher. He looks a bit like my father – his rotund belly like a mountain where he lies, bushy eyebrows and curved nose and sunspots on his bald head. A *kippa* dangles from its clip, hangs over his ear. He grasps at a gash above his temple, and blood is coursing from it still and soaking all his clothes in red. Some splotches are already a crusty brown.

'Where am I?' he keeps crying. 'Where am I?' again and again. 'There's been a mistake. I live at Ussishkin 28. Please. Take me home. My family is waiting.'

He claws at the paramedic and I really wish I had my phone to call my father.

'*Adoni*,' yells the woman at reception, her voice squeezed and grated through the grill in the protective glass. I don't have my *Teudat Zehut*, so I recite my ID number from memory as she types my details into the computer, bored and detached as she waits for it to spit out the sticker with my name and age, attaches it carelessly to a thin brown file which she slides back out to me on the other side of the divide. I limp through to the waiting area and the whole place is packed to bursting. All seats are occupied the walking wounded dutifully waiting their turn. Like me.

I push my leg out straight, use the wall to support my body as I slide down onto the floor. Somewhere smarts and I grimace: I've forgotten about my wrist.

'You still haven't told me what happened,' says Milli. She sits beside me, crosses her legs and pulls them in towards herself. She sniffs the antiseptic on the air, lifts the camera and begins snapping away with abandon. I am about to warn her to put it away, but then it occurs to me that everyone here has more important things to worry about. She doesn't bother with any of the trivialities – focus, shutter speed, aperture – and the purity is touching.

'I mean, I know you got fucked. Both ways. I can smell it on you.' She giggles. There's nothing to say, so I don't. I sit there and avoid eye contact with anyone, watching the bodies swirl around me like cars in a garage with insufficient mechanics. 'Why did you do it? I mean, I know you're married. Not that it matters, but still.'

I don't tell her that it does matter. That I feel remorse and shame. I fucked a stranger and now I'm in hospital, busted and broke, and all I want is for all the pain to go away.

A Russian lumbers through the doors from reception. He's filthy and his skin is slick and cratered, a frog's hide interrupted by heavy red sores. He slumps down beside us and I gag on the thick mix of urine, excrement and booze. He's prostrate but still murmuring and sometimes he shouts. It's unclear at who. Milli and I shuffle silently sideways, pivoting around an occupied stool to clear an exclusion zone between him and us, but still we cannot escape the stench that seems to have spoiled the air. A patch of darkness seeps through his filthy trousers, and he begins to laugh without self-consciousness. He seems to exist completely alone.

I can't take it any more. I pat Milli on the shoulder and she helps me to my feet and supports me outside. It must be long past midnight, but there is no respite from that choking summer heat that gut-punches me through the open door.

I was last here during one of those week-long winter storms. It was nearing its end and there was a freshness to the city that smelt like rejuvenation, that kind that only blesses us once, maybe twice a year. Lia was breathing heavily – in and out, in and out – just like she'd been taught. Her eyes were closed, and she was silent, calm and still. I couldn't contain my excitement and awe as I watched her, as we prepared to welcome our son into the world. The windows were still wet with the dregs of the rain as she groaned and grunted Ben into life.

I tore off my tee-shirt, held his naked body to my skin. Joy exploded through me as I felt him breathing, the clamped chord dangling from his belly. So much love: for Ben, for her. Overwhelmed by the miracle. So close to them, in those first moments of his life.

But there too was the fear. And as the terror grew, so did the isolation. I missed the life I had before, the connectedness Lia and I shared. When the whole world seemed just us.

What kind of a father does that make me?

Tears collect in my eyes again. A Filipina walks past and

pushes us into the road. She's speaking loudly in Tagalog into a mobile phone, pushing a wheelchair, ambivalent to the man housed within. He's an awful sight: slumped and cowed, tufts of salt-and-pepper hair shooting in all directions atop his head. A cigarette is clamped in his thin grey lips and its lit end sprays ash onto his chequered hospital gown. He whines pathetically with every revolution of the wheels, and his hands claw at a bandaged stump where, until recently, his left leg must have been. I want to say something, make him feel even a tiny bit better, but can't think of anything that doesn't sound pathetic, condescending, or both.

Milli points the camera at me and the shutter clicks, whirs, falls silent; the picture will be much too dark.

We skirt the Russian alcoholic and make our way back to the reception area. A nurse is looking for us and she is angry, though we are not necessarily the cause. Her eyes flick around the room even as she scans my file, snaps it shut, hands it back and beckons us over to a series of beds in the corner, each separated by blue curtains. She does not wait for me to clamber up before opening a barrage of personal questions, notes the noncommittal answers on her pad. Milli sits patiently to one side as the nurse takes my temperature and my blood pressure, then leaves.

We are left alone with the groans from the next door bed. I pull the curtain aside just a crack and see the old man from the gurney laid out beside us. Machines beep erratically. There's a mask on his face so his words are garbled and his eyes are like a cow's, raving and rolling in their sockets. He's no longer alone: a boy hovers beside him, softly caressing his hand. His features are dark but his face is white as the sheet upon which the old man lies, and he stares down blankly at the contortions of agony. Above them, a clock reads 01:30. It is earlier than I thought.

I push the curtain a little further to the side as if a clearer, more complete view will decode the mysteries of the curious scene. The man is most certainly a Jew – he's still wearing his *kippah* though someone has returned it to his head, but the boy is an Arab, and a young one at that, raised during the last Intifada. I have an aching desire to interrupt myself into their story, but suspect their relationship will not survive to see the sun rise.

This hospital is an airport: a transit point for arrivals and departures.

My curtain rustles and the doctor slips through. Like the nurse he doesn't look at me, only at his board, but at least he tries to crack a smile. He can't have shaved in a week and there's a hint of ginger on the tips of his brown whiskers. His eyes sit in deep-dish crows' nests and his pupils are far too large for the harsh, bright light shining down from the fluorescent tube directly above. He must be my age, give or take a few years. Underpaid and overworked, he looks like he would have justification to be in a tent on Rothschild preaching social justice. I feel so upset for him, angry even, on his behalf.

'You look tired,' I say, though the observation feels like an imposition.

A nurse is passing. Without breaking her stride, she says, 'His wife had a baby three days ago. That's why he's working nights.'

The doctor turns, and the two share the warmth of a smile, a fleeting instant of mutual affection as she disappears.

'Congratulations,' I say, but the moment has passed.

He looks at me crookedly and then quips, 'Good time tonight?'

I feel it only right to laugh; too hard. I stay quiet while he examines my head and my legs, but the pressure he places on my wrist makes me jump from the bed and rustle the curtain of our neighbouring opera.

'That doesn't look good,' he says, and he makes a note on his pad and then tears it off and points me down the corridor, past where the alcoholic is still lying on the floor, spread out like a sodden rag. The sign says X-Ray and before me are a middle-aged woman with no obvious injuries and a group of young boys. They are grinning like idiots despite their wounds, the bandages wrapping their legs and arms.

'Don't worry, *motek*,' the woman says to me with a kind smile. '*Yihiye Beseder.*' It'll be OK.

She is dealt with first, and the group is dispatched quickly. Then it is my turn to be ushered in through the door. It's stark in here: a metal table with the most inhospitable of padding for bum, head, arms and legs, and a recessed section shielded from the radiation.

The radiologist is an old religious man. He is small, hunched, a thick beard below his ringlets and his *kippah*, the threads of *tzitziot* oozing out from his untucked shirt. He drags over a chair and bends my arm this way and that, pulls down the machine and a target in lights appears just above the most painful part of my wrist.

He checks his work, nods, pats me on the offending wrist, and leaves me to head behind his little barricade.

There's a hiss, a click and whir, then he's back with a picture and a bit of paper. He pulls me by the arm and pushes me back outside.

'*Chag sameach*,' he says, Happy holiday, and I can't tell if he's being facetious. There's nothing to celebrate in this seemingly endless summer. If I want to ask, I've already missed my opportunity: the door has been slammed in my face.

The doctor is hovering by the reception so I thrust all I'm carrying into his surprised arms and stand there waiting for his prognosis. His worn-out, bloodshot eyes scan it all and then he tells me what he and I both already know. My wrist is broken. *Chag sameach.*

The nurse will sort me out, he says, and she does, seating me down beside the alcoholic to encase my throbbing arm in plaster and cotton wool. As she curls the wet white goo around my fingers there is an alarm that jolts the patients in the emergency room. Milli springs to her feet, grabs her camera like Robert Capa at Normandy, but then doesn't know where to go. As the alarm continues to blare, the Arab kid throws his curtain to one side. His mouth is open as if he's screaming but there's no noise emerging from his bloodless lips.

'I think there's something wrong,' I say to the nurse still working my arm, but she looks over her shoulder with a face that says that she's been here too long and that the boy's problem is not her problem. She is finishing, checks her work with little pride, and places a packet of painkillers on the tray by my side.

'One every four hours,' she says.

'Please.' The boy is yelling now, in that hard, clipped Hebrew of the Arab. 'Help him! Help him!' He turns back and after what feels like an age, doctors and nurses pile in with the weight of elephants going to die.

But not I, no; not Milli. The terror upon the boy's face is too excruciating to watch, and as I catch a glimpse beyond the curtain of the man in the grey rattle of death, I grab her around the waist with my good arm and, stepping lightly over the alcoholic so as not to wake him from the fathomless slumber that even the alarm could not disturb, we make our way out into the fetid night. We no longer wish to intrude in a narrative not our own.

The opening is heralded as a great success, and the write-ups that follow are roundly positive. For a while, Yonatan is a minor celebrity, among a few interlocking Tel-Aviv spheres at least. A Haaretz journalist calls for an interview to be published in the Friday weekend edition. They meet at a kiosk on Rothschild, laugh and flirt, and though the profile only appears in truncated form in April 2008, they fall into a relationship. The passion burns bright and hot.

Neither are capable of controlling their hands. Their life is a series of constant interruptions: blow jobs in dark alleys beneath the watchful eyes of Tel-Aviv's innumerable stray cats; oddly angled limbs pressed against misty windows, her car rocking on Tel-Baruch beach as the inky sea laps at the foot of the cliff and the aged prostitutes warm themselves with fire kindled in old steel barrels. Every conversation is concluded with sex, and their lust draws them into isolation, severs them from the city.

They are mid coupling when his phone rings. At first he ignores it, lets it ring through to voicemail, but it rings again and again. It interrupts first her orgasm, then his, then hers again. When he finally answers he hears his mother's rapid breathing, heavy and strained. Something is wrong.

The girl drives him to Tzfat in her car.

She soon gives up trying to draw him into conversation.

'I'll be here for you,' she says, somewhere around Afula. 'I love you.'

Yonatan finds his father in his hospital bed, pipes and tubes zigzagging across the blue and white hospital pyjamas that clothe his body. His skin is ashen grey, his imposing bulk diminished by the harshness of the blue institutional light. A machine above his head chirrups insistently.

Yonatan's mother hugs him. She seems so feeble, so fragile; she waits to be introduced to the girl but he is lightheaded, finds he cannot place her name. Instead, he watches dispassionately as they stumble through awkward introductions, takes a seat on the hard, easy-clean hospital chair and stares at his father, abruptly laid low. The girl sits politely beside him, checks her phone despite the lack of cellphone signal.

When Yonatan leaves to find a soda, she follows him outside.

'Do you have anything to say to me?' she says.

'About what?'

'What I said.' After a while: 'In the car.'

A bottle clatters through the machine. Yonatan bends down to retrieve it.

'I think I should go,' she says.

'That's a good idea,' he says. 'I'll be here for a while.'

She stands there, waiting, and he watches her. He can see her spirit harden.

'Is that what you want?' she says, finally.

We sit cross-legged under a tree, each blade of grass a shard of glass pricking my skin. My joints and tendons ache; I realise I haven't sat like this since I was a child.

The camera clicks again.

'Please stop it,' I say.

Kikar Hamedina is deserted and though a few shops in the inverted triangle buildings have left their lights on, it's a pitiful imitation of life. The black windows are befitting of an area populated by the city's aged well-to-do, returned from the suburbs to flee their giant empty homes. I lie on my back and watch the bats swoop here and there and here between the ficus trees. A waking dream in the darkness: of somewhere with space; huge deserts that can swallow me invisibly, that aren't mere scrubland, dotted with Bedouins in conurbations of unacknowledged shacks; oceans not seas and narrow straits. Where the guys on the outside looking in don't want me dead.

Milli offers me a can of beer but I don't want to drink. She's finished two Goldstars already and I watch as she works on her third.

'Thanks for staying with me tonight,' I say.

'That's OK,' she says. 'At least it wasn't boring.'

The drained can clatters as she tosses it over onto the pile.

'Are you happy?' I ask her. The question takes us both by

surprise.

She tilts her head up, stares at the bats.

'I guess,' she says. 'I'm nineteen. I'm in the Army. I'll be free in six months and then I can do what I want. I'll work for a while, make some money, then maybe I'll go to India. Thailand. After, who knows?' She shrugs. 'I don't really think about it like that, but I guess you could say that I'm happy.' She takes a sip. 'And what about you? You've got a wife, kids—'

'A kid,' I correct her. 'A boy.'

'So what set you off on this,' she draws quotation marks with her fingers, 'adventure?'

I think of Lia and Ben back home, of the empty space beside her on the bed. How everything changed when Ben was born. How all the failures and uncertainties, they suddenly mattered so much more.

'Life,' I say. 'You know.'

'Tell me about your kid then.'

'Ben. His name is Ben.'

'How old?'

'Six months.' Give or take.

'You must love him.'

'I do.'

It's there. It exists. Sometimes, as he sleeps in my arms, it's so pure and concentrated that it threatens to slice a hole through my gut. I hold him and smell his skin and feel the softness of his hair and I realise I know nothing about him and I wonder where the love comes from. I fear that it must be borne solely out of some sense of obligation.

'What's he like?'

I don't have anything to say, so I start slowly, with words that sound empty to my ears. 'He's happy. Smiles a lot. Always ready to laugh. Unless you put him down.' Then it comes faster. 'He doesn't like to be left alone, to feel like he's being excluded. And he started talking recently. Not really talking, but he makes these sounds at exactly the right time, you know? Like he's taking part in the conversation. And he's got these eyes, they just stare at you, like he gets everything. Like he sees right through you. They're just so… wise.'

It suddenly strikes me that I miss him very much.

'And your wife?'

'She's tough,' I say, and I laugh a little. 'Tough. But also sweet. And smart. And loving. And supportive. And a great mother.' I shake my head, rub my eyes with my un-cast hand. 'What have I done?'

Milli takes my hand in hers, strokes the back of my palm.

'Don't be so hard on yourself. It's fine. You're only human, and this is Tel-Aviv. Anything can happen here. People can fuck up. What's a little minor infidelity?' The word scolds. 'You love her, you love your son. Just pick yourself up and carry on. There's nothing here you can't forgive yourself for. Just don't tell her. It's better that way. She never has to know.'

She pulls me towards her in a hug.

'Thank you,' I mumble into her neck.

'It's fine. Really.'

I hug her closer until I am scared the brittle hardness of my cast will pain her back.

'You could've left me, but…'

A song I don't recognise erupts in her bag and I feel a tremendous loss as she pulls away, fishes around inside for her phone. I wonder who the song is by, realise I know little of current music, that my own tastes have been moving backwards in time.

The phone is to her ear and her head is cocked to the side so that she can wedge it between her cheek and her shoulder while she uses her free hand to open a fresh Goldstar. As she drinks, she wraps the camera's strap around its heavy, metal body and stuffs it into her bag.

'Hey Sweetie,' she's saying, '*ma hamatzav*? What's up?'

The sounds she is making are new: sharp, acidic, but tinged with a fake sweetness like sucrazit syrup. Up an octave, down a nasal passage, like a strangled bird. It doesn't sound like her voice, and her whole face has changed too: pinched in at its sharp edges, eyes wider and glassy; dead, with a long history of disinterest.

Her mouth opens wide and expels a violent banshee wail of laughter. I don't like this Milli nearly as much.

'*Yalla*,' she says. 'We'll be there soon. *Neshikot!*'

The phone drops from her ear, and the girl I know looks at me quizzically.

'What?' she says. 'You coming?'

'Where?'

'The Akirov Towers. Danielle's there. We're going to join her. Danielle,' she says, squinting at me with what may be incredulity, may be a bit of dust from this dustiest of cities in her eye. 'The girl I was with. Before. She went with Maoz? You know Maoz, right?'

Somewhere along the way my sense of humour has deserted me.

I don't want to see Maoz again. Perhaps she can go alone. I could just stay here and fall asleep under the stars. Or go home. I want to go home.

Against my will I let her offer me a hand, take my weight and pull me up. I push up with my sheathed wrist and the pain ricochets around my body like a stray bullet. It's as if the plaster has become a part of me, has grown nerves.

'You should take those painkillers,' Milli says, and her face is all motherly with concern, reminds me of Lia in the instant.

I can't, though. I forgot them in the hospital as the old man was dying.

The wave of pain subsides to a dull throbbing, and I find its physicality comforting. I focus on it as we walk, only to find a sharp little stone has wedged its way into one of my pink flip-flops. It stabs with each step.

I don't bother calling for Milli to wait as I hop on one leg and pry it away with my fingernails.

Yonatan's father's recovery from the heart attack is slow and arduous. He returns to his childhood home, eerie in its comfortable, secure familiarity. His own sheets, bed, room; the unalterable inertia of personal history. His mother exists in a twilight world. In that two-storey house perched atop the rocky hill, she cooks, cleans, lumbers about, complains, as if her husband of over three decades is out shopping; at the hospital she is mournful, silent, visibly diminished.

Yonatan is soon accustomed to the routine mechanics of his father's incapacitation. The laboured breathing, the beeping of the machines, the timetables of the nurses, the doctors, their checks and adjustments. When he awakens, begins to groan and yell to Yonatan from his bed, the new sounds come as a surprise.

From his chair in the corner, he can sense his father's anger, feels it build in the prostrate body. Hours pass before the dry mouth is lubricated enough to permit first furious words, and then furious sentences, fired rapidly.

'You're a disgrace. Fool. No wife. Nothing. To have such a joke of a son. Cursed.'

Round and round the words lick. A nurse enters, cleans the giant wound that slices his father from belly to neck like a gutted deer. Her intervention does not halt the torrent.

After a while, the words bounce off Yonatan like droplets of rain on saturated soil. He stands slowly, takes the time to stretch his back, his neck, leaves as a hum reverberates in his ear. On the way to the bus he stops for a coffee, makes small talk with the pretty girl behind the counter. At home, he pulls a hidden box from his cupboard, leafs through the old love letters it holds. They raise a smile, the memories of Efrat, of young love, teenage infatuation.

He is in the kitchen when his mother returns, watches as she immerses herself in her patterns of domestic denial.

'Thank you for staying,' she says. She doesn't look at him as she speaks.

She empties the dishwasher. Chipped and faded plates clatter as they are placed in overstuffed drawers.

'He's my father.'

'It must have hurt. Hearing those things he said.'

'I knew them already.'

She has finished the crockery, empties the cutlery now. Her back is to him.

'He's just worried about you.' A pause. Some clattering from the topmost drawer. 'We both are.'

'It's not your place, Mum.'

'I know.' Glass now. 'But we're getting old and all we want is to see you settled, living your own life. Maybe if you weren't so lost, if we didn't love you so much...' She leans down, pulls a step out from beside the fridge, stretches up to place the better cups onto a shelf at the top of the cabinet. 'Maybe then this wouldn't have happened.'

He tries to catch her eye, but she avoids his gaze.

'Mum,' he says. Something catches. 'Are you blaming his heart attack on me?'

She slams the dishwasher door, fumbles in the cupboard for a vacuum cleaner.

'I'm not saying that, *ahuv sheli*. I'm just saying that we love you. Your father and I.'

As she leaves the kitchen, she stops briefly by his chair, places a kiss on Yonatan's damp forehead. Then she is wrapped in the cloak of the Hoover's whir.

They don't speak again in the days he remains in the North. As soon as the doctor says that his father's riskiest days have passed, Yonatan walks himself to the bus stop at the foot of town. He no longer remembers the bus schedule, so he waits patiently, watches the sun drift down behind the hills of the Galilee, set somewhere over Haifa. The Eged bus creeps down the northern mountains and hills to the flat coastal plains of Israel's centre, to the phlegm-coloured urban lattice of Tel-Aviv's streets.

He opens the door to the musty smell of his locked apartment. When he closes his eyes to sleep that night, he finds his mother and father occupying the hallways of his head.

The doors whoosh open and the lobby is all deserted, like the roads on the short walk from Kikar Hamedina. The spotlights create translucent, glowing pools on the white floor. I shiver from the sudden change of season wrought by the air-conditioning. There's a lot of empty space and a lot of marble but only four rectangular chairs of steel and pleather, the cold welcome of fifty families.

A man in a sand-coloured uniform perches behind a sweeping desk upon a bolstered dias of black-veined stone. He stares at us suspiciously and it's clear we are an undesirable interruption to the calm and quiet of his night guarding the residents of these famous buildings, their name synonymous with ex-prime ministers and rich Russians. Our oligarchs and theirs. I shift self-consciously in my pink flip-flops.

He's a common guard dog.

'Can I help you?' says his mouth, while his whole being says 'turn around and don't let the doors bite on the way out.'

I can't seem to speak, but Milli is unfazed. She smiles politely and gives Maoz's name.

'He's expecting us,' she says. 'You can call him if you want.'

Her sing-song voice hits all the right notes and with a scowl the doorman points us towards the row of elevators and says: 'Eighth floor.'

I punch the numbers on the lift's key pad, enjoying the give beneath my fingers as I press the zero and the eight and the enter. We whoosh up and the digital numbers roll down like they're on an old circular roller. I'm mesmerised. The little detail is delightful in this city of maspik tov, good enough.

I'm reluctant to leave when the elevator slides to a well-damped stop, and I only follow Milli into the corridor when she has already knocked on the door several times. Loud techno music plays through into the hall. My head throbs; my wrist too. I should have ended tonight beneath that tree in Kikar Hamedina, ensconced in the anonymity of the city's nocturnal quiet.

'Look Milli…' I begin to say, but before I can finish, the music becomes louder and Maoz is standing, naked from the waist up, leaning against the frame of the open door.

There's a layer of sweat coating his skin and it glints in the light. His eyes are glassy but the pupils are huge and the irises are tiny, just like ten-shekel coins. He grins and I swear, in the uneven light, shadows sprout horns from his head.

'*Gever*!' he yells. As he moves to hug me I watch his muscles flex and relax, moving like a machine. I brace myself for the dampness of his hard body and grimace as my clothes lift and separate from me, stick to him. There's a faint, sickening sucking sound as we part, and then he looks at Milli.

'Come. Come in.'

White everywhere: the expensive furniture, the gleaming oven and fridge and cooker. They all look suitably displaced from a magazine, all glossy and sterile and unloved but it all feels cramped, as if attainability hobbled aspiration. Perhaps the other half don't live so differently after all; they just have concierges to limit who sees.

'Danielle?' says Milli, and Maoz points her down a corridor. She withdraws with a contrived curtsey. I share the living room with two others, and if I can't quite place one, I certainly recognise the second. It's a face I haven't seen for a long time; one I'd hoped I wouldn't see for a good time longer. Forever.

For a moment I hope she won't recognise me, but as her eyes flick up towards me from the mountain of ash and butts in the ashtray before her, I see she recalls only too well.

'Hello you,' she says, the hint of a smile in the raised corners of her mouth.

'Hi Anat,' I say.

I met her five years ago, five minutes after introducing myself to Maoz. We were all slouched outside the Tel-Aviv University Economics faculty in the dissipating late summer heat, squeezed into the sliver of shade provided by the building's brutal concrete boils. Shooting the shit, as you do with people you've only just met, and you're young and eager to live tall and broad. Anat demanded a cigarette, and both Maoz and I fumbled for our packets. I provided the smoke, Maoz the sex. That night at least.

She was always alluring. Still is. So different, so possessed; unflappable self-assurance cloaked in pale skin, wrapped in impossibly expensive clothes. I've seen people with all the money in the world wear designers and catwalk couture and look like a joke, but not Anat. She doesn't just wear wealth and entitlement, she breathes it.

Her grandfather had just died and she'd donned his fame like a bracelet that glittered in the sun and shade alike, bounced into the dark monochrome of our world and stated with impeccable sincerity, and not a trace of irony: I'm better than you.

'You look like shit,' she says to me, and I know she means more than my wrist and my battered face.

'Thanks.' I want to add something about how she looks bad too, but she looks sensational, and knows it. So instead I point to the man sitting next to her on the couch and say, 'Who's this?'

He shifts uncomfortably, wiggles in place and makes the leather squeak. He half raises himself from the chair and holds out a hand.

'Hi,' he says, a voice smooth and assured. 'I'm Roi.'

'My cousin,' says Anat. She doesn't look up from the

cigarette she has begun dissecting, from the plant stem she's sheering to remove the seeds. She's claiming ownership over him, like a puppy.

I seem to know him, but I can't quite place from where. He's short and bald and a little overweight.

There's a chair beside the window and I pull it up. Outside, the city is dark save hundreds of little lights which twinkle in tiny squares. Each is a window, each is a story, but it's impossible to piece together the humanity from up here.

A door opens and a girl enters from what must be Maoz's bedroom. Danielle is wearing not much, and the towel draped over her falls unnaturally and opens at some provocative places. She looks at us all, does a once-around as if searching for something and then turns back, disappears back into the room.

'So,' says Anat. Her eyes are narrow as they follow the girl on her trip. 'What have you been up to?'

The friendliness of her tone is disconcerting. I recognise that rough edge of hostility that always lurked beneath. Perhaps if I had recognised it before, I would not have been tricked into consoling her that night. I wouldn't have let her lure me into that giant bed with those soft satin sheets and the four pillows, two fluffy and light, and two as heavy and unforgiving as rocks. I wouldn't have kissed her as we curled together and rocked backwards and forwards and up and down in something like an uneven rhythm, wouldn't have rationalised away my friendship with my friend – yes, I called Maoz my friend then – as something false and unimportant when faced with what I thought looked and smelled and tasted, and felt, like love. In my narrative that night, I was her saviour: this poor little rich girl with her beauty and her money and her misery and her abusive boyfriend. I was her salvation.

Maoz stands behind her. The coke is doing its work and he is talking to the air, his arms swinging with pointless purpose. His muscles move even when he's standing still, even when his arms wrap around Anat's shoulders, when he presses his head beside her.

'Quiet, Maoz,' she says, jutting her chin out towards me. 'Yonatan's just telling me what he's been up to.' She slaps a hand to one side and catches his nose. The family of diamonds on her fingers, on her wrist, catches the light.

'I'm a photographer,' I say.

She looks at me with that self-same sneer that I awoke to that morning years ago.

'You wouldn't have seen his work,' says Maoz. He's up and thrusting like the chief at a Zulu gathering. 'Nobody has.'

They are perfect together.

'A photographer. Really?'

The other one – what was his name… Roi – is talking to me. Anat has finished rolling her joint and has lit it, shaken it, spat the first weeds from her mouth. The smoke is thick and curls around her gleaming eyes.

'Yes,' I say, agitated, searching for Milli who is nowhere to be found. I want to ask her to join me, to leave. I don't want to stay here but I don't want to be alone. 'You could say that.'

He asks me if I know someone. I don't, but he keeps pressing.

'It's just that she had an exhibition this evening and I could have sworn I saw you there.'

He's not at all like his cousin. He's measured, wary even, but there's no sign of malice. Still, his words trigger a cold electric panic. We are in terrible danger.

I nod, though he hasn't asked me anything further, and stand up to frantically search for Milli. The apartment has a corridor that spears off at a right angle and I can't make anything out past the corner.

'Sit down,' says Anat. I do as I'm told.

'So, are you a photographer too?' I say, playing for time.

'No,' he says, 'I mean yes but not like you. Not professional or anything.' I'm still looking for Milli so an uncomfortable silence falls.

He's blushing and I let him stew. I want to draw this out as long as I can, so I have an excuse to avoid any overtures from

Anat. So I can warn Milli.

'Well that's nice. Keep it up.'

Where is she?

'I'm in finance. Hedge funds, but I just love taking photos, you know?'

I nod, although I want to tell him to go back to his world of suits and healthy bonus cheques and Porsches and Ferraris and boats and planes.

The bedroom door opens and my heart catches in my throat. Only Danielle dressed in a tee-shirt which hangs down past her knees and whose sleeves stretch nearly to her wrists. She clambers over the back of the sofa, plops cross-legged beside Anat who shifts in her seat. She leans forward and helps herself to a cigarette from Anat's full pack. I want to warn her but it's already too late. Anat has been slighted and is hungry for blood.

'So where did Maoz pick you up?' Anat says.

'The tent city. He was giving a talk.'

Anat snorts. 'He doesn't believe in any of that socialist shit, deary. He's rich you know. Like me. Only says crap like that to sleep with girls like you.'

Danielle steps over the barb and continues smoking her cigarette, nonplussed.

'What did he have to say to sleep with you?' she says with infinite sweetness.

'You wouldn't catch me there with all those people. It's vulgar.'

Anat's nostrils flare.

'You're right. I guess we should all have had rich grandparents. Then we wouldn't have to worry about our futures and we could all live in places like this.'

Anat cackles. 'My place is nicer, *motek*,' she says. She doesn't realise that she's fallen for the trap. Alone in her victory, Danielle keeps smiling.

Milli comes bouncing down the corridor.

'Does anyone...' she begins.

Roi leans forward and touches my shoulder.

'Actually,' he says, 'maybe you could help me. I had a camera stolen tonight and if you could keep an eye out for it…'

Of course he'd have to say it, to breathe it into the world and set fate in all her mischief scurrying into action. No sooner has the last word set itself free than Milli's toe catches a side table and she yells in pain. Falling forward, she throws out her arms to protect herself. Her bag slides from her shoulder and crashes noisily to the ground, barfing its contents onto the white rug.

'Hey,' yells Anat, her finger already uncurled and her body sprung from the couch as she lunges towards the camera. 'Isn't that the one they nicked?'

Roi seems a bit puzzled, a bit surprised, a bit overwhelmed. He looks at me, all wide eyes, then looks at Milli, feels for an imaginary strap on his shoulder. It's obvious that he's put all the pieces together now, that he's connected the camera to my drunken tiff with the artist and our quick escape. He knows. Nevertheless, he seems reluctant to feed us to the lions.

'No,' he says, the word accompanied by an unsteady laugh. 'I'm sure it's not. It's too much of a coincidence.'

'Sure this is it,' Anat shrieks as she picks it up, studies it, shows it to him. 'See, that there says 0.95. Like yours. You said it was a big deal. Went on and on and on and on about it. You wouldn't shut up.'

Maoz is stretching his arms, fingertips locked together, eyeing the scene and pacing like a big cat. He takes the camera and the mood in the room is charged. I know high Maoz. I'm scared of high Maoz.

'No, really,' says Roi trying to back-pedal, to diffuse the clock ticking like the blood beating in my ears. 'It's not like they only made one. I'm sure there's some mistake.'

But there isn't, and he's too late. The night is too late. It's all too fucking late.

Danielle shrieks, jumps back behind the sofa and nearly knocks it over. She's clearly terrified for Maoz has pounced upon Milli, is grasping her hair and thumping her head against the floor. She yells in pain, but it's all drowned out by the horrible, savage screams escaping from his gullet.

'You little bitch! You think that's funny? You think that's OK? You fucking thief. You think you can steal from me? From her? From him?'

His voice keeps rising until it's straining and screeching and crashing against the ceiling of his stimulant-infested rage. We're all begging him to stop – all except Anat – but he's railing against Milli relentlessly. A sickening thud rises every time her head connects with the marble floor. Red is leaking from her, pooling like lacquer on the white. Her teeth have pierced her lip and it looks like they are smeared with a slick, glossy lipstick.

Danielle jumps over the sofa, over Anat. She tries to pull Maoz away, but he turns, shoves her back and she is sprawling too. Then Anat is on her, pinning her down.

I want to do something, to say something, to scream, but there are tears streaming down my cheeks and my voice has fled. Every last vestige of vitality has been sucked from me. All I can do is pull my legs in close and whimper like an animal.

'Stop it!' yells Roi. 'Jesus. Stop. Or I'm going to call the police.' But Maoz and Anat are not listening, or if they hear they don't care. Their eyes are cold and dark and red with the reflection of the blood which is now smeared across the floor.

Its colour stays with me even when I close my eyes. I hum to myself as I rock slowly backwards and forwards, backwards and forwards, backwards and forwards.

'You. Yonatan. Help me for God's sake,' says Roi, and I open my eyes to see him standing there over me, his arms outstretched, beseeching me. 'Do something!'

I rise to my feet but my legs feel wrapped in cement, and though I want to dive in, to help Roi drag Maoz off Milly's still writhing body, I can't. I can only watch, petrified. The motions are slurred and then I find that I am moving, but not towards them. No.

'Where are you going?' Roi's voice a desperate yell. 'Come back!'

A neighbour is poking his head from the next apartment and he may ask me about the racket, or he may just stare. The door closes behind me and with it all the yells and the beatings fade with each step as if a receding bad dream.

I don't want to wait for the lift so I find the stairs and climb down twelve flights as quickly as my bruised leg will allow. A few times I nearly fall into the wall but my cast-covered wrist protects me and I just keep going, one leg after the other, step by step. And still the tears flow because they can't be stopped and I'm still crying when I pass the concierge. He does not approve, but I have no time to consider how a bruised and battered thirty-year-old must look, crying as he limps from one of Israel's most prestigious addresses, because I have to get out of this twelve-storeyed torture chamber, and as far away as I can.

The doors slide open and as the heat hits me like a battering ram I try to fill my lungs with the damp air. Instead of cleansing me it suffocates me with the heaviness of all I've seen and I lean over and vomit in the lamplight.

Yonatan's work suffers. For weeks he sits in his studio, stares at the vast empty white walls, the empty ceiling, the cracks in the grey cement floor. He used to close his door to signal to the building that he was busy, now it is wedged open with a chair. Many of the inhabitants of the giant repurposed meta-slum have taken up near-permanent positions on the couch he dragged in from the street. They are a rag-tag collection: artists and musicians, the dog-eared husband and wife team who print the photographs he does not expose himself, time-worn prostitutes on their way to and from the sleepless brothel constantly expanding through the fifth floor.

Weeks evaporate in a haze of drugs and drink, always plentiful, payment for his infinite hospitality. His only rule: no injecting. He gathers everyone together, reiterates the point on finding discarded needles (used) in the bathroom. He no longer goes home, but rather sleeps on the sofa or on the mattress pushed into a corner, a mattress he does not remember buying. When he does leave, he ventures out only a few blocks, to the local *AM:PM* store, or the unsanitary lean-tos between the scuzzy garages for a falafel or a schwarma. Occasionally, he tries to wander the area's streets with his camera, watching the foreign workers, the micro-factories and openly for-sale sex. Inspiration is invisible in plain sight.

His father's words still reverberate deeply. The creeping sense of directionlessness has choked off his creativity, depriving it of oxygen.

One night, high on pungent, purple aquaponic weed, he signs up to the new Facebook social network. He uploads a flattering picture of himself and thinks of who to look up first. He recalls the love letters found forgotten in his parents' house; Efrat still goes by her family name. He clicks through her public photos. She is instantly recognisable, still very much the beautiful girl he was so besotted with all those years ago. He sends a friend request and waits, dulling the long-forgotten pangs of excitement that churn his stomach with another joint.

He awakes the next morning to find that she has accepted his request, has sent him a solitary smiley face. He returns to the computer constantly for the rest of the day, composing and recomposing a three-line message until he can bear it no longer and clicks "send". The hours until she replies are excruciating, but her reply is warm and sweet and riddled with nostalgia. Over the coming days they ping-pong back and forth, the conversation's constituent parts becoming shorter, more frequent, leaning into the intimacy they once shared.

A few whiskies with a neighbour sees Yonatan boldly suggest a dinner the following week. Several more whiskies follow. Time expands with no reply, a round hardness settles in his intestines. The computer finally beeps after a short forever, and Yonatan trips heavily in his haste to reach it.

He books a table at Hotel Montefiore, has his shirt laundered and pressed, buys new trainers from a shop on Bograshov Street. On the night, he arrives early. His heart beats fast as he takes a seat and orders an Old Fashioned to fortify his courage. He hasn't smoked weed in days and his head is too clear. She arrives and he stumbles to his feet, pulls out her chair. His hands shake. She looks fresher than her pictures, and as he leans in to peck her cheek, he smells that long lost scent, and all the forgotten emotions come roaring back.

She orders, he orders. They reminisce and flirt playfully as the courses arrive.

'Do you remember that night we broke into that old house on the Kinneret? What was it called?' he says between bites of his steak. Of course he remembers its name.

'Villa Melchett,' she says. 'We made a fire, cooked sausages and set sleeping bags down by the water.'

'We didn't just sleep,' he says. They both laugh and she covers her mouth with her hand.

'That was an amazing night,' she says. She looks down, plays with some scraps on an empty plate.

'I never told you, but that was my first time,' he says. 'You were my first.'

'I had my suspicions,' she says. 'But you always had a good game.'

Her hand rests beside her on the table. He moves his own forward so it covers hers.

'Why did we ever split up?'

She pulls her hand away, slides it beneath the tablecloth.

'Oh no no no no no,' she says. Her head swings slightly side to side. Her eyes are closed. 'Yonatan… We… I… I thought we were just teasing. Having a bit of fun.'

He listens quietly as she tells him of her fiancé, the wedding plans, their four-year relationship. 'I don't believe in marriage,' she says. Her smile is incandescent, and a cold chill descends upon him, spreads out to freeze even his fingers and his toes. 'But he's a hopeless romantic and I just want to make him happy.'

'So what are you doing here?' he says. The chill is in his voice too.

'I used to love you. I really did. And I missed you. I just thought maybe we could be friends.'

'Why aren't you wearing a ring?'

'Are you serious?' She rolls her eyes. 'It's Tel-Aviv in the twenty-first century, Yonatan. I don't need a symbol of someone's ownership over me.'

The dessert arrives, profiteroles to share. They eat without a word. When the bill arrives, she insists on paying her half.

'It was lovely to see you, Yonatan.' She holds out her hand for him to shake.

He returns to his studio, sits by the computer for hours considering whether or not to delete his Facebook account. He blames it for resuscitating their relationship, one that should have been left to die, but falls asleep before making a decision. The next day he begins packing up his things and then abruptly cancels his lease, does not even say farewell to those with whom he has shared so much of his recent time.

The old merchant on Allenby, down where the road kinks towards the sea, drives a hard bargain and, worn by his persistence, Yonatan sells the camera his parents bought him for less than he knows it's worth. He visits a shiny showroom in Ramat Hahayal where he buys a new body and lens kit specialised in capturing images in ultra-low light. During the day he sleeps, at night he prowls the city, photographing the destitute and despairing. He ignores the growing ranks of Africans, the Arabs and the Chinese workers, focuses his camera on Jews at the fringes of society.

Soon he is forced into Dizengoff Center to double his digital storage, and then double it again. Tel-Aviv, so compact and dense, so full of stories of love and joy, is equally as sodden with misery. The more he sees, the more he notices, the more he shoots. He keeps his distance, maintains a detachment that, he convinces himself, will improve the objective quality.

I steady my breathing in time with the lapping waves. In as the wave breaks and rushes ashore, out as it washes back to sea. The beach is quiet. I can see a barbecue somewhere towards the north, but my only company is a young couple upon the sand in the mid-stages of undress, their bodies intertwined like overgrown roots. Not long now till the sun rises behind us, and when it does they will first feel warm, and then hot, and then parched, and they will wake with a vicious hangover, and unquenchable thirst. For days they will be scrubbing sand from crevices.

We did that once, Lia and I. It was the night of my biggest show, the one she didn't attend, when I returned home to find her waiting, naked beneath her coat. She led me here, to this beach, perhaps to this very spot.

Such a perfect moment.

Riotous cheers cause my head to skip. I turn to see a group of teenagers, maybe twenty-somethings, sloping down towards the beach from the *Tayelet*. They are all wearing blue and white Taglit tee-shirts, all foreigners on a sponsored, choreographed sojourn to the Holy Land to kindle the flames of Jewish nationalism. They strip off while walking, toss their clothes onto the sand. Their young, tight bodies glitter in the coloured lights from the dying Clara atop the Dolphinarium, that blunt memorial to a history of cruelty: to the Russian children Hamas blew to scraps of flesh and bone and slurry outside; to the dolphins who died within.

A girl strips naked and dives into the water to bob up and down with the waves. The water is black and oily and swallows her body as her chubby arms wave above her head. 'Come on,' she says in shrill American English as a group of boys dive in and race out towards her.

There is a cry from the sea and I am wracked with the image of Milli on the floor, her blood pooling around her. I try and rationalise the aggression away. She shouldn't have stolen the camera; shouldn't have gone with Danielle to Rothschild; shouldn't have met Maoz. It all sounds cheap and hollow.

Out beyond the shore the girl looks as if she is drowning. She is rising and falling in great motions and her arms are flailing with a new urgency. She is shrieking. As I watch, she is surrounded by the other, male, bodies, and they all move in a choreographed dance, surging in, slipping away.

They close in around her and all move together back towards the beach. The sea vomits them onto the sand. A boy carries the girl aloft. She is shrieking and pummelling closed fists against his chest. He's so dark, like roasted coffee, and she is so white. She seems unaware of her nakedness. He is naked too, and his penis is erect. The others follow close behind, eyes transfixed.

'Put me down!' she yells. My eyes burn and my skin crawls with fire ants.

He tosses her on the sand like a piece of firewood and then stands there, lit by the sunrise just breaking in a crease behind us, all glistening. His legs bend and he falls upon her, his head between her legs. She begins to howl, still flailing and writhing. Another boy breaks from the group, crouches beside her head, fills her mouth, pins her arms to the sand. The others circle around them, arms crossed. Their bare buttocks and elbows and sea-slicked hair gleam between the long pregnant shadows stretched over them by the rising dawn.

The girl moans, and the sound is dragging back all the memories of the night. My soul and body are rending apart and a giant, insistent force drags me to my feet. I find myself crossing the beach. I'm almost blind, and my blood is pounding with despair and pooling in my shattered wrist. Despite the agony, I pull the boy from between her legs, shove the second from her head onto his back, utter some guttural, deranged groan.

'No,' it says. 'No.'

A familiar smarting in my cheek, and my mouth fills with sand. I have been hit today more than my whole life, since I was a child, scrapping in the playground. I spit it out but there is blood too and so it sticks to my teeth, my lips, my tongue, and to the roof of my mouth. My ears ring.

'What the fuck do you think you're doing?' says a female voice, hardened with irritation.

I can see pert, pink nipples attached to those large juddering breasts. They're connected to the plump rolled arms and the arms to hands with fingers and one, a central one, is facing me.

'I,' I begin; what am I going to say? 'I was helping you.'

'What made you think I needed help?'

'You were crying. Yelling. Trying to hold them off.'

She rolls her eyes.

'It was a game.'

I look around. A boy rubs his knuckles. The others whisper among themselves.

'I didn't know.'

'Not good at reading the signs, are you?'

I stare at her. At them. A smile breaks across my sand-encrusted lips, seeds a laugh that grows to a hysterical pitch. Everyone pauses, draws in breath. In the sudden stillness that falls upon us, I am the only sound.

I spit blood and sand into the centre of their little orgy and hope that some of it taints their perfect, glossy skin.

'Goddamn weirdo,' says the girl.

I turn and the boys dive back upon her, feeding on her as I walk away, back into the city, into the sun.

Yonatan's mother calls him once a week. He seldom answers, and when he does, the conversation lasts only a few agonising seconds. One night he feels his phone vibrate in his pocket and pulls it out to find eleven missed calls, all from his parents' home. There is no message. He calls the number he remembers by heart and waits nervously as it rings.

His mother answers as she always does: the family name, the last four digits of the family number.

'Is everything OK?' he says. His breath catches.

'Yes, of course,' she says. 'I didn't worry you, did I? It's just that your father wanted to speak to you, and you know how he gets.'

Before he can protest, before he thinks to hang up, comes the sound of rough clogged airways.

'Son, is this you?' The voice becomes faint, lashes at his mother in muffled tones. 'He's gone.'

'No, Dad, I'm here.'

Yonatan tries to fortify his voice.

'I want you to come up North.'

'I can't, Dad.'

'Rubbish. You'll come up tomorrow.'

'I'm very busy.'

A gruff laugh, half wheeze, half groan. 'Don't make me

laugh.' The laugh turns into a cough and an invisible hand slaps at his back.

Yonatan wants to protest, but his determination is feeble and his defences are broken before they form. It does not matter, for his father is not listening; he is nowhere near the phone. His disembodied voice says, 'He's coming up tomorrow,' and then the phone beeps and the line dies. The conversation, such as it was, is over.

Against his better judgement, Yonatan boards the bus at the New Central Bus Station. The city's squeezed brown box-work slips into the giant towers of the new peripheral wastelands to the North. When Yonatan was a kid, these were all sand dunes, fluffy rolling candy-yellow hillocks spotted with green tufty shrubs. Now the sea is blocked by rabid vertical suburbs. Mediterranean-view balconies, marble kitchen surfaces and subterranean parking garages. He feels too young to feel so old, so severed from his country.

A row of billboards line the coast road. 'Buy your dream' they say. A beautifully airbrushed head explodes through bricks and mortar, the numbers below either a phone number or a price. He would never wish to live in a place like this, towers in ill-planned, soulless conurbations. Nowheres, equidistant from somewheres. But even if he did, he could not. Even the undesirable is an unattainable, already drifted beyond his reach.

The sun is high when the bus lurches to a stop. It beats down on his head as he walks up the winding central road of Rosh Pina. His father is sitting by the broad window of the restaurant. The Sea of Galilee and the hills of the Golan Heights frame his head. The family legends are alive here. Before Yonatan was born, his father fought for these mountains, nearly died scrabbling up them. He holds a claim to them born from a bullet in the gut, from conquest and heroism. He fought for his home, repelled invading Syrians; Yonatan took pictures of a diminished people in their own front rooms to remind them of their inferiority.

'You're late,' his father says.

'Nice to see you too.'

'Your mother says I should walk on eggshells with you,' he says. He chews on an olive pit, rolls it around his mouth before spitting it into his palm, depositing it in an ashtray. 'But when someone's late you should tell them they're late. Life is more than politeness.'

A cough rattles up his chest. It seeps weakly from his nose and mouth. The eyelids are bloodless, the grey cast still overlays his face like a mask.

'I'm sorry I was late, Dad.'

They order: Yonatan the steak, his father a chopped salad with *tchina* and a boiled egg. It doesn't fit with the father Yonatan knows, but rather with the new variation – the frailty, the pallor, the mortality. He says, 'I wouldn't be a father if I didn't take an interest in my only son's life. And your mother says I should talk to you, so…'

He trails off, chokes down another mouthful of salad.

'What do you want to know?'

He gazes at Yonatan quizzically, purposefully, as if unpacking a particularly enigmatic crossword. Yonatan cannot meet his stare.

'Who are you?'

'I don't follow.'

'Who are you, son?' He speaks slower now, as if separating the words could clarify their meaning. 'Who are you? What do you want? Where are you going?'

Yonatan's fury threatens to punch a hole through the calm. 'How can you ask that?' It does not occur to him that perhaps he himself does not know.

'Your mother says I should be honest, so here, I am being honest. I am worried about you.'

'You don't need to worry.'

'First you go to that place – Thailand – and we don't hear from you for a full year, and then you drop out of university after barely a term.'

'That was my right. My choice.'

'Nobody's arguing with that.' The composed, compassionate tone is unfamiliar. 'But you still won't tell us why. One minute you're loving it, and the next you're gone. And we're supposed to just accept it? And now you're living in a tiny rented apartment. Really, our pantry is bigger. What do you have? Not even a girlfriend. Just taking photos. I mean, so you got into *Maariv* once, but you're not even shooting news now. Since when was making pretty pictures a proper job? Doctor. Lawyer. Work the land even, but no. You're behaving like a child but you're not a child. Of course I worry.'

'You shouldn't.'

'I'm your father. I have to.'

A pungent silence hovers between them. They eat their meal as the surface of the lake shimmers, molten silver gorging on the sun.

'So what do you suggest I do?' Yonatan says. The plates are being cleared. 'To fix my life.'

'You don't have a life.'

'To make a life then.'

'Well.' A wry smile breaks, colour enters the edges of his father's dry, cracked lips. 'There's a girl your mother and I met.'

'You're playing the *shadchan* now? Matchmaking? You know, three and you get into heaven.'

His father bats away the bitterness. 'Just hear me out. A nice girl. Good family. Just meet her, OK?'

He slips a yellow post-it note across the brown table. The sticky edge catches slightly. On it: a name and a number.

Business completed, they proceed to coffee in silence. They hug as he leaves.

'Your mother will be happy.'

Yonatan is back in Tel-Aviv by nightfall.

The garbage truck lumbers up our street and I follow in its wake. It stops every few metres and a sun-weathered Arab jumps from the running boards and loads another of the city's green bins into the slot. The arm rises, disgorges, falls before the bin is returned, vaguely to its place. The truck's progress is so laboured that I must hang a right and skirt Carmel Market, still empty of traders in the sweating dawn. The always-open *schwarma* is closed, its giant vertical skewers glinting metal, shorn of the shapeless layered slop of meat and fat. A black man scrubs the huge cookers as white fluffy soap water oozes from the ajar glass door.

I've already passed my building, but I'm not heading there yet. The Minzar is empty but I'm not looking for a drink either. The smell of alcohol which rises from my body in the rising morning heat is repulsive and I tell myself I will never drink again.

The crackhead's right where I left him, or thereabouts. He's slumped lengthways, back pushed up against the wall with a filthy pink rag over his head. A fat cockroach scurries up his swollen and boil-speckled leg and, beside it, a hand curls as if he fell into a deep nothingness mid-scratch. I fight the rising nausea, the urge to turn and walk away, and instead I stretch out a long finger and, holding my breath from the faecal stench that rises in waves, prod the most sanitary-seeming part of him.

'Hey,' I say. No answer. I poke him again and repeat, louder, sterner.

I prod him so hard that his whole body rocks, but he does not react. The cockroach scurries away. Perhaps he is dead. Sometimes, the familiar homeless disappear, after the boils and swellings and open wounds cover their limbs, after their legs are frequently amputated. I have never paid their absence any mind; there is always a replacement poised to claim their little hole in the city.

His ribcage rises and I breathe deep with relief and then gag. I reach into my pocket and feel the notes and coins that have accompanied me through tonight. I pull it all out and lay it on my palm. There, with the coins, is my wedding ring. I slide it onto my finger before counting out fifty-four shekels. I lean forward and tuck it into the pocket of his trousers, trying desperately not to touch visibly sodden fabric. I cannot repay Milli, today, but I will do something good with the money that remains.

The deed done, I stand there, waiting for some kind of relief to wash over me. Nothing comes.

My home is only a few steps from his home, and I count them off. Twenty-four, twenty-five, twenty-six. Past the recycling box filled with colourful plastic bottles, the giant bins, the Yemenite neighbour who chastised us, said that Ben should grow up with 'people like you'. With the code the door latch clicks and I swing it open. The downstairs neighbour is standing in the doorway, skeletal frame partly hidden in the shadow of his doorway. His dog lunges at me, strains at the leash, barking furiously as I push past.

'Hi Nadav,' I say. I know his name only from the mail that gets mixed up with our own. Both he and the dog are already back, barricaded behind a closed door.

I take the stairs instead of the lift and soon I am standing on the threshold of our apartment. I imagine that I am looking into a mirror and study my face with all the sand and the cuts and the bruises and the blood; I wipe my eyes and run my palms over my shaved head. There is sand inside my cast but it'll have to stay there till the next trip to the hospital.

She hasn't removed the key. It still lies hidden beneath the empty Mei-Eden water balloon. It's clearly visible but only if you're looking for it. The four prongs scrape as the door's pins retract into the frame, and I push it open. The air-conditioning hums and I feel the breeze from the fan in the bedroom wafting the cold air through the crack in the door.

The hinges squeak and I remember that I promised her I'd oil them all last week.

She lies in the bed, a shapeless mass, only a few wisps of hair visible under a soft duvet. I think I hear her move and so I whisper, 'Lia,' so light that it may have only been a thought. She is still.

Ben gurgles by the window and I freeze, hold my breath, wait to see whether he falls to the side of wake or sleep. There is a sigh and then he is quiet, so I padfoot over to him. His arms are outstretched to either side, his head rolled over to the left. There is so much white sheet beneath and around him, that he seems an island adrift in the ocean. So still; so peaceful; so young and new. I love him so dearly. After all that has happened, I feel physically sick. What an inadequate father I am.

A bubble fills on his lip. It bursts and a stream of clear spittle dribbles over the sheets. I reach into the cot and cup his head in my hands, feel the little ridge just below his crown, there from birth. The doctor said that his head shape will only settle after a year. He'll be walking by then.

My darling Ben.

I am so sorry.

A sliver of light seeps in through the blinds. Day has arrived. I strip down until I am naked, try not to let the sand fall to the floor. Somewhere deep within, the cast aches as I lift my tee-shirt over my head.

My clothes lie in a pile and they reek so strongly of alcohol and weed and sweat and the night that I carry the bundle into the bathroom and toss it in the washing basket. There's a collection of knickers already there, and Ben's things are in a little blue box to one side and though I need to take a shower to wash the night off me, I know that doing so would wake them both so I open a packet of baby wipes to

•

She hasn't slept yet, and the feigning of sleep doesn't come easy. The creaking tells her that he's returned from the bathroom and so she double-checks her eyes to be sure they're not open enough to give her away.

She takes no chances; squeezes them tight and then opens them just the tiniest sliver. She can see him reflected in the closet mirror facing her side of the bed.

The green glow of the baby's nightlight illuminates the bruises that litter his body. They're only now coming into their blue and purple own. He looks terrible and his arm is set in a cast. She wants to apologise. Just not yet.

She's glad she is asleep.

They'll talk. They have to.

She will talk. He will talk.

Just not right now.

She will wait till morning. Real morning.

Her body tenses as the duvet rises and he slides himself into bed as if this were a normal night. He drapes his arm over her, and she smells adventure and drama beneath the scent of Pampers wipes on his fingers. She is desperate not to deconstruct it all. His penis presses against her buttocks and she doesn't want to notice that his pubic hairs are matted and hard.

'I love you,' he whispers in her ear.

His voice is thick with alcohol.

'Wait,' she says silently, watching her lips move in the mirror. Just wait. And then, finally: 'I love you too.'

Yonatan's mother calls frequently, incessantly sells the "wonderful girl" he has already agreed to meet. Her spotlight curdles the milk. He feels he already knows her intimately, could draw a portrait of her, of her character, of their lives together. The post-it remains by the phone, the number undialled.

His latest exhibition opens on Gordon Street as the news of Operation Cast Lead and the Gaza incursion breaks on television and radio. As he catches a cab, he sees a homeless person reading the announcement in a discarded copy of *Maariv*. He cannot tell if the latest war is responsible for the pitiful attendance. There are few conciliatory words, and even the most friendly of critics cannot feign a smile. Though not stellar, the work sells relatively well, and the looming discussion with his gallery owners is temporarily postponed.

As the war rages, a letter arrives at Yonatan's tiny apartment on Fireberg Street. It announces an imminent rent increase of twenty percent. In a fury, he calls his landlord but realises almost immediately that he has no leverage.

'If you don't want to pay, there are a hundred who will,' his landlord says. His words are a smoked laugh.

Yonatan checks *Yad2* and *Homeless*, but the web, too, reflects the same rent inflation, so he looks at the sales listings instead. He has made some money from his exhibitions, but the full sum will barely cover the down payment on a two-room apartment. With no guaranteed income, there is scant chance any bank will provide a mortgage. He scours the want ads, realises with a growing sickness that no job will bridge the financial gap.

Thoughts turn to the girl: she is from Haifa, and Haifa is not Tel-Aviv. Haifa is cheap...

He calls her.

'Hi, is this Ilanit?' he says.

'It is.'

Her voice is soft and melodic.

'This is Yonatan.'

'Hi. My parents said you'd call. How are you?'

'Good.'

'Good.'

A pause. In the faltering conversation, he notices the background static on the line.

'So do you want to meet?'

'Sure.'

A dread cramp fills his stomach. He does not want to expend any effort on something already set.

'Do you ever come to Tel-Aviv?' he says.

'It's kinda hard not to nowadays. I'm actually there for work later this week.'

He thinks of asking what she does, but of course he already knows.

'Great.'

'Great.'

Yonatan struggles to think of something to say. The static seems to grow louder.

'There are loads of places around me,' he says. 'I live in Shenkin area.'

'I know.'

It is clear both are eager for the call to end.

They arrange to meet at the Stephan Braun on Allenby. He doesn't ask her how she plans to get to Tel-Aviv, nor how she plans to get home after; predestination hangs over him like a black cloud.

He arrives late to the date even though the restaurant is an easy five-minute walk from his home. He asks the hostess to point out his table and then slinks into the shadows to watch the girl as she checks first her watch and then her phone. She is pretty. Gorgeous even. Olive skin encases a delicate, elegant frame and flowing ringlets of onyx hair swirl across half-moon eyes and a warm welcoming smile. Her perfection fills him with delight, and then sadness, and finally, anger.

He turns to leave. As he passes the toilets, his shoulder knocks against a girl who leans heavily against the wall.

'Hey,' she says. 'Watch yourself!'

'*Slicha.*' He says. 'I'm sorry.'

They linger.

'Are you going in?' he says.

She thinks for a moment. 'No. I don't think so. You?'

'No.' Neither moves. He holds out a hand. 'I'm Yonatan,' he says, 'do you maybe want to get a drink?'

There are fine creases around the smile on her face.

'It depends,' she says. 'Where?'

Lia

'You must be Sharon,' says the voice. She notices the man long after the words have evaporated. 'I've heard so much from your parents. Seems you're doing great things in the pharmaceutical industry.'

She smiles politely. Her teeth grind towards the rear of her mouth.

'No,' she says, 'I'm Lia. The other daughter.'

'Oh, well,' the man says. There is no trace of embarrassment. 'I'm so sorry.' She isn't sure for what: for the insult, or for her brother's death. 'I wish you a long life.'

Lia curses him silently as he turns his back and walks through the assembled crowd into the living room.

He taps her mother on the shoulder, waits for her to turn to him before mugging her with already overly familiar mourning platitudes. She waves him away and returns to her task. Lia's view of the table is obstructed, but it's obvious that in her bereavement, her mother has withdrawn into the embrace of her disorders, working hard to line the *bourekas* into perfect, parallel rows. The mourners have paid scant regard to her diligent work, picking one cheese from here and two potatoes from there, inflicting chaos on her order.

The small house has filled quickly in this, the first evening of mourning after *Shabbat*. The familiar musty smell is invaded by cologne and sweat and bad breath. All the nooks and hide-holes are occupied by strangers. Each has dutifully set aside an hour, maybe two, before the week begins, to dip into her family's tragedy. Then they will step outside, take deep breaths, and drive off and away. The family's tragedy will be brushed off like lint.

The house feels too tight, the crowd too close. She hears her father's voice say, 'well at least now he'll have both of his legs,' and in the ensuing silence, the audience is uncertain whether it's an inappropriate joke, or he has lost his mind with grief. A few chuckle uneasily. Eventually a belly laugh erupts so loud that everyone present turns towards her father.

'Come on.'

Long fingers grip Lia's upper arm. She imagines the colour of the bruise-in-waiting as the fingers tighten and loosen, passing on silent directions down the hallway, up the stairs and across the landing.

The door shuts with a familiar thud and she's still thinking about her mother and her father as she sits on the faded pink sheets of a single bed. Sharon's single bed. Her older sister sits beside her and the old, worn springs roll beneath their shared weight as she fumbles inside her bag and pulls out a small ziplock bag.

'Did you see Dad downstairs?' Sharon says. She pulls a CD case from the rack and blows away the decades of dust and obsolescence that cover it. Aviv Geffen. She uses it to separate the green leaves from the seeds that will pop and fizz and burn unsteadily and ruin the sisters' best clothes.

'I heard him say maybe now Mickey's in heaven he'll have his leg back. The one they had to amputate after they cut him from the wreck.'

Sharon rolls a funnel from the thin tobacco papers and sprinkles the leaves inside. 'He said it to five sets of people. Laughed every time.'

'I heard him tell someone else that the injuries were no big deal. That he'd always been brain-dead.'

They both chuckle. Their father's humour was always improper, occasionally cruel, but Lia cannot bring herself to talk to him now, to alert him to the discomfort of his guests. When the machines were turned off, her brother's pulse slowed and stopped, the gap between them turned into a chasm with bubbling lava at its bottom.

Now she could never explain that his jokes were not jokes, any more than she could say that she loved him, heal his hurt.

Sharon slides a lighter's flame up and down the shaft of the joint. The paper crackles as it shrinks around the weed. 'And what about Mum?'

'With the *bourekas*?'

Sharon laughs; she's lifted herself from the bed and is tugging at the window, stubborn from decades of paint on paint. Finally, it gives and she slides it aside, pushes open the mosquito net with its flecks of stray colour. It gives a little beneath her hand.

She props a little bit of loose wood against the frame to stop it snapping shut. *'Boi.* Come on.'

Sharon crawls outside first; Lia follows onto the little ledge, the architectural oversight she claimed as her own. Immediately they settle into their historical positions: Lia faces the window, Sharon the street. Their legs are crossed.

'You want to light it?' Sharon hands her the joint but Lia hasn't forgotten the basic etiquette.

She waves it back and her sister puffs, first slowly, lightly and then with growing intensity. A thin but swelling cloud of smoke rises above them and hangs in the stale air. It is only June, but already the last relieving crispness has drained from the country. The wet heat of 2012's summer has begun its steady rise towards the unbearable, the charred and arid yellow all-consuming. Below them the landscape of their suburban youth spreads laconic, all so irrepressibly ordered and predictable: chest-high white walls and cars in neat tiled driveways. Hand-painted signs lean into the street as if drunk. They give the names of each family dwelling within each home.

'So when are you, Yonatan, and Ben moving to the suburbs?'

Sharon asks this with an outstretched hand. Lia accepts the spliff.

Never.

Her breath is too deep and she sucks in more from her first toke than she expected. The smoke cracks her lungs and she doubles forward, coughing and spluttering. Her eyes stream as the slight deadening oozes through her and takes the sharpest edge off her thoughts.

She hasn't smoked in an eternity and the assault is relentless.

'Woah there,' says Sharon. 'Take it easy. You don't want Mum and Dad to know you're stoned, do you?'

Lia laughs a crooked laugh. Two stoned daughters are trumped by one dead son.

'Why do you think Mickey never joined us out here?' Everyone but Sharon called him Michael.

'I don't know.'

In the hospital room: the machines drew graphs and assaulted them with numbers that they didn't understand. It was one of those days that the doctors said that he was doing well, but they were being too nice, their smiles too broad, their tone too conciliatory. Perhaps everyone else had that feeling too, because they all sat there in silence with their *cafe barads* from Aroma sweating onto their laps. Each was lost in their own thoughts, nobody talked.

Lia had thought of questions, things she wanted to know about her brother if he ever woke up. Like: Why did you never join us outside on the ledge? What's your favourite colour? Why do you always skin your chicken nuggets? Why did you get that horrible earring? Why did you take it out? Why were you driving so fast on that road? Everybody knows the Arava Road is not safe. That's why everyone flies to Eilat. Arrive at Sdeh Dov airport and thirty minutes later you're there. So the planes are terrible and it's kinda scary, but nobody's died yet. And it's so cheap. So quick, so easy, so safe. So…

Why?

The sound of prayer rises from the living room beneath where they sit.

Bile rises in Lia's throat.

'I don't want to be here,' she says.

'You want to go home?' says Sharon, and she offers her the joint again. 'I'll tell Mum and Dad you weren't feeling well.'

No, she doesn't want to go home, because although home means Ben, it also means Yonatan, and it means that strange, heavy normal that's been strangling them all for nearly a year now since he came home as day broke, with a shattered wrist and a pulped body. And she can't leave here, now.

'No.'

She refuses more of the joint. What she has already smoked is making her head swim. It's not strong – Sharon's stuff is never strong, always grown in natural sunlight in a box hung from the giant window of her beautiful apartment in Bazel – but Lia's body is no longer accustomed to its effects. Her mind is fighting to retain control, but everything is slowing down, becoming more deliberate, more laboured, and the downstairs chanting is falling into step with her heartbeat to form a rhythm that sounds like panic.

'I need to go,' she says, and scrambles to her feet. She's unsteady, and for a terrifying instant it seems she will topple and plummet from the edge onto the gleaming black roof of her father's car in the driveway below.

'Easy, Lia. You're twenty-seven. Not some kid any more. Way too old to throw a whitey.'

Sharon has her arm but she shakes it off, feels the manicured nails digging into her skin as she clambers in through the open window. Falling heavily through, she knocks the little wooden clasp and the window slams shut. She can hear Sharon struggling to pry it open.

'Lia, wait!'

She walks unsteadily, down the stairs into the crowded hall below. Every eye feels turned upon her, and each one burns like a cigarette.

'Lilush!' yells her dad, his voice carrying over the heads and the scriptures as she pulls the door open too hard and it smacks back to chip the plaster from the wall. The noise makes her jump.

She is finally outside and she's breathing hard. The inert heat of the night torments her lungs, thick like syrup, and it sticks in her throat. She falls to her hands and knees, retching and wheezing until vomit, yellow and steaming, pours out onto the yellow brick of the driveway.

'It's OK,' says a voice, and she feels Sharon's hand on her shoulder.

'What must they think of me? Just take me away, OK?' she pleads through tears and puke and she feels Sharon lift her to her feet and help her along the row of parked cars that, in their neighbourhood, can only signal a marriage or a death.

Lia cries in the car, all the way to the hospital. At first her father yells; after a while he is quiet. She tries to get Sharon's attention, but her older sister stares at the moon, hanging like an apparition in the blackening blue of the autumn sky. The radio is on low, the incessant voices without pause: Israel, Jordan, crows picking over the bones of the historic peace between "friends", how different the rest of 1994 will look, the beautiful future created in its wake.

Nobody in the car is listening.

At the hospital, Lia's father walks faster than his daughters. He stops at each doorway, each stairwell, urges them on with a stern look, one of impatient eagerness. His excitement would be infectious had Lia not been overcome by a sense of dread. The sisters do not enter the room with him, but rather huddle outside, ears rapt for the cooing sounds stealing out from within.

'We should go in,' says Sharon. Forever seems to pass between the words.

'I don't want to,' says Lia; to go in, to be left alone.

Sharon's footsteps are heard not seen.

One. Two. Three breaths. Then she, too, steps beyond the threshold.

The baby lies upon her mother's breast, pink and wrinkled

like a grape dried in the sun. Lia holds back tears. This interloper, so small, so unformed, has already stolen her life. She's now just two of three. A middling digit.

'Come and meet your new brother,' her mother calls from the bed. Sharon and her father are already crowded around, and the picture seems so perfect, so complete. Mother, father, oldest, youngest.

Sharon crooks a finger, strokes the tiny forehead and the face turns to her, gurgles, coughs and burps, and Lia wants to yell, to tell her sister to stop, but her mouth remains closed.

The doctor enters the room with the force of an approaching storm front. The family tenses, prepares, shifts nervously. He smiles but there is no softness in him; he barks orders at the attending nurse, the new mother. His imperiousness is masked as concern.

'Please put baby Michael – that is his name? – in the bassinet,' he says. Hearing the name for the first time moves Lia closer to the crib. The hospital staff are there for the mother, not the newborn in his clear plastic basket. For a few moments, she is alone with him, all other attendant backs facing her as she gazes down at the swaddled life. His pink boiled face pokes out from white cotton below, a blue cotton hat above.

Yesterday, he wasn't a person, not in any way Lia could understand. Now here he is, so tiny, so helpless. So new, as she must have once been. He is dreaming. Of what? His whole universe is a womb.

She reaches down, strokes his face, works her hand down the fabric to trace the outline of an arm, a hip, the gap between his thighs. She pauses there, feels an outline padded by the swaddle, by a thin nappy beneath. She holds her hand steady, grips first loosely, then harder, then too hard.

Baby Michael begins to yell and all eyes are turned back to them, back to her.

Lia's hands are already stowed safely back in her pockets.

Still Michael cries.

They've been driving for a while before Lia realises the congealed sick on her hands. She explores, finds more: orange-yellow mingled with the black strands of her hair, a few chunks clinging to the dimples on her cheeks. The traffic is unusually heavy for a Saturday evening, and the uneven tarmac is wringing her stomach with every bump.

'I'm sorry,' she mumbles. She is watching her sister from the corner of her eye as she scrapes away the worst from the fold between her forefinger and thumb. It tumbles down onto the matted Mazda carpet beneath her feet.

This car means a lot to Sharon, she knows; her first new car, bought after she returned from England. She has driven over one hundred thousand kilometres in it, and Lia doesn't know how there can be so many roads in their tiny country. Every one ends in either the sea, or the tips of machine guns.

Cars are crawling up the Ayalon Freeway that slices Tel-Aviv down its spine. Atop the city's mushrooming skyscrapers, red lights blink against the hazy blue-black of the night sky. The car's air-conditioning blows vaguely against their faces as they crawl forward only to grind to a halt again.

'Strange,' says Sharon, and she pulls herself forward with her arms around the steering wheel. Tilting her head up, she tries to peer over the line of red lights ahead. Lia stares at the firmness of her muscles as they tense to hold her up – her arms, her stomach, flat beneath her dress, the rivulets of bone and tendon in her shoulders. 'Shouldn't be traffic this time of night. Not here.'

'Maybe there's been an accident.'

She immediately regrets her words. No talk of accidents, not after everything. Too late. The car once again crawls forward. Lia listens to her sister's breathing and prays for her to say something, anything, although she knows nothing will do.

As the silence becomes deafening, the traffic funnels into a single lane. She tries not to look out at the carnage to their left, but she is powerless to resist the drama of the flashing blue and red lights, the mangled pile of metal and the four wheels upturned like the legs of a dying cockroach. She feels nauseous again, but then the traffic breaks like a fever and they are once again free.

She wonders whether Michael's wreck looked like that, then, on some anonymous strip of road, somewhere between the Dead Sea and Eilat.

Sharon says: 'Do you think they survived?'

'I'm sure they did.'

They enter the stretch of highway at the very heart of the city and have drifted into the outer lane and up the off-ramp. A white car cuts them off, its pin-prick headlights jerking violently left and right as it writhes through the mess of cars aiming for, or coming from, the kerb, dropping people off, scooping them up. Hashalom Train Station regurgitates its load after the Shabbat break.

Sharon pilots the car around the morass, turns it right onto Begin Road beside the triple towers of Azrieli, and Lia lets out the breath she doesn't realise she's been holding. Home was to the left but now there's a central reservation and a tunnel and a dozen no u-turn signs between them and turning back.

Yonatan came to the funeral, but he didn't stay for the shiva.

'I think Ben is too young for this,' he said, and she couldn't argue. It was the first night since his birth that they had been apart, and every second of his absence wounded her.

Only a few lights are on in the Yoo buildings, in the new neighbourhood of skyscrapers wedged between Namir Road and the Ayalon. Panoramic views of the national commute. They are quickly running out of real Tel-Aviv, and Sharon turns left onto Rokach Boulevard towards the giant chimney of Reading Power Station and into the parking lot of the Namal, Tel-Aviv's old port. The car slips into the vacuum like a single pea in a Tupperware box.

Nowadays Lia seldom comes here. The Namal is too far North, too busy with local tourists, too prettified for her and for Ben; all wooden decking like some me-too luxury Tel-Aviv apartment project. Fortified and nipped and tucked, the once anarchic mayhem of its disused industry is now squeezed into little soundproof boxes of genteel coffee-shop and restaurant chains where the prices are high and the quality is low. Only the sea lapping the disintegrating concrete barrier is comforting, some connection to the past. A reminder of the nightclubs in ramshackle warehouses with their endless parties, and before that: holding steady a ship, when Jaffa was the city and Tel-Aviv was the satellite, the upstart. When Jewish trade was boycotted from Jaffa's port, when battle lines were drawn and the docks were built, and the young city struggled to survive.

The night is still early, and a boy flits by on a balance bike, skids on a puddle of sea spray and falls while his mother checks her phone. 'Look after your child!' she wants to yell. 'Is he hurt?' She wishes Ben were here with her, asleep in his stroller.

Most people around are revelling in their youth; men with hair so gelled Lia is fearful of the proximity of their close cigarettes; women in tight, tiny clothes. They shout and bray and pout and pose.

Unconsciously, Lia reaches down and touches her belly. As Ben grew inside her, she'd smothered her shirt flat against her skin and twisted left and right in the mirror, studying, learning, remembering, every line, every curve, like a blueprint. Then Ben was born, and they went home, and then every day she studied herself anew. 'Tomorrow,' she told herself, 'tomorrow you'll be back.' She never was though, not completely.

Sharon pulls her forwards, tucks her hair behind her ear and brings her face forwards to whisper into her ear.

'You look beautiful,' she says. 'Forget it, OK?'

There is no queue at the Galina. Lia shuffles forward, follows her sister, nods at the gatekeeper as his eyes slip over her. It's an ugly bar, long and thin wedged between a family restaurant and a fast-food joint. Metal barriers pen them in like cows and Lia is already dreading it filling up, fearing the unfamiliar press of bodies with nowhere left to go.

They pull up two bar stools and Lia lets Sharon order for her. The bartender has no time for her, separates the sisters with an elbow on the counter. She doesn't mind; she wears her invisibility like a comforting blanket, wrapped tightly around her. He makes small talk, drools over Sharon, and she plays along, batting her long eyelashes and running her slender fingers over her cheeks. He grins and gawps and doesn't turn his back for an instant, even when he's pouring liquid from bottles and chopping limes and adding ice and shaking the metal tumblers until finally two overflowing glasses appear before them, straws and little pink umbrellas poking out on top.

'Thank you,' Lia says to Sharon.

'It's OK. I doubt we'll have to pay for them.'

'No, not just for the drink. For getting me out of there.'

'Really, it's OK,' Sharon says. She lifts the glass into the air, motioning for Lia to follow her lead. 'To Mickey.' Their glasses clink; Sharon drinks but Lia only pretends, sucking liquid into the straw until it brushes her lips and then letting it slip back down. 'I'm actually happy we're here.'

Sharon removes the straw and lifts the glass to her mouth. Tilting it back, she finishes it in one go so all that is left is the ice to slowly melt alone.

'You should drink yours,' she says, but Lia doesn't want to mix alcohol with the weed that is still in her system. Together, they will only drag her down and open a sinkhole through which all her vitality will seep. So instead she fondles the glass, running her finger up and down the six decorative indents that run around its side, playing with the bubbles of condensation as they try to drip down to the wood surface.

Sharon says, 'It's just so strange. So wrong. All these people coming to Mum and Dad's house. Did you recognise any of them?' Lia shakes her head. 'No, neither did I. Most of them, anyway. Do you think he knew them? Did they know him? Mickey I mean. Yet Mum and Dad were running around like it's some dinner party, making sure everybody's having a good time.' There is quiet. 'Do you think they'll be alright?'

Lia doesn't want to answer, so instead she says, 'Did Richard come?'

A long silence. 'He called. Said he was sorry about it all. That Mickey was like a brother. Then he wished me a long life.'

'The bastard.'

Sharon laughs, too loud. She scratches at an eye with a manicured nail the colour of new blood. 'But what about Yonatan?'

'Yonatan,' Lia says, the name rolling around her mouth like an ice cube or a shard of glass. Now, finally, she does pick up her drink, sips it down properly, moves the straw aside and tips it back as the level drops. 'Yonatan.'

He came. He left.

If that was Yonatan at all.

'He's so changed,' she says. Since that day that he packed up his camera, fired his gallery, and not a week later left the house at eight in the morning to a new job in some grey tower in Petach Tiqva. He said he didn't want to talk about it. So they didn't.

That was nearly a year ago.

She slides her hand over, wraps her fingers over Sharon's. They are so delicate. She holds them tight.

'So go on,' Sharon says. 'How are you both? Make me feel better. Let me believe in true love.'

The question is unnerving.

Lia's about to say: 'How do I start?' but another voice speaks first.

'Hi,' it says in British English, thick but not syrupy. 'Can I buy you a drink?'

She leans over, points an accusing finger, but it is too late. Sharon is gone. All her sister's features are contorted into a chillingly placid, open smile. It all happens so suddenly, the change absolute.

Lia cannot make out their conversation over the insistent and invasive music. The laugh that curls around Sharon's turned back is featureless, without mirth or joy. The soundtrack to a late-night comedy show whose actors are long since forgotten, the live studio audience decades dead. It must be working though, for the tourist's face is a vision of delight, broadly lit by the fluorescent bulbs that make the coloured bottles pop behind the bar, and illuminate the tiny rivulets beneath Sharon's foundation. He isn't unattractive, but his good looks are too obvious; the stubble on the chin too tended, his hair too naturally floppy. He's definitely from somewhere else.

Lia's drink is drained, yet still she sucks on her straw, tugging at the melting ice water swirling away at the bottom. She watches Sharon tease her hair, pout her lips, giggle just a little bit.

He looks a little like Richard, Sharon's exotic, rich, successful, handsome fiancé. Now ex-fiancé.

Lia raises her cup to her head, presses it against her forehead. It is cool, and provides some respite from the muggy night.

Sharon never told her Richard had left. It was Michael who dropped by unannounced to share the news. His garbage-tin exhaust boomed and burped as he reversed into the red and white space that blocked the corner beside their building.

'I'm worried about her,' he said, and in Lia's memory, she concentrates on that kind smile in vivid technicolor. It stretched his lips out so that they seemed to widen his face, to touch his ears and show off that cracked tooth, earned from a foolish jump into the shallow end of a wealthy friend's swimming pool in Savyon.

He suggested a meeting, the three of them all together. 'Next week,' he said, 'when I get back from Eilat,' and she teased him about some girlfriend who neither she, nor the family, had been permitted to meet.

Michael always cared so deeply. And now he's gone.

She sighs, stares at the fine lines that spread from the corner of Sharon's eye as she turns away from her suitor and momentarily lets the smile slip. Lia counts, one, two, three before Sharon turns back.

Yes, Michael was right to be worried, but Lia can't take on that responsibility. Her life is already saturated with worry.

Her thoughts pool tension in the strings of her neck, ready to snap and drop her head down to the floor. She can no longer bear to sit, ignored on this stool, and so she turns and faces away from the bar, distractedly scans the bobbing heads of the rapidly-filling Galina. She notes the exits and plans a possible escape. She feels too old and ugly to be here, too vulnerable to be alone. She pushes off, begins to walk through the tightly packed bodies. She touches an arm, brushes a buttock, smells the perfumes and aftershaves. The people form fluid walls around her, wedge her into smothered solitude. She walks aimlessly because all she really wants to do is sleep.

A shoulder smacks hard against her cheek. She mumbles a '*slicha*', looks up into a face she recognises but cannot place: long eyelashes, Demerara sugar skin and tight curls of black hair.

She just stares up at the brown eyes, the hook nose, the lips, pink like the flesh of a blood orange, trying to pinpoint where this piece fits into the puzzle of her life.

The panic at home laps up the stairs in waves of shrieking.

Lia's mother screams and cries; Michael, now all of one year used, abandoned, instinctively creates a rolling echo.

Lia's father left this morning to find Sharon; he has yet to return.

The whole country is gripped by tragedy: the assassination of Prime Minister Yitzhak Rabin – not by a bestial Arab, but by a traitor within. A real Israeli, a fellow Jew. Sharon has been missing for a whole day and Lia's parents, haggard with anxiety, have already exhausted all leads.

Lia is sure she is dead.

Without trepidation she opens her older sister's drawers, rifles through her notebooks and plays with her toys. She wonders how it will be to have a room of her own, to graduate from the youngest, to the middle, to the oldest, like leap-frogging years at school. She wills a few dry tears to fall, begins reorganising their shared space as their mother sobs beyond the stairs. If a prime minister – the symbol of the state, all power and glory and the leader of the eternal Jewish people – can be killed, certainly there is no chance for an insignificant pubescent girl from Kiryat Ono, an unglamorous suburb just a stone's throw from the West Bank.

By the time Sharon is thrust forcefully into the back of the family car, Lia has already colonised much of her sister's side of the room. Their father finds her in Kings of Israel Square, soon to be renamed in honour of Rabin. She is just one of the faceless throng, a new generation emerging brutally into the crushing reality of the modern Middle East. The vigil will remain for days, for nights, a chimeric groundswell of mourning and hope, just real enough to evaporate into the outline of a corporeal memory that will remain, for decades, singed on those present.

Lia feels nothing at Sharon's return. They are both sent to their room without dinner, and the expected reprisal for her raid into Sharon's territory never arrives. They lie in bed, both awake.

'What was it like?' Lia asks. Sharon breathes heavily; it takes a while for her to reply.

'You should have been there too,' she says. Her voice is drained of emotion. Her arms are crossed, her eyes stare at the ceiling.

'You should have told me you were going.'

'I shouldn't have had to.'

Lia turns to face the wall.

No more words are said that night. For weeks the sisters say barely anything to each other at all.

It seems to the family that Sharon is indelibly altered after the assassination. She joins the local branch of the Ha-noar Ha'oved youth movement, spends every afternoon there after school. When she returns home, she lectures and berates her family, spitting ideological axioms Lia does not understand. She speaks of freedoms and rights, of historic struggles and the historic brotherhood of man. She exercises her liberty by boycotting Friday Shabbat dinners, cuts her hair short, pierces her ears in asymmetrical patterns. Her shorn locks do not hide the purple hickeys that crawl up her neck; the swinging gold loops frame them like targets for their father's fury.

Sharon sticks a 'Peace Now' sticker on the bumper of their parents' new, grey Mitsubishi Galant, their father's symbol of professional success after a series of brown Subarus. When he steams it carefully off, she disappears and does not return until morning to chastise and ridicule and attack him with well-practised phrases. Pride is the territory of the small man, she says. Not advocating for peace is equivalent to wielding the dagger for war. There is alcohol on her breath.

Lia cannot make sense of the arguments. 'We are not at war,' she says to her sister that night, 'so doesn't that mean we're at peace?'

Sharon scoffs.

Lia is relieved when Sharon demands her own room. Their father's study is magicked away and Sharon's things are apparitioned to the front of the house while Lia is at school. Whenever she passes, Sharon's new door is always closed.

As the 1996 election draws near, Sharon and her youth movement claim ownership of the major junction leading into town. It follows Lia's route to and from school and she hates passing, feels threatened as she watches her sister and her friends pouncing from the pavement to devour the paused cars. They do not ask permission, but act as guerrilla fighters to burnish bumpers with the words of Bill Clinton: *Haver Ata Hasser* – friend you are missed – uttered in Hebrew at Rabin's funeral. A rallying cry. Lia hides, waits for the lights to turn green, for the cars to flee. Then she darts into an adjoining street.

One night, Lia finds Sharon, unusually, sitting in the living room, watching the television with a pillow pulled close to her knees. She has paid little attention to the details of Operation Grapes of Wrath; Lebanon seems very far away from the daily monotony of her life, but something about Sharon's expression makes her sit and listen to the news, to the story of Qana and the 106 Lebanese civilians killed in an Israeli missile strike on a UN compound. The screen shows footage of the devastation, cuts to the acting Prime Minister Shimon Peres. Lia points and asks, 'Wasn't he the one for peace?'

The day of the election, Sharon disappears from the house

before day breaks. She does not return that night and it is with a weary resignation that nobody looks for her or utters a word of concern out loud. Their father nurses one drink after another as the clocks tick and the votes are counted. He is asleep on the couch before Lia's mother ushers her up to bed.

Lia wakes early. She heads to the kitchen in search of something to silence the rumbling of her stomach. Sharon is sitting at the kitchen table, a newspaper in her hand. She smells rancidly sweet of weed, and the heavy makeup she has taken to wearing is run on one side, smudged on the other as if interrupted whilst wiping away tears. The house is still.

'It wasn't supposed to be like this,' says Sharon. Her eyes follow Lia as she moves towards the fridge. There is no trace of emotion in her voice.

'What happened?' says Lia.

'There won't be peace.'

Lia doesn't know the correct response, is intimidated by the prospect of engaging her sister in conversation. She is relieved, therefore, when her mother, bleary-eyed and cheerful, invades the kitchen's wake-like calm.

'Hi *hamudot sheli*,' she says.

'Go fuck yourself.'

The words are abrupt, violent, launched at their mother like a rocket. Sharon's chair is tossed to the floor, the kitchen door slams. Her footsteps fade and then reverberate over their heads. Another bang. Michael cries.

'What was that about?' says Lia's mother.

'She says peace lost.'

Their mother picks up the newspaper still resting on the table, scans the headlines. Bibi Netanyahu's smiling face smothers the front page. She sighs. 'Oh Sharon,' she says. 'There will never be peace. Not here. Not with them. Life is not that simple.' She rubs her eyes, pinches the bridge of her nose. 'You kids. Always so idealistic.'

Lia nods, but she doesn't understand, can't comprehend. Not when she is in her home, with her bickering family, and there is water in the tap and electricity in the plugs and television and school and homework. How can this be war when there is peace, or at least a kind of peace, in her tiny, unalterable world.

The music at the Galina is heavy and pounding, and the boy towers above her. He is tall; slender without being skinny. His eyes are deep brown, almost liquid black. It's those eyes that Lia thinks she remembers, and in the shooting tubes of light that zip over their heads and shine off the tight-fitting gold loop of his earring, she cannot tell where she has seen him before.

'Dani,' calls a voice from the low chairs to their side. 'Let her through.'

She doesn't want to pass. She wants to continue standing there, to study his face and his body, to sift through all the sand and find him buried in her memories. She must have met him recently. He's so fresh and so young, still not at the age where years fly by.

Lia steps forward, places an open hand on his shoulder. It's an unintentional movement, as is the little squeeze she gives his flesh, feeling the solidity, the tension. The boy slinks backwards, and her hand is left hanging limply, unsupported in the air.

'No, please,' she says as he turns away. 'Wait. I know you. Really, why do I know you? Where do I recognise you from?'

The seats erupt into howls of laughter. They're laughing at her, but why? Is it her age? Her confusion? Her mourning clothes? They should go to hell, these cruel animals, with their slim flesh wrapped in fashionable clothes and trinkets.

'Look man,' says one, his trousers too tight and his shirt too loose. God he looks good. 'You've got an admirer. Lucky you. Looks a bit old for you though. But you never know.'

Someone else adds: 'He might like a sugar mommy,' and their laughter erupts again.

She feels a flush of anger, but the boy leans forward so close that she can smell the mouthwash like boiled star anise on his breath and says, 'Please, go away.'

Her mouth hangs open. If she knew who he was and the connection between them, then perhaps she could argue. But despite the faint acknowledgement, he's still a stranger, and so she does what he asks, turns and weaves back through all the dancing bodies to the still-unoccupied stool beside her indisposed sister. She cannot take her eyes from the boy even as she orders another drink, swallows it down thirstily. The night seems reluctant to pass.

Somewhere nearby, Sharon says, 'Where else have you reported from? Really. That's so cool.'

The opinionated, determined woman is still in hiding. Lia focuses all her attention upon the boy. Dani, that's what they called him. She knows him, she's sure; wherever he fits into her life is completely removed from this drunken reverie.

She watches as across the bar he leans in, laughs easily while his arms gesticulate dramatically beside a girl. Everyone laughs. At first she assumes it's a come-on, some clumsy flirting within a close, incestuous group, but no. One by one he leans in, hugs each person in turn, says things she can't make out. Those sitting furthest away he merely gives a cursory wave and then he turns, makes his way towards the exit. Lia is gripped with panic, terrified that if she lets him leave she'll lose...

The recall strikes her.

Yesterday morning. That was when she saw him, for the first and the last time, walking among the mourners through the dusty expanse of the cemetery. When they reached the impatient hole in the earth, he hovered at the edge of the small crowd. Dressed in a cheap, shiny black suit, he was crying real, scalding tears.

'Sharon,' Lia says, voice cracked and quick with desperation. An outstretched finger taps insistently at her sister's back. 'Sharon, please, I need to ask you something.'

The violence of Sharon's shrug sends her arm flying and it knocks her empty glass on its side. Numb, Lia watches it roll one way then the other until it finally tumbles over the side of the bar. As it crashes to the floor she understands. She doesn't have time for permissions.

She dunks her arm elbow-deep into her sister's bag, and though it threatens to fall from the stool, it doesn't. She pulls out the plastic car key and runs from the bar.

She trips on the low heels of her shoes and so she pulls them off, endures the little pebbles that bite into the soles of her feet. As she unlocks the Mazda, she tosses them into the passenger seat. The car lurches forward as she frantically scans the line of vehicles ahead. The muscles of her chest are tight as stone but her heart is pounding and straining within. She glimpses the boy's twisted head in the foremost car, waiting for an opportunity to merge into the traffic streaming past on Rokach Boulevard.

She swings the car erratically, far too fast, and flicks a righteous middle finger at the concert of car horns that she leaves in her wake. As she swerves onto Rokach, she narrowly avoids a speeding van and a scooter as she struggles to maintain control. The scooter darts from her path and slows, but no damage has been done. In a second he will overtake her at the lights, and they'll both wave and put it down to one of the infinite near misses of life.

She tries to maintain an even distance between her and the dirty red paint of the boy's car, poking out beneath caked yellow dust. Slowing down and speeding up. Passing the Carlton Hotel, she is cut off by an ancient brown Subaru like her dad used to drive, a relic from when they were the default and only choice, when the Arab Boycott had teeth. It boxes her in as the light goes from green to yellow and finally red, so she guns the throttle, flashes her lights at the group of people at the junction, threatening to cross, careers violently and barrels on by.

She can still see him up ahead, driving slowly, responsibly, indicating and sticking to the speed limit, to the line markings, to the lights. With the sea always on their right, the waves breaking lazily against the sand, she settles in behind him once again, waiting for him to turn left into the heart of the city, weave through the maze. Maybe he'll pull the car into the parking lot of a nice refurbished Bauhaus building around Shenkin, or drive endlessly around the block by a development off Ibn Gvirol Street, in search of the mythical empty parking space.

But he never does turn left, just keeps driving south past the Opera Tower, site of the state's first parliament; past the mosque and the giant car park, all that remains of the Egyptian Officers' neighbourhood of Manshieh; past Hatachana, the Ottoman train station now an outdoor shopping mall that feels like the terminus at Auschwitz; past Charles Klor, the park with no trees.

Where is he going?

Perhaps to the gentrified, Jewdaised, northern neighbourhoods of Jaffa? But no, instead of turning right out over the sea and up to the clock tower, he keeps straight on Sderot Yerushalaim and she settles into her seat for the drive to *Bat Yam* through Tel-Aviv-Yafo's Arab desert.

She is gazing out of the window at the rows of crumbling buildings and decaying stores that line the side of the road, is not paying attention when his indicator blinks. She's got sloppy and the buffer has disappeared, and it takes a hard stab of the brakes to avoid clipping his bumper. She tosses the car around the corner in a tight arc.

She feels tetchy. The air-conditioning pricks the sweat beads on her skin like tiny needles. She's never been here, never wanted to be here. All the furniture of state is so familiar –

the concrete houses and the white and blue and red and white marking the parking from the no-parking – but many of the shop signs are in Arabic and the atmosphere is so sketchy, so threatening. His car now provides comfort so she follows close, her headlights blinding. Silently, she begs the boy to turn away and lead her from this wilderness.

He slows, indicates in an empty street as if he is politely guiding her. She watches him pull into a driveway which may just be pavement, continues to the nearest cross street, pulls around the corner as he switches off the ignition. Driving halfway up the road, she conducts a dirty three-point turn. The gears crunch like an assault rifle. As her car creeps back towards the corner, Lia just catches a glimpse of the boy entering the house. The door swings back, closed.

The scene doesn't make sense. Dani, Daniel: a nice name. The name of a friend of Michael. A nice Jewish friend.

She wants to put the car in gear and drive away, drive north or south of here where things are congenial and familiar, but instead Lia finds her hand under the steering wheel. The engine splutters into silence. She has to know, and so she doesn't think, she just does: somehow she is in front of the house looking up at a heavy naked yellow bulb that swings above her head. Her finger is prodding a bell that protrudes from uneven masonry.

The sound is rough and loud, and it rattles the house like a hollow frame. Footsteps carry from the other side of the door. They stop abruptly, replaced by mechanical thuds that descend from the top of the doorframe, locks being opened in series. Finally, the door cracks open and two bloodshot black eyes stare out at her through the hand-span's crack. They squint, hovering just above a gold chain that glints in the lamplight.

If Lia kicked out now, she could probably force the door open, send the man flying, enter the house. The chain is thin and flimsy and would snap easily, but its presence is a statement: she is not a welcome guest.

They stand in silence, neither willing to pre-empt the other. But then, as she opens her mouth to speak, he speaks first.

'Who are you? What do you want?' The voice is hard and tight. How often does a visiting Jew late at night foreshadow anything other than disaster?

'My name is Lia,' she says and her accent suddenly sounds so Hebrew, so mouthy and measured compared to the throaty, guttural sounds coming from the other side of the door. 'I would like to speak to Dani, please. Daniel. If that's OK.'

The eyes narrow further.

'There is nobody here by that name.'

He is already shifting his weight, pushing the door closed and moving his hands down towards the first lock. She can't let him reach it.

Lia tips her body forward, leans her weight full against the broad wooden door. It gives slightly and creaks on its hinges, weary with age, edges back just far enough that she can wedge a foot behind it. This door is old, the house too. Older than the state and at least as old as Tel-Aviv.

She yells out in pain: the man has yanked the door back and slammed it against her foot, grazing the top of her shoe and cleaving off some skin. A reflex pulls her leg back, and by the time she decides to fight through the agony, it is too late. The locks are thudding in time with the blood in her ears.

'Please,' she yells, rapping her knuckles against the worm-eaten wood. 'I saw him enter this house. I need to talk to him. Please.'

The footsteps recede, heavy with victory. A little sliver of blood drips down over her foot.

Lia watches Sharon recalibrate her life after the 1996 election with distant curiosity. She leaves the youth movement, lets her hair grow back, removes half her piercings. The holes become but faint shadows. One night in the hours that are both too early and too late, howls from the street shake the house to life. A voice wails and yells and begs like a wounded infantryman trapped in no man's land.

Lia tiptoes out onto the landing, wary as all the lights are already on. Her parents are barrelling towards the front door. She doesn't follow them, instead rushes to her sister's room where she pushes through the unlocked door.

Sharon's window is wedged open and Lia crawls through onto the ledge. Down below them in the driveway a ghostly outline stands in the twin beams of a car's headlights. His arms are outstretched like those of a martyred Christ.

'Amir, go home,' Sharon hisses. She seems unaware of Lia's presence.

In the leaking fragments of the light, Lia can just make out tears falling from his eyes. He has foregone all dignity.

'Why did you leave the movement, Sharon? Why did you leave me?' His voice is a wail. 'I love you. I always will.'

'You're drunk, Amir. Go home.'

'I'm not drunk.' He stumbles forward. 'I need you. Marriage

is a bourgeois concept, but I'll marry you if you want. Anything for you. Just don't go.'

He collapses into a heap, yowls, cries and groans. Somewhere below them, the front door opens and Lia sees the head of her father, his body wrapped in his weathered flannel dressing gown. In his hand he wields a broom.

'Inside, now.'

Sharon shoves Lia back into the room and the slamming window does little to muffle the aggravated yelling of a car tearing away, out onto the street.

'Who was that?' asks Lia.

Sharon is sitting on the bed, silent and still as the dead. Her eyes are damp, but all emotion is scrubbed from her face.

'Nobody.'

Their father's footsteps are heavy. They beat a furious rhythm up the stairs. Lia knows better than to be there when he arrives.

In a dark, dank Jaffa back street, what hope Lia entertained for some explanation seeps down through her body and bleeds out through the cut on her foot. She has lost, and it is an achingly familiar sensation.

Perhaps she will never know the connection between her baby brother and this Arab boy with the Jewish name. The round sound of the last lock clicking fades into silence and she wants to yell, to scream and to pound her fists against the door; to prostrate herself like a dog or a Muslim, and beg. Instead, she just stands there, rooted to the spot with her numb, dead limbs. Her arms hang limp by her side, her legs are barely able to carry her weight.

Slowly, without real purpose, she turns and stares blankly out across the empty street, at the street lights spraying jaundiced pools of uneven yellow on the tarmac. She gazes right, then left; she can't remember where she parked the car. She must move, must do something, and so she places one foot before the other.

A yellow rubber ball barely misses her head. She watches it bounce once, twice, three times before rolling into the gutter and disappearing down a drain. The whistle that floats down adds to her confusion.

'You,' comes a whispered shout, 'there's a place around the

corner. I'll meet you there in half an hour.'

She turns towards it too late; two large wooden shutters have already clanged shut, and as the stillness returns she's unsure whether the voice was real or a product of her frenzied imagination. This part of town, this house, with its crumbling arches and its jagged weathered stonework that probably pre-dates British Palestine and the Balfour Declaration, is so bizarre and threatening. The voice wasn't real. None of this is real. This isn't her Israel, the country she knows.

She scans for Sharon's car, but just as she plips the alarm, heads for the noise, as the locks have sprung open with a well-oiled thud, she pauses, weighs options. With a willpower she must summon from deep within, she walks away from the car in the direction mandated by the voice which, like everything of consequence in this land, may not have existed at all.

Lia is one of the first in her year to experience the swelling and stretching of puberty. She feels self-conscious, isolated by the changes in her body, only approached by the most presumptuous of her male classmates.

She watches with awe as Sharon becomes a model pupil, seemingly without effort. Her love life is the talk of the school, a never-ending stream of eager suitors. Whispers promise a future in the army's fabled 8200 intelligence unit, the reserve of the country's rising or risen princelings. Her earlier incarnation seems extinguished, her activism and idealism excised. The edginess has been replaced with a cloak of impermeable perfection.

Sex arrives early and quickly for Lia, a foolish confusion of opportunity and affection in an alley not far from her home. She uses no protection and after fixing her skirt, checking for popped buttons on her top, she spends the evening searching for a pill to bring the event to a close. In the school corridors the next day, the boy ignores her.

Another election is announced in May 1999 and for the first time, Sharon is eligible to vote. Lia accompanies her to the local polling station, set up in the school they both still attend. Lia is not permitted to enter the cordoned-off voting area, and so she watches as her sister disappears.

When Sharon reappears a few minutes later, Lia inundates her with questions. Who did she vote for? How did it feel?

'It's anonymous for a reason,' she says.

Although Ehud Barack, a decorated general and Yitzhak Rabin's heir apparent, is elected in a landslide, Sharon exhibits no trace of joy in the result. That evening, when the family camps around the television to watch Bibi Netanyahu deliver his capitulation speech, Sharon has long withdrawn to her room. Lia runs upstairs to tell her sister that peace has won, but there is no answer to her knocks upon the door.

The summer passes quickly and, in the North, the IDF withdraws from the last occupied sliver of Lebanon. A few human interest stories pepper the media, follow the country's former allies as they are massacred or flee to Israel; in Kiriyat Ono, Lia's life settles into a tedious routine. Her days are spent behind the counter of the local mall's sweets-and-cigarette store, her nights filled with American teen soaps and gossip on the phone. Her father complains of her tying up the line but refuses to purchase a second. Free from school but not yet drafted, Sharon too has found a job in the mall, up the escalators at one of Israel's local-brand clothing companies.

Lia parries the advances of her lecherous boss, makes a point of befriending all the younger mall workers during her breaks. She explores the building, discovers quiet nooks and crannies throughout the administrative floors on the upper levels, smokes weed with her sister for the first time.

Sharon only agrees to smoke once her shifts are finished. She arrives early and leaves late and it is not long before she has progressed to store manager. Her fellow staff keep their distance.

Towards the end of summer, Lia is summoned to an army base for evaluation. She is excited, feels the long-anticipated future breathing imminent and close. In an airless room, a computer spits out questions of logic and a girl barely older than her sister quizzes her on her personal details, her history, her life. She takes no interest in the answers, treats Lia like an idiot, explains it is only to make sure she is not one.

'If something happens to you,' her interviewer says, her voice flat and bored, 'who would you like to receive the compensation money?' It takes a moment for Lia to realise she is speaking about her own death.

She stumbles, mumbles something incoherent and vague before finally mouthing the names of her parents. The interviewer ticks a box, slides over a booklet.

'The last thing,' she says. 'Read these and tick off all the things that interest you.'

Lia skims the pages. She ticks the box that says 'helping people'.

It is the only one of which she is certain.

It feels to Lia as if the golden hands of her Swatch, bubbled with rust, have stopped. She watches them intently, willing them to turn. The old man with the sag on one side of his face, and the glass eye on the other, hasn't taken the eye that moves off her yet.

She is the only woman in the coffee shop. The only Jew too.

This is how she always imagined Riyadh or Beirut or Damascus, those chauvinistic, medieval fiefdoms, not somewhere minutes from her home. Most of the tables are full but there is scant conversation. Men smoke bubbling *nargilot* and grunt, bathed in the glow from the muted television hung on one of the walls.

It hangs at an uncertain angle, flanked to one side by a too-slick portrait, she assumes depicting the family patriarch. On the other, an indelicate painting of Al-Aqsa's gleaming dome. The mosque sits amidst a Jerusalem cleansed of modernity, cleansed of Jews.

She has ordered a cup of coffee, and it sits on the table, untouched. *Black coffee,* she called it. *Arabic coffee* is racist.

It is time to sip. She grips the crude porcelain handle with two fingers, but her hands are shaking and the top of the muddy sludge rolls and tumbles over the cup's thick lip. She puts it back down, but the unintended crash against the saucer seems to draw everyone's gaze away from the television.

The voice said it would meet her in half an hour, but already nearly forty-five minutes have passed. She is certain he's not coming and, worse, she's sure that the voice never existed, that her sanity's thread may finally have snapped. It has been a tough month. Tough months; a tough year.

She should leave. This is no place for her.

Lia scrambles to her feet and is half-way to the door before a pair of shoes blocks her path. Black leather, rubber soles worn at the heels to reveal the gait. The cheap shoes of the working man, like those that now sit by the entrance to her home.

'Where are you going?'

Dani whispers in Hebrew, but he follows it with a yell in Arabic aimed behind her. It is deeper, more masculine: testosterone unrestrained by the good sense of women. He yells again and then hisses, barely audible, in her ear, 'Sit down, you stupid woman. They think you're trying to leave without paying.'

She's about to protest but he's right, and so she lets herself be guided back to her seat, hunched and embarrassed like a child caught mid-crime. Here he seems so different from the boy in the bar. There, his motions were fluid, his dress ostentatiously current. Here his movements are less fine but bolder, more robust, dressed in the muted colours of the Arab. The earring has disappeared, the hole now no more perceptible than a freckle.

'You speak English, right?' he says in a thick American accent, spiced with the deep south. 'No Hebrew, please.'

'Who,' she begins but he doesn't let her finish.

'So you're a sister. Which one? No, don't tell me, let me guess. Lia. Definitely Lia.'

'How did you know?'

'Just something about the way he described you.'

He pulls a pack of red Marlboros from his pocket, taps the bottom twice and lifts one to his mouth. Two cigarettes in the pack are upside down, the strips of tobacco sprouting irregularly like leaves. He slides a gold Zippo lighter across the table.

'I doubt we'd be sitting here if you were Sharon,' he says, beckons for her to pick it up. 'Do you mind?' Lia clicks the lighter wheel and the cigarette crackles as the flame sears and singes and burns. 'They say you lose half your sex appeal if you light your own.' He takes a deep breath and the cigarette end shimmers bright red. He shrugs. 'I know it makes no sense, but we all need our superstitions.'

'You know it's illegal to smoke inside.'

'We're a long way from central Tel-Aviv, *motek*,' he says and to make the point he blows a thin line of wispy grey smoke in her face. It smells like Yonatan used to, and it makes her cough. 'That's where you live, right? Kerem Hateymanim.' He pauses, takes another deep breath, cracks a sadistic grin. 'Among Arabs.'

Everyone is watching her again. She is crying. He knows so much of her life.

'Who are you?' she whispers, wipes her nose, her eyes with a wrist.

'Why should I tell you?'

He leans back, spreads a long arm over the back of the empty chair by his side. She is shaking. She cannot meet his gaze, so instead she looks outside into the overwhelming dark of this Arab town.

Blue and white lights flash; a police car prowls the street. It doesn't aim to be invisible, anodyne, like the white and blue Skodas just up the coast in Tel-Aviv proper. This jeep is grey, the windows covered with chicken-wire, the body with armour. It is hard and threatening.

She takes a deep breath.

'*Achi*!' she yells in Hebrew, to the glass eye. She thrusts a hand into the air and clicks her fingers as loudly as she can manage. 'Brother, another cup of coffee, and one for my good friend Dani too.'

'What are you doing?' he hisses. His face drains of colour and his knuckles, too, are white, as his hands grip the table.

She says in English, calmly now, 'I'll ask you again. How do you know who I am?'

She has him. He knows it too. Slowly, he withdraws.

'Mickey told me about you. About all of you.'

'Told you what?'

'That you were sad. That your marriage was collapsing. That you weren't capable of fixing it.'

'He said that?'

'I just met you tonight. Who else would have told me?'

'And why would my brother talk to you?'

'Let's just say we were close.'

Glass Eye places two coffees on the table and leaves with a brusque grunt. Dani says something to him in Arabic and then stubs out his spent cigarette before picking another from the packet. The action seems contrived, and he looks so young, younger even than he must be. Once again he slides the lighter over. She watches the flame dance in the wetness of his eyes and she suddenly realises what's been obvious all along. A great jagged boulder settles in that hole in her heart.

'What's your name?' she says. Her voice is stripped of its previous edge.

'Dani.'

'What does Glass Eye over there call you?'

'Not Dani,' he says with a sad smile. 'That's what they call me over there. You know, in your city.'

'Were you two... You and Michael...'

He exhales a curtain of smoke that hides his face. She does not see his features though she knows that he nods.

'How long?'

'Who knows.'

His shrug tells her that *he* knows. To the day. Probably to the hour, the minute too. 'A few years, I guess.'

'Did you love him?'

'What do you think?'

What does she think? That sat here under the arches of this Arab coffee shop in this Arab town with this Arab stranger, she feels further away than she did when she visited the vast expanses of Patagonia. Yet this boy across from her – the kid making her so nervous that her foot keeps tap-tap-tapping against the cheap tile floor – is bringing her closer to Michael than she has ever been.

'How did you meet?'

'At a club. In a bathroom. How it's done for people like us.'

'So you—' She doesn't know how to say it tactfully, so she doesn't. He glares back.

'Of course not. We just held hands.'

'Then? In the bathroom?'

'Sweetie,' he says, shuffling in his seat as if preparing himself for a familiar judgement. 'We're already filthy, disgusting animals. Don't pretend as if it's the sex that's wrong.'

His hostility is returning, but this time she wants to reach out and comfort him. She wishes to show him she isn't like these backward bigots around them here; that she comes from a place where who he is – what he is – is accepted.

So she says, 'Your English is really good. Where did you learn it?'

'Dallas,' he says and she wonders how he can be so well travelled before she remembers the TV show, all big 80s hair and a catchy theme. 'They used to play it on Jordan 2 with Arabic subtitles. I watched it when we could pick up the signal, when the weather was good.'

'Seems unfortunate for a man,' she pauses, swallows her words, '...like you, to speak Southern. Doesn't seem a particularly appropriate choice.'

They both laugh and perhaps a few bricks have been loosened in the wall between them. Lia knows they'll never get further here; she needs to free him from these barbarians with their *nargilot* and their doctrines.

The fear arrives anew: she doesn't want him to refuse her. Nonchalantly as she can manage, she reaches into her bag, pulls out her wallet and says:

'How about we get out of here?'

High school seems alien to Lia without Sharon's presence floating through the halls. She feels a new freedom from association, but also nostalgia for a lost companionship. So when Sharon invites her to play truant one day in September 2000, soon after the start of the new year, she leaps at the opportunity. They catch a bus at the nearby airport and steal together up Route One to Jerusalem. Atop a broad hill they offload, queue among the religious and the tourists for a taxi which patiently wades through the gridlock of the city's streets. The familiar bitter honking of traffic is accompanied by cracks of gunfire and light arms that both sisters prefer to ignore. The Arab taxi driver peers at them in the mirror. They diligently avoid his gaze.

Their destination is a small, stone house in a quiet, middle-class neighbourhood. The road overlooks the walls of the Old City and the Temple Mount and as they exit the cab, they can see plumes of smoky white cloud rising into the pale blue sky above the golden mosque.

'What the hell is going on?' says Sharon quietly to herself.

An old lady greets them with a warm handshake. She sniffs the air as if catching the cause of the troubles on the wind.

'Poking those Arabs with a stick by going up there.' She beckons the girls to follow her. 'Ariel Sharon's a monster for sure, murdered all those Palestinians up in Lebanon in Sabra and Shatilla. But he's right, you know. They only understand force. Why can't we pray at our holiest place? Our Temple, their Haram Al-Sharif. That Al-Aqsa mosque was only built there to deny us our rights, y'know.' She tuts. 'He's wrong, but he's also right.'

A crack of gunfire responds like a round of applause.

There is a car tucked behind the house. The driveway upon which it rests is scarred with discarded masonry and overgrown weeds. This is what Sharon has come for, and she studies the ancient Autobianchi with an earnest diligence. One day the body may have been black, but now it straddles the monochrome spectrum in patches even to white. The roof is potholed with blotches where the clear coat has been mauled by the sun, exposed rusted metal visible in droplets through the battered paint.

'May I?' says Sharon, as she gestures to the ignition. The woman shrugs, gazes absentmindedly across the valley to the walls and the golden dome beyond. She spits on the ground.

'That Ehud Barack,' she says. 'We never should have trusted him. He's no better than that terrorist Arafat.'

The car sputters into life on the first twist of the key. Joy flickers on Sharon's features, but it is little more than a phantom, dissolves in an instant.

Lia stands dutifully aside as Sharon and the woman talk money. She immediately goes in low, but the negotiation is half-hearted and the payment finally agreed is barely more than the opening offer.

'To tell you the truth,' the woman says, 'I'll just be happy to get it off my property. Nobody will buy the house with that heap of junk leaking oil into the *calaniot*.' Hastily, she adds, 'It doesn't leak oil, dear.'

The cash has yet to be paid.

'Are you leaving Jersualem?' says Sharon.

The woman's shoulders fall heavily. 'There's no place here for normal people,' she says. 'Not any more.' She waves her hand over the neighbourhood, points accusingly at the surrounding buildings, at a religious family crossing in a neat line before the house. 'Just the *dossim* and foreigners here now. You know, we used to have friends all around here. Families. Artists, doctors, lawyers. Kids. Good people, all of them. All gone now. The religious crowd into the bad parts of the city, just like the ghettos in the war. The good parts, like here, are all being bought up by rich Jews from America. They only want their part of the holy city for two weeks a year and the rest of the time it's a ghost town.' Gunfire and grenades go off beyond the wadi. 'Crazy people and Arabs. That's all that's left in Jerusalem.'

Sharon has the money ready in an envelope. As the woman speaks, she removes a few notes, stuffs them into her pocket. The woman does not check the contents before she hands over the keys.

As they are set to drive off, she leans over, raps calloused knuckles on the glass. Lia cranks down the window.

'Where are you girls from?' says the woman.

'Tel-Aviv,' Lia half-lies.

'Tel-Aviv,' the woman repeats, nods. 'I'll probably end up there.' She chews on an empty mouth, then straightens. A vertebra cracks. 'Things will reach there too,' she says. 'In the end.' She nods again, gives a little wave. This time it is a goodbye.

On the way to the road to Tel-Aviv, they pass a column of armoured cars. A few Humvees follow behind, their soldiers decked in olive green combat gear, sitting bolt upright, open to the elements. They look like cyborgs.

The Autobianchi is gruff and uncouth, its tinny engine clattering through the gears like a phlegm-laden larynx. The odour of long-since extinguished cigarettes gives Lia a headache. The ancient terraces and valleys open around them as they descend to the coastal plains.

'Mum and Dad were going to buy you a car before you went to the army,' Lia says.

'I know,' says Sharon.

Within an hour the Autobianchi is parked up in Kiryat Ono. It will not break down once before it is sold, a few days after Sharon is discharged from the army.

Lia feels nostalgic, being beside the sea. The washing water, the sand in all its rolling uncertainty, always shifting. She feels it beneath her feet, between her toes.

She recalls the army, waiting for the sun, a swollen orange orb, to set behind the horizon of the Red Sea, for streaks to lash out in pinks and reds across the sky. Those moments after the sunset were always her favourite.

She remembers the night Ben was conceived, feels Yonatan's sleeping breath against her shoulder blade. In, warm; out, cool. The juices of them together mixed with the tiny little shards that filed at her legs, her buttocks, her back, ferreted their way into every fold of her body.

At the beach she feels at peace.

Dani tosses another spent cigarette onto the sand. 'I miss him,' he says. All his bravado and drama has drained from him like water. 'Sometimes I think that we've just had a fight. Or that he's having one of his straight days. That I just need to wait a while and then he'll call.'

'Straight days?' Lia says.

'He wasn't very good at being gay.'

'It never occurred to me, you know.'

'That he was gay? Or that gay people had days they didn't want to be gay?'

Both.

'Sometimes I thought maybe he wasn't having problems with being gay, just of being gay *with me*. He'd get so angry, so bitter and hateful, and then I'd suck his cock and we'd hug and kiss and hold each other after he came.' He gazes into the distance. 'He'd say he loved me.'

A wave breaks in a line of salty foam. Overeager, it crawls slowly up the beach, laps against their feet before thinking better of it and slipping back out to sea.

'I didn't think it was a choice,' she says.

'I'd say that to him and he'd laugh – you know, that beautiful, sexy, I'm so much smarter than you laugh – and he'd tell me I couldn't talk about denial.' He coughs a laugh, heavy and sad. 'He had a point, but I could never come back after that. It just killed it, you know... the conversation.'

'It can't be easy for you.'

'Being an Arab? Of course not.' His voice becomes coarse like gravel. 'But you're a fool if you think my being an Arab was easier for him.'

'Why didn't he tell me?'

He shrugs. 'He said that he thought about it a few times. Said he was planning to tell you, Sharon, your parents. Even went as far as convening some grand family meeting to announce the news. That was when it was best. When he was telling me he couldn't imagine life apart. Then, afterwards, he wouldn't talk about it any more. I kept trying to convince him, because it's exhausting, really really exhausting, to be with someone who's always like "yes, I'm gay, let's be together", "no, I'm not, fuck off, you fag".' His wet eyes reflect the moonlight. 'As if I'm not dealing with enough shit without him claiming that I turned him. That it's all my fault. What bullshit.'

Of course Lia would have welcomed him with open arms, hugs and kisses. It wouldn't have changed anything, only added a new layer of intimacy, a special quality to their confidence, to their relationship. So she'd called him "gay" once or twice, but there wasn't any malice in it. Not intentionally.

'He was such a happy kid,' she says, empty words to break the silence. It's not a real, bottomless silence, though. That's the beauty of the sea. Even here on this unfamiliar beach; Ajami's waterfront, strangely unloved, unkempt.

Do Arabs even like the beach?

'He wasn't happy,' says Dani. 'Not happy at all. Not for a long time.'

She bats it away. Michael had just finished school, just got back from a boy's holiday to Greece with his friends. He was training by the beach nearly every day, pushing his body on, further and further, harder and harder. That dream of his, to be accepted to the commandos. She can still feel his eager excitement; an afterglow of his life.

'It was all a lie,' says Dani. He's studying her face intently, and she feels exposed. He clears his throat, spits a long trail of thick yellow onto the sand. With one foot, he moves the beach to cover it. 'It was all an act for your benefit.'

'You don't know what you're talking about. He couldn't wait to go. Was even gonna do *gibbush matkal.*'

'You really think he wanted to go to *Tzahal*? To fight people on their own land? To risk his life in some war without a goal? Maybe he'd fail the test, end up manning a checkpoint to stop grandmothers from visiting their grandkids. That's the dream, right?' His hands gesticulate. 'All you fucking Jews. I told him the truth; what it's really like for the Arabs over there, and even for us Arabs over here in what you call "Israel proper". He didn't want to hear, but I told him again and again and again. No, he wasn't excited about the Army.' He takes a deep breath, sniffles, closes his eyes, wipes his nose. He is crying again. 'I have a clear conscience. On that at least.'

All his pain, the anger, it's just frustration painting a picture of what he wants to believe. The Arab hates the Jew as the sun rises in the east. A natural order to the world. This boy may have ravished her brother, but he is still an Arab.

He can't understand what it is to love your country and cherish your people. Of course Michael must have known that bad things are being done in the territories – every sane person does – but the root, the cause, it's not us. There are crazy Jews across the Green Line in Judea and Samaria, in the West Bank or whatever people want to call the Land of Israel – those religious crazies in their caravans. The real settlers, not the young families in search of subsidised rents and good schools. But no Jew has ever blown himself up, wilfully, to murder the innocent, mothers and children; to invite reprisal and further pain.

War is war, but the Arabs have no humanity.

'You think I'm lying?' he says. It is a statement set up as a question. Lia doesn't want to hurt him. He probably really does think Michael came around to his point of view.

Two stray cats squeal and both Lia and Dani turn. They don't see anything in the wet gloom. Maybe they're fighting. Maybe they're screwing. Maybe that's just the way they talk.

'You look like him you know,' he says.

'That's what they say.'

'More than that. Your mannerisms. They're like his. Like how you're picking at your nails.'

She looks down at the raw cuticles on her finger.

'I really miss him,' he says, and she watches a tear break loose and fling itself weightlessly upon his cheek. He sighs. 'I woke this morning, and I was going to call him. For a tiny fraction of a moment, I forgot he was gone.'

He gasps down air and the words are bloated, heavy. 'The day he had the accident, it was unbearable. We'd been planning the trip for months, but then we had a fight and he said he didn't want me to come to Eilat. Then later, he called from some gas station outside Arad and told me he loved me, that he missed me. I asked him if I should fly down and he just said "We'll see". Then he said he'd call me when he got there, and when he didn't I knew something was wrong. I think I was the last person to find out. From *YNet*. A fucking traffic report.'

'I'm sorry. It must have been horrible to hear like that.'

Not that there's a pleasant way.

'I nearly didn't make the funeral.' He says. 'I had to lie to my work to be able to leave.' He laughs through his nostrils and the sound is cold and bitter. 'I say I had to, but they probably would have been OK with it all. That's the thing about lying: you don't know when to stop.'

'I saw you there.'

'I know.'

'You were crying.'

'When his body half slid into the ground and then stuck on the gurney, that's when it all became real. There's his fucking body, this lump of meat in a shawl, and it's sweating in the heat, but still there's no Michael there any more.' He pauses, takes a long slow breath. 'I drove to Park Yarkon and cried and screamed like an animal till after nightfall.' So much for Arab pride. 'This is all I can manage now,' he says and flicks the moisture from his fingers. 'I'm all spent.'

She nods, waits. How pitiful he is. This is a mitzvah, to let him talk, let him mourn, let him be who he is, unfettered, unafraid. Just be with his grief.

'Does it feel better?' she says. 'Today?'

'No. I'm afraid of when it does, though.'

He tilts his head up to catch the tears which once again threaten to fall. The cigarette shifts in his fingers and he releases a nail to scratch at his three-day beard as his eyes remain desperately open, staring out at the shadowy horizon.

'Then it will feel like I'm losing him. All the details... the smell, the touch. The sensation. Of him. I can still feel them now... actually on my skin... in my nose, my mouth. But I know they're getting ready to slip. To disappear. And... I'm terrified that when they go, all that will be left is this hole that just... aches.' He shifts a fistful of sand into an open palm and lets it fall, slowly, rhythmically, through his fingers.

He's lost the fight and his tears are flowing freer than ever. Lia is struck by an immense warmth towards him in his vulnerability. He is suffering so much, as much as she, maybe more. What is a higher rank of love, of pain?

She shifts her weight to one buttock, leans over across

the sand between them to place, perhaps, an arm around his shoulder. Her ringtone rends open the Ajami quiet. The opportunity is lost.

'Your phone?' he says, turning to face her.

She yearns to salvage the intimacy, to complete the embrace that may have been, but he says, 'You should get that,' and it's too late.

Sharon's voice is frantic, whispered, consumed with a panic it's trying to disguise.

'Where are you?' she says breathlessly. 'They stole my car. Those bastards stole my car. It'll be carting around goats in Rahat by tomorrow. Can you hear me? They fucking stole my car!'

Lia catches the laugh just in time. Somewhere in the background there's another voice, and it is whispering between heavy breaths. She imagines bony, masculine fingers prying her sister's impossibly thin waist, the sandpaper stubble grazing her neck.

'It was me. I took your car.'

She could have drawn it out, waited for a more opportune moment, but now she has hung herself, and in the silence of the line Lia imagines her sister tensing, straightening to her full height and placing a hand on the man's wayward probing knuckles, holding them still.

'Why would you do that?'

There is fury there. Lia knows she won't press, not now, and that little space allows her to run with a story, lay out the facts as she creates them.

'I just needed to do something and you were so wrapped up in your boy toy it was like I didn't exist.' It is true. Or at least true enough. 'I didn't want to interrupt.'

There is another silence, then:

'It's not like that.'

Lia knows she's won.

'Where are you?'

'Still at the Namal.' Of course: Lia has her car. 'But we're heading to Rothschild. There's a protest planned and Chris wants to go. He's covering it for his newspaper.'

The voice in the background: 'Radio. It's for radio.'

'Fine. We'll meet you there.'

'We?'

Lia watches the man-child lost in the rolling of the sea. He is staring out at the crescent moon that seems to hover inches above his head.

'I'm bringing a friend.'

The little nearly-dead Autobianchi is Sharon's vehicle to slowly, methodically, extricate herself from their lives.

As the Ehud Barak government collapses, as the last-gasp peace talks in the once Israeli-occupied Egyptian casino town of Taba extinguish with a whimper, as Ariel Sharon becomes prime minister in a landslide equally as impressive as Barack's before, Sharon becomes a living memory. She rents an apartment in Tel-Aviv's old north, her windowless bathroom facing the park and the Yarkon River. Word arrives to Kiriyat Ono that she is to be drafted, as expected, to 8200. The apartment enjoys easy access to the Ayalon highway and her daily commute will be a leisurely twenty minutes back and forth up the coast to Glilot junction. She asks her family not to see her off.

Lia's home is no longer Sharon's home.

The Second Intifada roars into life. *Piguim*, "incidents", usually suicide bombings, come thick and fast throughout the country. Lia claims she does not visit Sharon due to the security concerns, and while it is true that Tel-Aviv is heavily targeted, her words ring hollow in her own ears.

The family has planned a trip to the North for June. Sharon declines to join. As news filters through of rising tensions with Hizballah on the Lebanese border, and rolling flashpoints emerge even between Jews and Arabs in Israel proper, Lia's father adjusts plans. The majority of the country's citizen-Arabs reside in the Galilee, so they head south to the Dead Sea, their grey Mitsubishi following a red Volkswagen equally stuffed with the family of a work colleague. Lia's father becomes skittish as they turn just before Jerusalem to follow Route One. They pass the Maale Adumim settlement, and cut down through the Judaean desert, deep into the West Bank.

'Crazy idiot,' mutters Lia's father. 'I didn't avoid the Galilee to end up in the Palestinian Territories.'

'Why didn't you go via Ashdod?' says her mother.

They are surrounded by green and white Palestinian licence plates. Silence fills the car. Ratty old Mercedes sedans belch thick diesel smoke; yellow, sun-worn Ford transit taxis veer dangerously between lanes.

Lia stares into the passing vehicles. Maybe this is the first time she has seen real Palestinian Arabs. Not 1948 Arabs, not migrant workers waiting beneath highway underpasses for either work or a ride home – gone now that the Oslo Accord borders, recently drawn, are closed for war.

'Dad, are they going to kill us?' says Michael beside Lia. He is looking into the dilapidated Subaru that rides beside them. An Arab family gazes back: father and mother up front, daughter and son behind.

'No, son, they won't,' says their father. There is little conviction to his words.

The sense of relief is palpable when they cross the checkpoint to the Dead Sea. From there it is only a short drive to the Ein Gedi oasis where the two families fold themselves from their cars and size each other up. Only the fathers have previously met.

Alon, the oldest of three sons, is tall and slim and nineteen years to Lia's seventeen. His clothes seem painted onto the slab-like creases of his body. He is to be drafted in weeks. Lia is immediately smitten. Each family has its own bungalow; two bunk beds pressed up against the wall, a toilet and a shower. Spartan, efficient. There is a patio in front, decorated with a table, chairs and a parasol against the dusty desert sun. They share the little encampment with a party of middle-age Russians; the lisping warble of their voices filters through the walls.

They leave their things, prepare shoes, clothes, chilled water bottles in insulated packs, hike up through the canyon to the waterfall. They are quickly overtaken by the Russians and the parents ridicule their immaculate clothing, the women's makeup, their coiffed hair, so inappropriate for the activity, the place, the heat.

Lia maintains a constant proximity to Alon. When they swim, she grabs any pretext to connect skin with skin: she falls dramatically into his arms, kicks him playfully beneath the surface. Michael sticks to his sister like a limpet, shadowing her every move.

Exhausted from the exertion and armed with the superficial familiarity of fast friends, the two families eat dinner together in the cafeteria. They share a table and pick at the vats of hummus, rice, schnitzel and day-old salad, slop them onto chipped stoneware plates. The Russians file in, and their raucous laughing drowns the families' voices. They pass around vodka bottles and shot glasses brought from home.

Lia watches them, marvels at how different they are from the grey, faceless wretches that piled out of plane after plane, airlifted to the Promised Land from the decaying carcass of the Soviet Union. Their boisterousness gives Lia a pretence to isolate Alon from his family and she lures him away with a malabi, leads him to a lonely table by the window. An unwelcome foot grazes hers; Michael sits in the chair by Alon's side.

Her brother has grown into a young boy of great sensitivity, crushed by an innate kindness, often abused. Lia usually enjoys his company, but not now.

'Is it OK?' he says.

She says no just as Alon says yes, and so she bites down on her tongue.

The families relocate to the patios of their cabins. As the

night wears on, their numbers thin until only Lia, Alon and Michael remain outside. Even the Russians have retreated to bed, and the night is windless and ominously still, as if the desert is holding its breath. Only the stars above them glisten, oblivious in the celestial blackness.

Lia feels her time slipping away, senses the drive home in the morning, the squandering of fleeting opportunity.

'I really like you,' she whispers to Alon. Her hand rests on his leg.

She does not expect Alon to shuffle backwards, to push her back. Her muscles fall limp.

'Stop,' says Michael. 'Lia, he's telling you no.'

'Why are you even here?' she yells. 'What? Do you like him? Is that it?' Breathlessly, she adds, 'Gayboy!'

She immediately regrets her words, wants to apologise to her brother but he seems beaten, will not meet her gaze.

'I really like you,' says Alon, 'but I've got a girlfriend.'

Lia is not listening. She is only concerned with Michael.

A phone begins to ring in one of the adjacent bungalows. Soon, another and then another. A flock of electronic songbirds has descended. There is a long, heavy pause before screams rent open the blank blackness of the night.

The Russians flood patios around them, a flurry of confused activity. Some run, some stand stock-still. Others turn and twist as if lost, confounded by the solidity of the very ground itself.

The light comes on in the hut of Lia's family; her father pushes open the blue door. He is rubbing his eyes, and her mother follows, her telephone pressed up against her ear.

'What happened?' says Lia.

Her father doesn't know, and so they wait for her mother to close the phone, to provide the context.

'*Pigua*,' her mother says. 'Suicide bombing. A nightclub in Tel-Aviv.'

'Which one?'

'Pacha. At the Dolphinarium. Do you know it?' She does,

well. As the details emerge, she can perfectly visualise the Arab joining the queue, the explosion popping off his head and ripping through those waiting, shredding muscle and bone and murdering twenty-one teenagers, splattering their mutilated carcasses across the tarmac.

A Russian woman barrels from the cabin next door. She falls to the floor and her brutish yells congeal into one harrowed sound, as if her soul is being ripped out through her mouth.

Most of the murdered children are Russian.

The traffic is crawling up both sides of Rothschild Boulevard. They circle and circle in an endless loop, and Lia curses the tall buildings that tower over them, for they've robbed the city of its unplanned open spaces, and with them the parking lots. The few that remain have boards outside: "Full" they read, but they may as well say "Good luck".

A blessed sliver of blue and white pavement, and Lia squeezes the car into a tiny space on a parallel street. She knocks bumpers with the car in front, the car behind. This must be a lovely spot during the day, the bougainvillaea creeping across the dilapidated facade of the pre-state building, grand and decrepit and dignified. For decades, these "eclectics" were ridiculed, scorned; florid Euro-Arab bastardisations, an embarrassment to the White City and Tel-Aviv's stark Bauhaus aesthetic values. Now they are coveted, and it's a surprise to see one not surrounded by brash advertisements, being nipped and tucked and prepared for an expensive new lease of life.

Sharon's car has the wrong permit sticker – blue rather than red – but it'll be gone before dawn brings a flood of traffic wardens and their ticket books. Lia locks the doors, pulls the handle just to double-check, and then weaves her arm through Dani's as they dodge the traffic to the central walkway. This southern part is quiet; only a few teenagers loiter with the homeless on the benches that line their route.

Dani pulls the collar of his polo shirt up so the logo is visible from behind. From his pocket he pulls a leather bracelet and fixes it around his wrist.

'Don't forget your earring,' she says.

As they walk north, the density of people increases. She's arranged to meet Sharon by Tony Vespa, but there's no sign of her or the tourist. The smell of reheated pizza smacks them as they hover by the stairs. Lia briefly considers calling Sharon but there is no rush. She has no plans, nowhere to be. There is nothing and nobody to tend to.

Absentmindedly she strokes an arm, feels Dani's dark skin. This strange boy who isn't her brother.

Someone barges past. The corner by the theatre is packed. The television trucks piled onto the pavement have funnelled all the pedestrians into a manic bottleneck and chain-smoking drivers watch the angry yells with disinterest.

'What's going on?' she says to someone leaning against a lamppost smoking a joint.

'There's a protest planned. It should start soon.'

'Protesting what?'

'The city. The police. They arrested Daphni Leef. Didn't you hear?' No, she hadn't heard. Daphni Leef, accidental founder of last year's social protests, when thousands of people called this boulevard home. It seems like a different age. 'She tried to set up a tent. Because, you know, nothing's changed. But they arrested her. Broke her arm. It's a disgrace.'

So many people are milling around by the corner, and it all strikes her as the aftermath of some big cataclysmic event. A terrorist attack maybe, like the ones when Lia was a teenager.

Dani is fidgeting nervously by her side. He shifts constantly, checks his watch compulsively, glances at the police that crowd around the central reservation linking Rothschild, Marmorek and Habima Square. He tries to avoid drawing their attention.

His trepidation is amusing. Paranoid naivety. Now is not the time for lectures or lessons, so she places her hand softly on his shoulder and bellows comfortingly into his ear over the ruckus.

'Habima,' she says, and points across the road to the new grand plaza. The sound of an orchestra rises faintly from the speakers in the submerged garden. Here Dani should be able to breathe. Lia likes this place, comes here often, late in the afternoon when the long shadow of the theatre provides blessed shade for all the mothers escaping the tiny apartments they can barely afford. Each vies for a space in the criss-cross of colourful flowers and saplings, coveting a picnic spot *down there* as children run and play and fight until bedtime, when everything is still again. She loves watching Ben, exhausted from the frantic movement here and there, drift off into sleep in his stroller as they walk down Shenkin, headed home. She tries not to wake him as she changes him into his pyjamas, lowers him into bed. He has to sleep in the *mamad*, the safe-room with its foot-thick walls and its metal curtains and the reinforced door that doesn't shut properly and is so heavy it must be pushed open with both hands. Safe from everything but a direct rocket hit. Sometimes her imagination is agony; when he is in there, she cannot hear him cry.

More police huddle around the tree perched above the spherical grassy knoll. They laugh and backslap like bored teenagers. Aside from them, the square is strangely empty, the periphery of the intense action elsewhere. A single man sits alone, feet in the pit. His chin rests lightly on his palm. The other hand pushes a black baby stroller back and forth by his side. He lifts his head. Lia's breath catches.

Dani is watching her. 'Is that Yonatan?' he says.

Yonatan's presence here, with Ben, floors her. Dani takes her hand and she lets herself be led over to a cement bench beside the escalators that lead down to the car-park bomb shelters.

Lia feels the bench behind her knees as she lowers herself onto it. She wants to run over and grab Ben to her, hug him, smell him, feel him and his life in her arms, but she's terrified of what to say to Yonatan, how she will explain her presence. She cannot take her eyes from him, like that first night at the bar to which they both fled, using each other as an excuse to escape their own lives. When she kept searching for mirrors and glasses through which to watch him without watching. Then it was all oblique, distorted, but now there is no barrier between them and so she is gorging on him, complete.

She feels the rush of warmth, of a fizzy lightness in her head: affection, love, adoration, also concern. He seems so thin, so insubstantial. A bicycle tyre deflated, unseated by a blunt trauma to the wheel. His shoulders are hunched forward, his spine a question mark. His hair is grown out. No longer the neatly-maintained stubble, it is a greasy mop, uneven and patchy. Something seems to be disintegrating within him.

'Is he what you imagined?' she says. Smoke from a new cigarette that Lia didn't light wafts around her face.

'No,' says Dani, 'I expected someone proud.' Ash glides towards the ground. 'And maybe a bit *misken*.'

She uncurls a finger, points it at her husband. 'And how would you describe that?'

He thinks for a moment.

'Broken.'

She wants to wrap her arms around Yonatan, to cup his head to her breast and feel him there. She stands.

'Did Michael like him?' she says.

'Yes and no,' says Dani. 'I couldn't tell. It was about you… when you were good, he liked Yonatan, and when you weren't…'

She begins to walk. With every step she feels a part of her confidence withdrawing, burrowing further into the cloistered shadowy recesses into which she's long retreated. Finally, she towers over Yonatan, clicks first one shoe and then the other against the wooden slats that begin the plunge into the ground.

In his stroller, Ben is deep asleep. He is wearing the little blue and white sailor suit Yonatan's mother bought him, and Lia always hated. The outfit was topmost in the closet, at head height. The first clothes Yonatan would have seen. He looks ridiculous.

His head is turned to the side, cupped by his upper arm as

he breathes lightly and his pacifier bobs up and down on his lips with every breath.

'Your mother would be happy,' she says. It is a joke, yet it sounds so caustic and accusing.

He looks up.

'Hi,' he says. 'What are you...?'

'I just couldn't stay at the shiva,' she says and then waits. He doesn't push further, so she points down to the sleeping baby. 'I missed him. How is he?'

'He's been good. Ate. Made a mess. Watched "Pim Pam Po".' As Yonatan speaks, she bends down and kisses Ben's temple, gently so as not to disturb him. 'He complained a bit when I dressed him but then fell right to sleep when I put him in the stroller.' There is an uncertain pause, then: 'You don't mind I hope.'

'No,' she says. 'Of course not.'

'Who's your friend?'

Dani waves, the red end of his cigarette tracing an arc in the night.

'Just a friend of Michael's.'

'Right, right. From the shiva?'

'Something like that.' She doesn't dwell. 'Sharon should be here soon, too,' she says.

The conversation is already stuck, but she wants to break it free, doesn't want to let it get sucked into silence. 'Listen,' she says, 'I just. I just want to... To talk to you.' She is stuttering, but his eyes are wide so she pushes on, forces the words to continue. 'I know that something happened. That we haven't been... doing too well. But I want you to know. That I love you. That I want to fix it.'

A commotion erupts behind them at the intersection. Yells of either excitement or anger mix with the sound of people in motion. Her phone rings. Sharon's voice is struggling to be heard above the din.

'Where are you?' she says.

Lia is drafted soon after finishing school. A few days after her eighteenth birthday, her parents drive her the short journey to Tel-Hashomer military base, a place she has passed nearly every day of her life, but has never entered. Michael said his goodbyes at the front door; Sharon, recently discharged, is backpacking in Bolivia before the start of her degree at Bristol University.

Surrounded by the other new recruits and their families, her father hugs her. Her mother is crying.

'I'm so proud of you,' he says. Lia does not know why.

She is immediately shipped off to Camp 80 in Pardes Hanna. There, she shares a room with seven other girls, and a bathroom with several dozen more. Their barracks are nicknamed 'The Hilton'; apparently it is unusual to reside in a building, not a tent. The physical exertion is gruelling. She learns to shoot M16s, is taught about weapon classes, about chemical and biological arms, their horrors masked beneath layers of oblique technical jargon.

A girl in Lia's room suffers a bladder infection, a consequence of the strict voiding regime to which they all must adhere. The treatment turns her urine bright red and the ailment compromises her already sketchy bladder control. During a particularly punishing drill Lia watches as the girl's trousers are stained with what looks like blood. The red drips down and pools on the sandy concrete at her feet.

That night, there is little conversation in the room. Lia falls asleep to the sound of the girl's sobs. Soon after Lia takes up her permanent posting at the Southern Naval Command in Eilat, she learns through the grapevine of the girl's death: an army-issued bullet through the head, spraying bone and soft tissue across the wall of her parents' living room. It does not feel real.

Eilat itself is hot and dusty. Its buildings crawl up the craggy beige hills like gnarled desert ibex. The town feels small and provincial and isolated, even after Lia's own suburban childhood. As a *Mashakit Tash*, Lia is a glorified social worker. Her days are a drab trickle of *miskenim*, the military's unfortunate and unwashed, a product of universal conscription among the Jews, Druze and some Bedouin volunteers. Often, she promises to help them with their commanding officers, even makes a few cursory exploratory phone calls to check the validity of their claims of abuse and incapacity. They come to nothing, and she waits for her days to end, to head to the shore and gaze out disaffectedly over the Red Sea. Hemmed in by mountains that channel the clear, cobalt water down towards the Straits of Tiran, to Egypt, to Jordan, to Saudi Arabia, on a clear day she can see all the southern front of the country's perpetual war, laid out like a map.

It is on one such clear day that she is introduced to Ben-El. Shrunken and fragile, the boy is employed slopping out vats in the kitchen. With too few hot meals in his own history, he wilts before her in his chair. His voice is hoarse and brittle, his face is too emaciated for his nineteen years. He tells her the story of his life, and instinctively she knows he is not embellishing the misery. His tale is one of historical slights: the family, refugees from the Arab world, the peripheral development town, the deprivation and unemployment, the factory closures and the men driven to drink and drugs. He speaks of a large household in a tiny home, of five siblings to a room, and their father, dead before his sixtieth birthday. His mother, he says, is so poor that without him working, providing a measly sum, she cannot feed his brothers and sisters, let alone herself. Through tears, he wishes for a war so that he may be killed and in his death, money be paid. Then, his family will eat.

By the shore, Lia fails to settle her mind. She kicks a large rock down into the water. It cracks the thin red lacquer on her toenail and she scrapes the rest off. She sneaks into town alone, drinks cheap vodka from a tumbler and swears to anyone who will listen that she will help Ben-El, do her bit to right all those wrongs.

She arranges a visit, takes a bus to the featureless Negev town. The landmarks comprise a discount supermarket, the rotting hulk of an abandoned soft-drink bottling plant, a central roundabout dedicated to someone of no note beyond the municipal limits. Furtive eyes glance at her from the shadows of the pavements as she searches for the correct street. Ben-El's mother lives in a rundown five-storeys building, crumbling balconies piled with discarded white goods and children's toys. Their garish colours are all that distinguish the block from the street, from the desert behind. The apartment comprises two rooms. In one, mattresses line the floor, dirty clothes heaped in a pile to one side. The other houses an ill-equipped kitchen and a couch.

'Where do you eat?' Lia says. Ben-El's mother points to the floor. 'And how many of you sleep in the bedroom?'

'The children.'

'All of them? And you?'

'I sleep on the couch.'

Ben-El's mother offers Lia tea and she accepts. As she drinks from the chipped cup, she notices that both the fridge and the cupboards are bare.

In the bus on the way back to the base, Lia cries.

Immediately upon her return, she recommends that Ben-El be permitted to seek work part-time. A week passes with no word, and then a month. Imagining the family starving, she hounds Ben-El's commanding officer, but time and again he brushes her off, laughs, tells her it's in the *Mizrachi*'s nature to procreate thoughtlessly.

'Barbarians,' he says. 'They live in caves. And you're asking me to reward them?'

She becomes emotionally erratic in public, takes to cutting herself in visible places on her arms and legs. At first it is an additional means to the end: she is methodical, wipes away the blood and sterilises the wounds; after a while she no longer bothers and her arms and legs are a series of proliferating red scars. She is insubordinate to her superiors, and bursts into tears whenever confronted. Finally, they agree to make an appointment with the *kaban*; the *kaban* passes her on to the psychologist. There, she complains of panic attacks and depression, spits the words through gasped tears. The psychologist listens patiently, scribbles short notes in a file. She attends the final hurdle, the 'psychiatric committee' where a thin, greying woman, all alone in a stark office, asks roundabout questions about her condition and well-being. Finally, she takes off her glasses, rubs the red spots on her nose where they sat. In a voice long drained of sympathy, she asks, 'Are you going to kill yourself?'

When Lia doesn't immediately answer, she asks her again.

'Are you going to kill yourself?'

Lia wants to say yes but she cannot find the words. She is unable to push past the image of the girl from basic training, slumped in her parents' living room, brain splattered on the walls.

'No,' she says.

Her profile is reduced to forty-five, only borderline fit to serve, and she is instructed to collect her things and to immediately check out of the base. A shameful silence wafts behind her as, one by one, she notifies her colleagues and the relevant administrative departments of her reassignment. She is moved to the Navy's southern Mediterranean base in Ashdod, theoretically close enough to home so that she may commute daily. But the bus journey is too long and her parents are so ashamed of her actions that they refuse to buy her a car. Ashdod, the port city, depresses her even more than Eilat, and the Mediterranean with its rolling foam and soft yellow shore is not infused with the exoticism of the Red Sea.

Within a month she has been sent again to the *kaban*. This time, when the question comes, she answers yes.

Sharon joins them just before they are forced from the junction down and onto Ibn Gvirol Street. The tourist trots behind, shoulders back, nose high with impudent authority. He seems less concerned with Sharon than with the grand movement of the collective through the streets. Around them circle drums, and chants of '*Tzedek Hevrati!*' and 'Mayor Huldai Go Home!'.

'Where's my car?' Sharon says. Lia can't hear her, instead reads the motion of her lips.

She stabs her finger in the vague direction of behind them.

Somehow they have been carried into the middle of the few thousand protesters, all pushed in close together. Lia feels limbs without context banging and brushing against her.

'This is Chris,' says Sharon, pointing at the tourist. He's looking out across the crowd.

'It's not as big as I was expecting,' he says. 'Not after those protests last year. What was it, half a million people? When I was in—'

Lia turns away. He's right, though: it does seem small. The energy is here, but it all seems so insignificant; the temper tantrum of a small child. She yearns for a proper demonstration, like those she failed to attend in her youth: when Rabin was shot. Or before she was born, against the slaughter of Palestinians in Lebanon by Israel's allies.

The chants shift, the rhythm massaged like the key change midway through a pop song. The crowd's steps hurry in time. Lia is caught off guard and she stumbles forward, over polka dots and long brown hair, pink skin. The girl uses a megaphone as large as her head to break her fall as she tumbles in three stages down towards the rutted asphalt. The graze on her knee is not yet red with blood, and Lia apologises frantically as she bends to help her to her feet.

The girl brushes herself down and whispers into the megaphone. It screams, 'Thank you!'

The crowd roars and she grins with Colgate-white teeth. How clean and preened and pruned this girl is; she doesn't look like Lia imagines an angry protester should.

She licks a finger, scoops up the blood that has begun to drip from the wound.

'Battle scars,' she shrugs and grins those huge teeth. 'They think they can just stop us from protesting, can arrest people and kill this city's freedom. I expected some cuts and bruises, just not friendly fire.'

The girl leaps onto tiptoes and scans her surroundings. She sees Yonatan pushing the stroller, leans over and peers inside. 'Yours?' she says to Lia. 'That's fantastic.' She powers up the megaphone and it clicks and crackles as she presses it to her lips.

'The next generation,' it yells. '23rd of June is the night we safeguard this city for them!'

They're lost in a sea of cheers. Yonatan grimaces and Dani falls back but not fast enough to avoid her attention. She is on him, obliterating the space between.

'*Ahlan wa sahlan*,' she says.

'*Ahlan biiki*,' Dani replies. He is not enthused.

'Thank you for coming,' she says. She hugs him, and the stiffness of his body shows that he does not know how to react. 'This is your city too.'

A juggler separates them, sweat flying from his jerking body. By the time he moves on, the girl with the megaphone is gone.

'Bit unusual,' says Chris, peeking into the cocoon of Ben's stroller. 'You must feel very strongly about all this to bring a baby to one of these things.'

Yes, Lia wants to reply. So much. So much that I don't even know why we're protesting. What we want. Why we're here. I feel strongly about all these things, yes.

Sharon speaks before she does.

'We all do,' she says. 'It's horrific. What they're doing here. What's happening.'

From the way she's talking, they're all chanting, Lia feels as if they're in the *shtachim*, in Hebron or Jenin or even East Jerusalem, places of certain heritage but questionable legitimacy, not here in Tel-Aviv, in the bubble where people like them – like Lia, Sharon, Yonatan, Dani and Ben – are all free to not care, to live their lives and have their brothers die, without interruption or oppression.

'And what about you?' says Chris to Dani. 'Did I hear Arabic? Are you an Israeli Arab? Or, sorry, do you prefer the term "Palestinian"?' He seems excited by the revelation. 'What's your story?'

'I'm a friend of their brother,' Dani says.

'Brother!' says Chris with a deep belly laugh. 'It just gets more interesting! Shaz, you didn't tell me you had a brother. How many more secrets are you keeping from me?'

'He's dead,' says Dani bluntly, openly, without a hint of shame or uncertainty, in that trick Southern drawl.

Chris stumbles. His whole demeanour is that of a man unaccustomed to missteps, to being dealt a sideways blow. 'I didn't know.'

For a while they walk in silence while the protest's energy swirls around them like a cyclone of locusts. Lia sees the faintest hint of a smile on Dani's face and she feels a great affinity towards him. He too, it seems, is not a fan.

'When did he die?' says Chris. Sharon shrugs her slender shoulders.

'Thursday,' says Dani. 'In the ground yesterday.'

His brashness proves too much for Sharon. She grabs his arm roughly above the elbow, squeezes it hard so that her nails create little bloodless pools on his skin.

'Oh yeah?' she says. Globules of round spit fall upon Dani's placid features. 'And who the fuck are you?'

A cold smile draws across his face. 'I was the guy fucking him.'

Sharon's eyes are slits squeezing out the world. Her nails draw outlines of red.

Lia catches her husband's name on the air, called out in a soft, feminine voice. She turns, watches as a girl, so young and so pretty, walks towards Yonatan, slowly, hesitantly. She is wearing a floral dress. Her long mouse-blonde hair is tucked behind her ears to emerge once more and cascade over her shoulders ending just above a tattoo of some algebraic formula. Half a dozen hoops climb like spiders up her left ear.

'Hi,' the girl says. She has stopped a safe distance away.

'Hi,' says Yonatan.

'You've grown your hair,' says the girl.

Yonatan lowers his head self-consciously. He shrugs.

'Not on purpose.'

His hand rises to her face but she steps away from his fingers. The line of a thin, faded pink scar that sits uneasily between the smudges of black that indelicately line her eyes. It's not immediately obvious, but now Lia can't unsee it. There's more too: a slight lilt to her features on the left side of her face, as if the mechanics were not properly lubricated.

Yonatan's eyes crease, his face scrunches.

'I'm so sorry, Milli.'

'I don't want to talk about it.'

'But you have to know. To understand. Something happened to me. I didn't mean—'

'Stop.'

'I should have done something. Should have helped to stop it. Not a day goes by where I don't think about what I did to you. That I don't hate myself.'

'You didn't do anything.'

The lightly concealed anger of her face belies the conciliatory nature of her words.

'Please,' he begs, 'just tell me you forgive me. I keep running that night through my head and it's like real pain that doesn't go away. What I did... didn't do.'

She takes a deep breath, looks around. Lia meets her eyes, and in a brief instant, realises this stranger knows who she is.

'What do you want me to say? That it's all OK? You left me there. I nearly died.'

'I went to the police. I gave a statement.'

'Nothing, Yonatan. You did nothing. Don't kid yourself.'

'At least...' He scrambles in his pocket. 'At least let me pay you back. What I owe you.'

She shakes her head. 'It's not about the money. It never was.'

Dani lets out a yell and Lia turns to see Sharon grabbing his arm. When she returns to her husband, the girl is gone. Yonatan looks like a walking corpse.

'Who was that?'

'Just someone I knew,' he says.

'Don't lie to me,' Sharon yells behind them.

'I'm not.'

Lia turns, sees her sister's face almost pressed up against Dani. Both her hands grip his arm.

'Sharon, calm down,' she says.

'So you're telling me,' she hisses, 'that my brother – my little baby brother whose nappies I changed and for whom I always covered with Mum and Dad, who I helped raise and watch grow and is now dead; that my brother, was gay? And he didn't tell me?'

'I already told you.'

Dani is wincing in pain, but his smile is resolute.

'Liar!'

'Shaz, come on. Stop it now,' says Chris. 'You're making a scene.'

'We're in the middle of a demonstration,' Sharon yells, 'how can I make a scene?' She rounds back on Dani. 'He would have told me.'

Lia passes Ben's stroller to Yonatan. By the time she and Chris can separate Sharon and Dani, the main body of the protest has left them behind.

A red Volkswagen narrowly misses Sharon's shoulder and the group moves onto the pavement.

'She's definitely the family bitch,' mutters Dani, now a few steps ahead, loud enough that Sharon can hear.

'Maybe,' says Lia, 'but she's family.'

They walk in a hostile silence. Lia senses Yonatan's presence growing by her side.

'Hi,' he says finally. She can almost feel his hand touch hers.

'Hi.'

The pad-pad-pad of their feet and the stroller's one squeaky wheel form an uneven rhythm.

'So that's his boyfriend. Didn't think that would be his type.'

Lia's little laugh is swollen with grief.

'What, a guy? I didn't think that was his type either.'

'Actually, no. Not that. I always had my suspicions or – no, that's not right. I mean: I never *didn't* think it was a possibility. It's just who he chose. The thing is that it's *this* guy. He's just so—'

He turns his head, glances quickly back to where Dani has dropped back, now lopes behind, fiddling with the ring in his ear.

Arab, she thinks but doesn't say. Perhaps that's not what he's thinking, and she doesn't want to be *that* person if it isn't.

The conversation parks itself again. Yonatan's presence is comforting.

Rabin Square opens to their left. It has been seventeen years since Sharon was lost here.

Up ahead, the main crowd has amassed in front of the stacked tupperware of city hall. They're surrounded on all sides by police cars, and the blue and white lights cast an ominous and hypnotic glow over the scene. The atmosphere is the city in concentrate: a tinder box awaiting a spark.

So when the first frenzied screams rise just as they reach the perimeter of that porous siege, their wrongness seems irrevocably right.

Lia's profile is lowered to twenty-one and, psychologically unfit to serve, she is released from her military duties. At home, her parents barely acknowledge her presence except to tut, avoid her gaze, make clear their shame. Her friends are still in the army, so she is eager to escape, begins planning her trip abroad, hurries her preparations. She works as a hostess at a restaurant in a local gas station, pools her salary with the little cash saved from her summer jobs, her meagre army pay. She is not brave enough to go East, to India or Thailand, so her trip to South America will be short, ticking off the must-sees from her Argentina list: Buenos Aires, the Iguazu falls, Tierro Del Fuego and Lago Argentino. The wide open spaces unnerve her, the scale of everything – the sky, the pampas, the glittering mountain lake – a contrast to home, its ends always close, always sensed, even if not seen.

Throughout, her travels feel unearned.

She settles into the Israeli enclave of Bariloche, counts her remaining cash to see how long it will last. She goes on jeep excursions, fishing trips, mouths 'Nazis' at the old German couples that populate the town. She befriends Yaron, a quiet Argentine-Israeli from the affluent once-agricultural community of Rishpon, travels to his family's historic estancia in Entre Rios Province. There she is introduced to Yuval, his childhood friend from the neighbouring town of Kfar Shmaryahu. He is as rich as he is attractive, and she is touched when he begins subsidising her further excursions. It is only implicitly suggested that she share his bed.

She never tires of the stories of his family's immense wealth and the associated trinkets, the offshore companies, the mega-deals and network of far-flung homes and famous associates.

When Yaron and Yuval head home, out of money, she too books her return. On her way back to Israel, Lia has a layover in England. She takes the train from Paddington Station to Bristol Temple Meads where Sharon waits, cowering from the rain beneath stone arches. Fresh from her trip, Lia finds her sister's life grey and depressing. Her shared student accommodation off the Gloucester Road has damp rising up the magnolia walls and the pungent scent of curry wafts from the restaurant next door. Her housemates, Indian and Chinese, utter barely a word. Their eyes flit left and right, unable to settle.

That night Lia drinks too much at the Student Union bar. The rain drizzles on the window. For the benefit of those within earshot she raises her voice, regales them with stories of her rich, successful friends, her elaborate plans and glistening prospects. Sharon listens. The party thins. The next day Sharon says she has lectures and leaves early. Lia makes her way to the station alone.

Back in Israel, she looks through the prospectuses of the universities local to Tel-Aviv. She visits the Herzliya Interdisciplinary Centre, up the coast to the north, keeps an eye peeled for Yuval who she knows is due to start soon. The campus feels more like a congratulatory construction site than a place of learning, each building named after a famous benefactor, a who's who of Israel's business elite. Yuval's family name graces a glass and concrete cube, and she flushes with a misplaced sense of pride. In the office, she takes the prospectus for a BA in Business Administration.

Television vans and besuited security personnel block the car park's exits. Dark sedans litter the streets and obstruct the road. Time ticks; she knows she will be in trouble for returning the family's Mazda 6 late.

Waiting helplessly, she turns on the radio. Ariel Sharon, the Prime Minister, fills the car, his voice deep and fatherly and self-assured. He is speaking barely a hundred metres from where she sits, and in this speech to the annual Likud-affiliated Herzliya Conference, he will outline his plans to "disengage" from Gaza, an idea first mooted by former Prime Minister Peres a few months before. The operation will remove thousands of Jewish settlers from that godforsaken strip, and leave over a million Palestinians to their own hermetically sealed fate. At the eleventh hour, he will suffer a stroke and his successor, Ehud Olmert, will drag the settlers out by force.

Lia finally arrives home at nightfall. As she hands the car keys to her father, she tells him of her decision.

'You disgrace yourself in the army,' he yells, breathless. 'You get kicked out with a twenty-one profile, and now you want us to pay an extortionate sum for you to be educated at Reichman, a finishing school for tycoons?' His face is bright red and a vein pops on his forehead. 'And what's wrong with the public universities? Tel-Aviv, Hebrew University, Bar Ilan? Even Ben Gurion? Go to the goddamn desert if you have to. What makes you so special?'

Michael hears the screams, descends the stairs. He works to diffuse his father's anger, ensures that a calm of sorts can be restored to the charged living room. Through gritted teeth, and with Michael overseeing, they work out a compromise of sorts. Lia will attend IDC as she wishes, but the fees will be a loan of sorts (the terms to be determined). During her studies, her parents will not contribute a shekel to her life. She may live at home, but from that moment, she is on her own.

So much noise. So many noises. The drummer is still drumming, the girl in the polka-dot dress is shrieking through her megaphone. Something else too.

A wave of terror washes over the faces around Lia.

'What's happening there?' she says.

Dani's not listening. He's on tiptoes, rocking forward and backwards like one of Ben's jack-in-the-boxes as he squints out over the sea of Jews.

'Dani,' she says again but it's no use. He digs into his shirt, pulls out a gold star of David, rolls it between his fingers.

Lia feels a blow; someone shoves her roughly aside. Blue and black clad police stream through the crowd and it splits for them, protesters scrambling out of their way. They surround her, separate her from the others. Somebody has knocked Ben's pram. He is screaming as Yonatan fights to right it. Each shrill cry is a sabre blow.

Lia is gripped by rising panic. She tries to move towards Ben, towards the stroller, but her path is blocked. Yonatan is there and she watches him lift their child, cup his head against his chest. The proximity of Lia's distance is torture. She needs Ben, needs to hold him, but she's blocked by uniforms on all sides. No matter how she scrambles and drags at the bodies, she can't get past.

Somewhere close, somebody is screaming in pain. The crowd have moved on from pithy catechisms. They are chanting 'Fuck the Police'. The joviality has evaporated.

Her fists rain down against the stiff blue cloth of a policeman's shirt. She yells, 'Get out of my way! Give me back my son!'

Someone screams, 'You fucking fascists! This is Tel-Aviv, not Silwan!'

A hand grabs at the shoulder of her dress and pulls her backwards. Struggling to break free, her elbow shoots back and connects with something a little less rigid than bone. There is a yelp, and she turns to see Dani's face in the street light. His hands are held up to his nose and blood streams through the cracks in his fingers. The thick droplets drip down onto his shirt, onto his trousers and a layer coats the six-sided star swinging against his chest upon its cheap gold chain.

Lia takes a deep breath to steady herself, gazes out over the furious activity, so many individual spots of mayhem, tries to plot some course to Ben. Everyone is packed in so densely, and she's surprised to glance across the square, across Ibn Gvirol Street, to see an old, stooped woman shuffling from the supermarket with her hands full of plastic bags. She is oblivious to their struggles.

She takes a step towards Yonatan and Ben, but two policemen flank her, hold her back. A blow strikes the back of her knees, and her legs give way. She tumbles onto the gritty asphalt, rolls over to gaze upwards. Faces peer down at her, hands grasp for her arms, her legs. She flails frantically against them as the ground claws at her back.

Fingers close around her ankles. Her dress rises and her shoulders and elbows feel warm and sticky with new blood as she is dragged across the rutted paving stones. There is no pain, instead the discomfort fizzes outwards from the spots of blood until it coalesces under her arms where other unfamiliar hands now grip. All of her weight is now rising, and her head lolls backwards. It is weightless but heavy, hanging suspended in the air as her feet and arms move out of sync to strangers' rhythms.

She is crying, and yelling. For Ben.

The crowd is still chanting, but Lia can no longer make out the words. Tears flow with every upturned breath, choking her. She needs her Ben, her precious son, the one good thing she's done with her stupid pointless wasted life.

Her limbs head in different directions. Her pallbearers can't seem to decide to where she's headed. The world looks different: inverted and incomplete, obstructed like a movie watched through frightened fingers. The latest chapter in the story of mothers separated from their children.

She sees Sharon, hanging like a bat above her. Her face is flushed with a raw anger as she yells at a uniform. It juts out her lip, pushes it upwards. Marbles of spit fly from her mouth. Everything's happening so slowly, all her movements are so exaggerated, so strange. It is so clear now, from this vantage, how distant they've become.

Lia's legs are thrust apart by two men's hairy wrists. Her panties must be visible to the world, and it feels as if some real violation is imminent. A reserve of energy explodes outwards and she lurches like a ship on a squall, all axes out of kilter and reeling in all directions. Pressure releases from a wrist as a grip slips. The other soon follows and then there's a voice that's not entirely unfamiliar, that says in English:

'Oh for fuck's sake, you're dropping her on—'

There is a loud crack and spreading warmth and

Despite its reputation, the Herzliya Interdisciplinary Centre is not the easy, coddled institution Lia's father expects. Her life becomes a stream of obligatory lectures and seminars from morning to night, intense courses in economics, finance, marketing, accounting. All the numbers make her brain hurt. To answer even one question in ten incorrectly on the regular tests is considered a fail. The nights she is not working as a hostess at the same gas station restaurant she follows Yuval and Yaron to the Gat Rimon, the Mizuari, the Tamar, the Erlich. Tel-Aviv's clubs become familiar to her, and she drinks vodka from the bottle, dances on private tables to pounding music.

Many mornings she wakes in Yuval's bed. The sun glares in her eyes, reflected off the Mediterranean through the floor-to-ceiling windows of his seafront Herzliya Pituach penthouse. There is no formality to their relationship; she keeps a toothbrush and a few tampons in her bag. She knows not to call him during their nights apart, and one night, when she has to make her way home alone after watching him disappear from a club with a blonde, her brown roots showing, she loathes him, loathes herself. She resents her circumstances, the money she hands to the cab driver, cash slipped from Yuval's wallet while he showered. The next day, she attempts to speak to him about their relationship, but is terrified that what she thinks they have will prove a mirage. That evening, she calls in sick to work, remains at home.

She has broached the subject of her poverty with her father a few times, but he refuses to be dragged into conversation or concession. She is left cursing an empty seat on the couch. The hostess job and the shift work she takes at the local mall pay little, and though her hours are flexible enough to maintain her academic timetable, they are sporadic and ensure only that her purse is always empty, and that she cannot progress from the lowliest position of employment.

Just as Lia is completing her second year, Sharon returns home, accompanied by her boyfriend, Richard. He is charming, handsome and urbane, and the family is instantly smitten. Lia is certain he will be a temporary fixture, but when Sharon scores a job at a large pharmaceutical company, both of their names are on the lease of the large, airy apartment they rent on a shady street in the upscale Bazel neighbourhood. Richard's job is in London, but he spends most weekends in Tel-Aviv, often arriving in time to join the family's Shabbat dinners at their parents' suburban home. His dedication to her sister only underlines Lia's loneliness, and it is after one such dinner that Lia finds herself outside Yuval's apartment, a small suitcase in her hand.

'Can I stay here for a while, please?' she says. Although he does not say no, the word yes is never uttered either.

After a week, the atmosphere in the flat is noxious. It is clear what must come, but before the inevitable, the radio and television tell of rockets falling in Israel's North and despite the scheduled exams, a substantial portion of Lia's male classmates disappear into the call-up, into the latest war with Lebanon.

The stillness in Yuval's apartment is surreal. Lia lounges on the furniture, makes a concerted mess that she quickly cleans up, alternates between watching the perpetual rolling of the sea and the televised updates from the front. Yuval and Yaron, childhood friends, are both in the same infantry battalion, and every time she sees a soldier in camouflage on the TV, muddied and heroic, she wonders if it is them beneath the grime. The official list of casualties is of only tangential interest. Only through the tears of a classmate does she learn of Yaron's death, shot in the neck during an ambush by Hizballah fighters.

It is surreal to prepare for the funeral at Yuval's apartment, all alone. She attends dressed in a too-short black dress that she usually wears clubbing, hangs around the outer rim of mourners, among the not-girlfriends, the not-really-friends. Yuval is there beside Yaron's family, his expression morbid and blank. She notices that his left hand is heavily bandaged, wonders why he hasn't yet been home.

She waits for him in the penthouse. She will shower him with affection, heal his wounds and soothe his pain. She will love him; he will love her. She waits and waits, but he never returns. His mobile phone has been disconnected.

The apartment's landline rings a few days later. A cold, professional voice asks Lia to kindly vacate the premises within twenty-four hours, thank you. Yuval, she is told, is taking a break from education, is moving to an unspecified city in America for an undetermined period of time. The apartment has found a buyer and is to be sold. Please leave the keys on the dining-room table, thank you again.

It takes Lia only ten minutes to collect her things. Holding her small suitcase, she closes the door behind her as the sun sets out to the sea.

She will not see Yuval again for nearly two and a half years.

Lia is lying on something soft when she comes to: the sliver of grass between Ibn Gvirol's traffic. Just opening her eyes hurts, and there's a sharp smarting at the back of her head. She tries to sit up, but a fresh flash of pain from her ribs floors her.

'Easy. Easy.'

A pair of hands holds her from the shoulders, tenderly this time. They ease her forwards. She can smell Yonatan's faint manly smell behind her.

'How do you feel?' he says.

'Like shit.' It's agony to breathe.

'You were bleeding. From the head,' he says. Her hand leaps upwards, explores the matted hairs that stick to her scalp. 'It looked quite bad but it's stopped now.'

She points down to her chest. 'What about here?' His gaze on her breasts feels inappropriate, and a melancholy accompanies the ache.

'One of the guys fell on you as he dropped you. With his knee. It was probably an accident.' He shrugs. 'Probably.'

Her mind swirls in the thick soreness. She tries to stand but her movements are all confused. Every motion, every emotion, sends a nuclear blast rippling outwards from the back of her head. It's crippling, and with each wave her body dissolves into the force.

'Where's Ben?' she says.

Her voice is two octaves too low.

'He's here,' says Yonatan. 'He's asleep. He's fine.'

All her will evaporates, and she allows him to guide her back down.

'Can I see him?'

The stroller squeaks as it's pushed towards her. Ben lies pressed to one side against the black fabric, his pacifier bobbing like an apple on a wave, in time with his breath. Yes, he seems fine, but still she wants to cry. Experience is never benign.

People still mill in front of the municipal building, mere footnotes after the fact. The police cars have thinned slightly, but those that remain still spray blue and white light. A few addicts have drifted into the corners of the square. A bank's window has been smashed, and a few black men in fluorescent orange are scooping the shards into little rubbish carts.

'What did I miss?' Lia says.

'They got angry. Never fuck with an indignant crowd or they'll break your windows.' She taps him lightly on the arm. She misses the feel of his skin. 'They arrested a few people and dragged them into the *Irya*. That sent everyone over the edge. Turns out they don't like the police much.'

'And me?'

'Well, they did try and arrest you.'

'But they didn't.'

'No, they didn't.'

'Why not?'

He seems reluctant to answer.

'I stopped them,' he says finally.

'How?'

His face is all scrunched up.

'One of the police guys. Noam. I knew him.'

'From where?'

'Does it matter?'

Yes it does.

'We were in the army together.'

The army. Of course.

'The same unit?'

He sniffs the air. 'No. Noam I know from *milluim*.'

She doesn't want to talk, doesn't want to hear about Noam, about her husband's connection to a man who assaulted an innocent woman. None of this was supposed to happen. Not in Tel-Aviv. Not to Jews in the Jewish state.

She removes her hand, uses it to try and steady her head.

She just wants to go home now, to change Ben's clothes and kiss him as he wriggles himself comfortable in his bed. A dilapidated white van pulls up beside them, stops at a red light. Electronic music blares from tinny speakers strapped to the roof. The door slides open and four *Braslav Hassidim* jump out, white shirts loose, ringlets flowing from knitted *kippot*. They dance furiously between the cars and then, when their light turns green, they fold themselves back into their van and are gone.

She tries to move once more, first one leg then the other, pushes through the pain. Yonatan offers her a hand. She is wobbly, but vertical.

'Can we just go home?' she says.

Slowly, they begin shuffling south. Lia is limping and must lean on Ben's stroller for support. A hundred eyes follow them from the al fresco tables of The Brasserie, heads bent low over steaks and chips and intricate cocktails. Waiters weave between the seats. Lia wonders how she must appear to the diners, distant as if on a giant screen, new pictures beamed in from the chaotic insurrections in Cairo, Tunis or Ramallah. Another place, another country, nowhere near home.

'Where is Sharon?' she says.

'She continued with that guy. Followed the protest.' Her sister's absence cuts her deeply.

'And Dani?'

He laughs. 'You've got a lot of strength for a small girl. I'm pretty sure you broke his nose. Haven't seen him since.'

'Did you notice that *Magen-David* around his neck?'

Yonatan shakes his head like the Indians: not a yes, not a no. 'Crazy Arabs.'

He laughs. She laughs too. His arm rubs between her shoulder blades. She leans into his touch.

'About before. About needing to talk—'

'Yonatan,' she says. 'Please. Not now.'

'I'm really sorry.'

'Let's not do this now.'

'But I just want to explain—'

'Really,' she says. Her head is throbbing and she feels dizzy, must come to a complete stop. 'Please. I'm begging you. Later. Just not now.'

They walk on in silence. His hand remains on her back.

'I love you,' he says.

Lia's graduation takes place on a beautiful day in June. She dresses in white and blue as mandated, dons the blue robe and the square-topped flat cap. Despite her fears, she doesn't trip up the stairs as she climbs the podium, enjoys the spatters of applause that greet her name. She whoops dutifully as she and her classmates fling their hats into the air, a photo finish to immortalise their achievements after years of hard work. She goes out to a party with the few close friends she has made; as 2008 and 2009 slowly pass by, so they will drift apart.

The day's optimism seeps away like a slow leak from a tyre. The much-vaunted economic boom Israel is experiencing post-Intifada seems to be passing Lia by. She attends interview after interview, but the only jobs she secures are secretarial. Their mind-numbing repetitiveness, low pay and long hours mock her education, temporary positions in sombre office towers in the peripheral towns of greater Tel-Aviv. After months she is depressed, after years resigned. She is constantly searching for better, for more, but all attempts to improve her lot end in failure.

After an argument, her father says, 'See what your expensive business degree gets you?' and she runs to her room and uses a pillow to muffle her cries.

Sharon's life, in contrast, is a frantic race up the professional ladder. The momentum is dizzying. At Shabbat dinner, Michael suggests that Sharon help Lia find a job at her work, but when the invitation arrives to an interview, Lia does not reply. The sisters never speak of it again; they don't speak at all.

It is Michael that shows Lia *The Marker* that morning, Haaretz's incestuous hybrid of business news and social gossip, with its repeating cast of characters. She is late for work, but still she pauses to gaze at Yuval's face winking at her from the cover.

'You know him, right?' Michael says.

'You could say that,' she says, skims the headline and the article. Yuval's family are to add the Israeli franchise of a large international clothing conglomerate to their vast business portfolio. Yuval himself, back in Israel, is to personally lead the project.

On the way to work, she gnaws at the nail of her index finger. The blood tastes sweet on her tongue. She wants to find some way to call him, but the memory of his empty apartment, the closing door, undermines her determination. She gets off the bus a few stops early, sits upon a bench and struggles to work her way through a possible conversation word by word. A hysterical calm settles, and in the tranquility of overwhelming panic, she searches the internet for Yuval's family offices, clicks on "call".

A woman answers. Breathlessly, Lia asks for Yuval. She is put on hold, lightheaded as she clutches her hand to her head. Another, younger voice answers.

'Hi,' Lia says, eyes tightly closed. She is told that Yuval is otherwise engaged. Still, she pushes on. 'I'm an old friend. Could you ask him to call me please?' She gives her name, her number, rings off. She bends over, retches onto the ground at her feet.

At work, she cannot concentrate, digs her letter opener into the fleshy part of her hand between her forefinger and thumb until it oozes clear liquid, then blood. That night he has still not called back, and she slices a razor into her thigh, just high enough that nobody will see.

She invites a colleague from work to a dive bar on Allenby, down near the sea where the hotels offer rooms by the hour. She flirts shamelessly with the bartender to secure more free drinks, and after too many shots begins talking to a tourist from Germany. Soon the conversation bores her, and when her friend leaves, she drags him into the toilets. She pulls his trousers down to his ankles and then collapses into a weeping ball on the sticky floor. He is quick to leave her be.

Despite her doubts, the call-back does arrive. Lia struggles to maintain her composure, keep her voice level as she hears Yuval's voice. He sounds the same but airier, a well-groomed contestant from a reality TV show she watches when she cannot sleep. When she asks him for a job, he doesn't hesitate.

'Of course,' he says. 'We're building something amazing here, Lia, and you'd be perfect. I'd love for you to be a part of it.' They set a date. When the line goes dead she finds the phone is shaking in her hands.

The meeting is a week away, and Lia cannot contain her excitement. She feels as if her adult life is about to start. When she tells her family at Shabbat dinner, Michael beams at her. He presses her for details about Yuval, of their relationship. Her parents applaud and suggest a celebratory dinner in Tel-Aviv straight after the meeting.

Sharon is silent throughout. As they leave, she touches her sister's arm.

'Just be careful, OK?' she says.

'Wait!'

Sharon's cry carries over the rumble of traffic pouring over and across Kaplan Street. She waves frantically, drags Chris forward by his hand, ignores the little red man and the clack-clack-clack of the blind-aid. They dodge the oncoming cars. The strap of her dress is ripped. The fabric flops down across her breast, revealing the black lace of her bra and the clear outline of its padding.

'You're OK,' Sharon says, panting heavily. She covers her bra with her hand. 'Thank God.'

Chris pushes past her, digs his fingers into Lia's hair and pulls her head towards him.

'You had quite a knock there,' he says, inspecting the wound, 'but you should be OK.'

'And how would you know?' says Yonatan.

'Oh, I've seen it many times,' he says. He brushes a lock of hair from his eyes. 'Greece most recently. A cameraman got a tear-gas grenade to the head. That was nasty, let me tell you.'

'I thought you were with radio,' Lia says. The thudding in her head is growing louder.

'We're all journalists,' he says, curtly.

'He's been everywhere,' says Sharon.

'Yes, I guess you could say that.' He takes a deep breath,

puffs himself up like a blowfish and rocks his head back as he counts each on his pristine fingernails. 'There was Sudan, of course. And South Africa, Zim, Georgia, Burma – or rather Myanmar although you still have to call it Burma for most people.' His sigh is theatrical. 'But you know, I'm getting a little itchy because these last few years it's all been about the Middle East. First the American invasion of Iraq and the chaos that caused, then that whole revolution-that-wasn't in Iran, now the Arab Spring and the civil wars in Libya and Syria. Too much hummus.' He says it with the Arabic pronunciation, soft and sticky. He laughs. 'I just couldn't understand how you guys have managed to be immune. That's why I'm here, you see. To get a feel for what's going on. That and, you know, Palestine's always good fodder for a story. And there are few other places where you can cover a war at lunch and then go to a bar for dinner.'

He laughs, but none of his expected adoration arrives. Even Sharon seems disinclined to pick up the conversation.

'You should have seen it,' she says, abruptly changing the subject. 'They blocked the Ayalon. The whole highway south. All the traffic was honking horns in support and flashing us victory signs. Lia, you should have—'

Chris interrupts. 'Shaz, really... I was talking. Manners, dear. You can't be surprised at what happened tonight. Not when you take a global view of what you're doing. This colonial project you've got going. It really was just a matter of time before your barbarity came back home to—'

Lia doesn't see the shove, doesn't witness Chris tripping, sprawling. She just hears his droning, abruptly silenced.

'Get up!' Yonatan yells.

But Chris just lays there, stunned.

Yonatan turns to Sharon.

'What is your problem?' he yells. She takes a step back. 'Every time. Every time you find some bullshit prick who's more interested in his hair than you.'

'That's not fair,' she says quietly.

'Just shut up and listen to me. I'm not done. Richard was an asshole and everyone – I mean everyone – knew it was doomed. He was sleeping with Natascha, that assistant of his, in London and God knows who else. And yet you just accepted it. Do you think anyone was surprised when he left? Nobody, Sharon. Nobody.'

Lia touches his arm, tries to will him down. 'Yonatan, stop it,' she says.

'When he left, we all thought, "OK, maybe that's for the best. Now she can just find someone decent and live a nice life and be happy." But this guy? Seriously? Some voyeuristic shit who comes here, all self-righteous and holy, into *our* country, into *our* city, and lectures *us* about *our* lives? Like we don't know how messed up it all is. Like I don't know, after my own wife was assaulted. He thinks we need him to tell us?'

'Hey,' says Lia. She grabs him with both arms, tries to pull him to her. He's scaring her. 'It's OK.'

'No it's not OK. Don't tell me it's OK.'

'Calm down. Leave him. Let's just go.' She grabs his waist and tries to steer him away from the petrified body.

'Such a big man,' Yonatan says as he turns away.

Sharon is slowly pushing the stroller away from them, away from the altercation. Lia cannot see her face. As they turn to follow, Chris slides to sitting, stares blankly at the cars filing down the street.

Lia and Yonatan catch Sharon and Ben at the giant junction between Ibn Gvirol, Karlebach and Marmorek streets. Ben groans and stirs, presses a curled arm into the buggy's folding sprockets. He pushes his head into the crevice of his elbow and settles once more.

'Are you sure you don't want to get your head checked?' Sharon asks Lia. She cannot meet her gaze.

She points out towards the Cinematek, to the little doctor's clinic on Ha'arbaa Street. Bad nights have ended there before. Like a hospital, but in miniature, with its not-quite-retired-yet Soviet doctors. One stage removed from proper care, from a proper emergency.

No, all Lia wants is to go home, to cleanse herself in a never-ending shower. Then she will be able to dream. Michael will still be alive and her marriage will be strong. The world will be love, and there will be no death, and no police, and no Jews and no Arabs, and no sanctimonious foreigners dipping their toes into her life. Everything will be flat and she will feel nothing. Those are good dreams.

Lia leans over, brushes Sharon's shoulder with a kiss.

'I'm OK,' she says. 'Really.'

They pass a man crouched on the ground, a collection of spray cans lined up beside him. Lia watches as he stencils a series of hearts that climb the wall and seem to break free into the night. At their centre is scrawled, 'It's not perfect, but it's all yours.'

Lia closes her eyes, walks with the blackness. She can feel the presence of her sister – her only remaining sibling – her husband and her son so close. She feels them treading through the flat, markerless landscape in unison. Somewhere far from here her parents are rolling sleeplessly in bed. They come to rest, facing apart.

She is alone.

Is this what it feels like to be loved?

Yuval's office is on the twentieth floor of a post-modern tower in the centre of Tel-Aviv. His family's name is emblazoned in illuminated letters above the main entrance, over the top four floors. As the glass elevator rises, Lia gazes out over the turquoise of the winter Mediterranean. The numbers tick up and she wonders how she could ever have found boredom in any sea, so churning and exquisite.

She checks herself in the mirror, adjusts her cleavage and her hemline, and then with a pang of panic realises that under her coat she is wearing the same dress she wore to Yaron's funeral more than two years before. She squeezes her eyes closed, repeats to herself, 'You'll be fine.'

The view from Yuval's corner office encompasses both the city and the sea, brown and blue crashing together. He stands as she enters, comes to her and places a kiss perilously close to her lips. He motions her to a chair and she notices the skin of his left hand is rough and rolled and discoloured. Like leather, wetted and heated to harden on open charcoal.

He asks her about her life; she tells of her graduation, skims over the stasis of the years since. He is friendly, affable, polite. Throughout she sees him rub his burn repeatedly, as if his mind is fixated on something, somewhere else.

'So,' he says, the pleasantries dispatched, 'you want to work with me?' Lia feels her mouth stretch into a smile and she wonders what was there before. 'It's really amazing what we're doing here,' he continues. It is a speech he has no doubt given countless times before. 'The amount of trust the company is putting in me. It's a great compliment, and they know I can do it. Their head office in France, they approached my father, and he sent them to me. They asked him if I could be relied on, and he guaranteed that I could. And, well...' He opens his hands, the good one and the misshapen one both, and gestures at the airbrushed models in unrealistic poses that adorn the walls. 'It'll be amazing.'

She sits passively, waits for him to continue but he just stares at her until she has no option but to speak.

'I'd love to build this with you,' she says.

He claps his hands together, and Lia wonders if it hurts.

'Good. It's great you called.' He rifles through the papers on his desk. 'I really think this will be perfect for you.'

Lia feels her smile break once more. This time it is one of relief.

'Here you go,' he says. He slides a form across the table, twists it so the text is facing her. She reads a few lines and then squeezes her eyes closed. She does not need to read any further. 'You can pick the store you want to work at,' he continues, 'and the shifts can be hours that suit you. And we're arranging a special card that will entitle you to incredible discounts.'

She slides the paper back across the desk. Her smile has hardened to frost-burned stone. She thanks him, tells him she will think about it and, when he kisses her goodbye, she turns her head so that his lips catch her ear.

As she waits for the lift, she watches the staff toiling in their little cubicles. She feels stupid, to have thought for even a brief moment that Yuval's future triumphs had space for her.

The sun has already set as she loiters outside the Stephan Braun, too close to the last week's dive bar. Her parents are already inside. The TVs in the window of the electronics store across the street are all showing the same pictures of flare-up in Gaza. In a fit of suffocating bitterness, she hopes the army will go in, that Yuval will be called up once more, that this time it will be his life ended.

She enters the restaurant, skirts the hostess, mills around by the bathroom. She does not know how she will break the truth to her parents, to Michael, to Sharon.

Exhausted, she leans against the wall.

A shoulder nearly sends her sprawling to the floor.

'Hey!' she says. 'Watch yourself.'

A man, handsome in a dishevelled manner, stares crookedly at her.

'*Slicha.*' He says. 'I'm sorry.'

They linger. She does not go in, he makes no effort to leave.

'Are you going in?' he says.

She thinks for a moment. 'No. I don't think so. You?'

'No.' He holds out a hand. 'I'm Yonatan,' he says, 'do you maybe want to get a drink?'

She smiles. There is only relief in an alteration of the night's course.

'It depends,' she says. 'Where?'

Nadav

Don't panic.

You're not there, not involved. Not this time.

The TV buzzes and flickers. There are tanks on the screen, and they're streaming down in a huge ball of dust, covered in kids poking from the roofs and smoking and talking on their phones. There are more kids on the ground, sitting in a line by the fence, flicking rocks, looking excited, looking bored.

But don't panic. They're not you. Not this time. That was over a decade ago. Now isn't then. Everything that happened has been forgotten. You've been forgotten. The you then: young and stupid and a pawn in the game. That person's dead.

The angry yells of the couple upstairs soak through the ceiling. They've been fighting so much recently, the pitch constantly increasing. The remote's batteries are dying, and there are no more in the apartment, none even in the freezer. The mute sign is hovering green at the bottom of the screen, floating atop whatever the ticker tape is repeating and repeating and repeating and repeating.

The phone begins to ring in the other room. It's Mum or Dad, it has to be, so there's no reason to move. No reason to pick up and say "hi" and explain it all again; how it was up there, and how they should have left this modern ghetto when Rafi was still a kid, saved him while there was still time.

Today, November 15th 2012, could be the day he becomes you.

The ringing stops, and the couple upstairs are silent and the apartment is still and empty and all the walls are too cold and too white and the floor is ice under socked feet. Winter in this city is brutal: built on sand and accustomed to sun. Now, with the rain and the grey, it's damp and desolate, hunched up, waiting for it to pass.

A new shot on the TV: a reporter stands on a dune. There are tufts of green and yellow on the ground by her feet – the desert blooming in the winter's rain – a cloud of grey behind. A rocket, either outgoing or incoming, impossible to say. To kill or not to kill? The answer's self-evident, no? Always – kill kill kill. What was the question again?

Remember what it was like that day, back during Operation Defensive Shield? The first sight of Jenin from the tank, peeping out from that reinforced bucket of bolts. No. Never. Push it back. Don't listen to Dr. Katz. Don't face it. He says it'll grow into a monster, but it's always been a monster. It was what it was; it made you who you are.

Sitting outside the city, all grey and yellow and resting amongst the sad jaundiced greens of areas apparently neither ours nor theirs. Everyone was smoking, leaning on the tanks, bitching or bragging about some girls. Who were those people? Who knows? Time and separation erases even friendship from memory.

Then word came down and cigarette butts were stubbed out under black boots, and everyone clambered into their dark little coffins of protruding steel. Base. Functional. No concessions to humanity's vagaries; a sore back, an explosion of claustrophobia that those pokes, prods, teases, tests failed to identify. A flaw in us would have saved us all with a glorious twenty-one profile. But there were no flaws and it was all perfectly crafted – clinical, efficient, effective – for one purpose. As the turret crashed down, it shut out the world. A device speeding off into that hornet's nest to do its work, to fumigate.

The television flashes a creamy, murky white. The reporter ducks, holds the helmet tight on her head and points upwards. The camera zooms into the jagged grey of a rocket against the washed-out background of the sky. It stays there, motionless, stripped of a point of departure, or a destination, as if suspended against a painted background, as harmless as an exhibit in a museum. See, children, this is how we used to kill each other.

Something so deadly, created and crafted by man to destroy man, reduced to something so banal, so ugly. That's the beauty of the machines of war: it's impossible to grasp their power, their severity, unless witnessed in the instant of death.

You know that. You shouldn't forget that.

You can't forget that.

The beginning of the rocket's flight doesn't matter; it's the landing. What goes up comes down – law of nature, law of physics. Law of death. This one will fall in a field or on a house; a house with a garden and a roof and rooms and a kitchen and groceries in a fridge, and a person filling and emptying and cleaning it. And that one person will maybe be blown head from neck and legs from hips and arms from shoulders, and their extinction will reverberate like an atomic blast rippling out to maim a whole family, a whole community, a whole nation. All because some guy pushed a button or squeezed a trigger or dropped a mortar into a tube.

Did he know? You knew, though you didn't. You didn't think twice. You saw the man walk into the screen, all white and red and yellow and hot and alive, and then you lined up the little cross and pressed that trigger and there wasn't – shouldn't have been – a connection between your actions and him pirouetting, falling back, there on that screen. No longer being in the world.

You did that.

I know.

The rocket disappears in a puff of brown and green and grey. This time it fell in a field, a failed murder, but as the camera settles there's a row of red roofs just visible in the distance, partly obscured by a thin strip of sad trees. How can they live like that in the South, cheek and jowl with Hamas? In the North too, so close to Hizballah. Here in the middle there's Fatah, but they're cowed, for now at least. The centre, the eye of the storm. But them, there – always about to die. About to die but not yet dead.

You can die today. Maybe. There are razor blades in the closet and the boiler's on. There'll be warm water enough for a bath. For that.

Die. Enough.

The television sucks itself into a silent black hole. This is not your war. This is a war of the periphery, not of you. You are Tel-Aviv and this is not of Tel-Aviv. Those poor people of the Negev, pity them. But they are in danger. Them alone. If they're about to die, it means you're not.

There's no Coke in the fridge. The Mei-Eden cooler is empty too and the water from the tap tastes terrible today. Out of habit Sufi's leash is already in hand. Put it back down. The coat is too thin and it's cold outside, the murky, mottled sky accompanied by a wet, cracking wind. Nobody makes eye contact at the *pitzutziah*, they're all staring at the screen above the till as water is collected from the fridge and paid for, six bottles wrapped tight in their clear plastic prophylactic. The weight on the walk home pulls down on the shoulder blades and the thin strip of plastic digs through bony fingers. Every shop streams the war in silence, like different frames of the same cartoon, until the key is in the door and the silence of the black apartment is complete once more.

It's so quiet. So painfully, thunderingly quiet.

Like it's been since Sufi died.

What would she be doing now? The tap of her nails would be slow, lazy, working their way across the tiled floor, stopping only to lap-lap at her water bowl before turning around and around and curling into her bed. Or, if she'd been left alone then those steps would be frantic, unfocused, random but rooted in space like a scatter graph. Eager to be stroked, to be scratched. Eager to be loved.

But Sufi's dead. She died in your arms and you buried her yourself in a grave that you dug with your own hands under a tree in Latrun because you don't have a house, a garden, and your life's been on hold for a decade, the decade since *your* war, the one where you killed and could have died.

Her bed still remains in the corner; everything else has been recycled in the Tel-Aviv way: trauma placed on someone else's front step. The bag was overflowing with memories: her bowls, brush (wiry hair still twisted in the bristles), her food, the brown knit monkey that she could no longer bite without leaving smears of blood. Everything was gone within a few hours, objects repurposed, stripped of history.

Dr. Katz said to get another dog. Mum and Dad and Rafi too. But she wasn't a refrigerator or a car, something to be replaced like a disposable white good. She was warm and soft and her belly sagged into rolls of loose flesh that would shudder as she stretched and sat upright, when she looked at you and broke your heart.

You're alone.

There are enough pills in the bathroom cabinet.

The phone rings again and even from afar the word *Mum* and the smiley happy photograph from a birthday or a holiday is visible across the room.

'Your brother's phone's switched off. He told me he was heading down towards the border, and now his phone is off.' Her voice is frantic, clawing. 'You said they took yours away. You know – before you went in.'

Now she's concerned. After all these years of saying "that's just how it is" and "you're overreacting; Yoram, tell your son he's overreacting" and "you made it out OK". Now she's worried.

'Mum, they do that. It doesn't mean anything. They take your phone away just in case. So you can't give anything away.'

The box was overflowing with phones. Real phones. Simple, shiny plastics in black and silver. No Twitter. No Facebook. No internet. Connected only to the ones we loved, to those that loved us, but even they were too much. Love, concern: both dangerous threats, hindrances to surprise, shock and awe, death without dying.

'It'll be alright, Mum.'

'Do you mean that?'

'Of course I do.' Lies. Liar. You liar. 'He'll be home in a few days, just you watch.'

'If you hear anything, you'll let me know?'

'Of course, Mum.'

More lies. They contact the parents first. The knock at the door; the three soldiers outside.

The phone beeps. She's gone.

Gaza. *Azza*. They said it was beautiful. Not the city, not the camps, not the evacuated settlements, but the bits without people.

The woman upstairs is shouting, and I can just make out her husband's name, Yonatan, in the din. It's as if the ceiling is shaking. A child cries.

Mum and Dad will sit by the phone, sit by the TV. But why? What happens in Gaza will happen there whether the television's on or off. Rafi will sit in that tank and scour the horizontals of the street and the verticals of those buildings and he'll kill or be killed whether they wait by the phone or not.

But food, food will not wait. Hunger and thirst and anxiety about life and about death, they don't wait, they don't relax with a coffee or take a cigarette break. Decisions: eat, drink, hang yourself; live, die.

A knot falls into a stomach. It grumbles and growls like an angry dog, like Sufi's warning when she heard a strange noise. The apartment door slams shut.

Shafts of sun crack through the thick cloud smothering the city. It looks sad, yellowy-grey, sleepy, except where the sunlight hits. God's angels passing to spare the first-born. Only some of the first-born. The passage between Kerem Hateymanim and the market is heaving. A bum lingers by the roundabout to nowhere, sheltering from the imaginary heat beneath its solitary palm, lounging and fondling his balls. A family on a day trip unfold themselves from a giant white SUV that the father has double-parked.

The Minzar is full and Gadera 26 is spilling out onto the street so onto The Bun. There's a space at the bar, all the better to stare straight ahead without the danger of potential involvement. Conversations float, mingle.

'We should just kill them all.'

'There should be talks.'

'I just want to emigrate. There's no future here.' A stolen glance at a blonde girl with a hole in her nose and cuts on her arm.

'Where would you go?' says the man next to her.

'I'd go to Germany. Berlin.'

'Really? After everything that happened there?'

'Berlin is great,' she says. 'And I can get a passport. My grandmother was German.'

'You're lucky. I think I can only get Hungarian.'

'Eastern European. Not sure I'd bother.'

They both laugh.

'Still, it's EU. Means I can go to London. Or come to Berlin.'

Somewhere else. A place with wars then, not wars now.

The girl talks of her dream: a third-floor walk-up in Kreuzberg, feeling the creative energy and building a new life. She forgets that Kreuzberg was where all the Jews once lived, where all the Jews were emptied out from, into carts and ovens to be sprinkled as fertiliser on the ground.

The Udon is good. Wholesome and comforting like another nation's chicken soup but without the baggage. You could be in Tokyo, with its glowing fish and its radioactive air.

The brown broth burns as it's gulped down the gullet. The belly rumbles, the beast not entirely satiated. How long since the last meal? Hours, yes; too many, maybe even a day. So long.

'Here, have this.' The owner places a shot of something clear on the bar.

When it's pushed away, he shrugs and works his way down the diners, offering it to each customer in turn until the girl with the incomplete nose smiles and nods. He just wants someone to drink with, he doesn't care who.

Not that he'll ever be alone with a place like—

What's that? A faint sound – too faint perhaps to even be real – infringes on the ordinariness of a weekday lunch. It bounces off the music that's playing but no one else in the restaurant seems to notice. Only the Berlin girl's chopsticks hover in mid-air, and a thick noodle slops back into her bowl. It spills broth over the black wood of the bar. She too seems to be sharing the same instant.

Do you remember anything? Yes, of course you do, you're being dragged there now. Running. Running through the bedroom, through the open doorway. Mum is standing there – she's younger, straighter and her hair is blonde, not faded grey. You've forgotten she was blonde. She's bending over and you think she's going to hug you but she doesn't, she grabs your arm between the elbow and the shoulder where it's soft and fleshy and vulnerable.

'Don't, please. It hurts.'

But she's not listening, she's sniffing the air, smelling the sharp, shining fear carried on that noise. She pulls hard and you nearly fall, nearly tumble forward but you don't because you don't want her to be angry with you, even when your body's not straight enough to balance down the stairs you still tackle them, and you're relieved when you only tumble down the last few. The room is white-washed and humid and all the sounds reverberate because the walls are so thick. It smells of mould.

There's a television there, and it's bigger than any television now. Not the screen – that's tiny – but everything else behind and around like it's got to work harder to paint the same pictures. On it, planes are taking off and planes are landing and good-looking, tanned people in neatly-pressed beige uniforms are talking in a language you don't understand. Letters in the corner of the screen read in red: "CNN". Then the aircraft carrier is gone and there's a man holding a young boy, and he looks different, darker with a bushy moustache like a bad guy from a comic book. Everything around him is gold. So much gold.

'He's a bad man,' says Mum, but that's obvious. Too much gold to be good.

The only word you recognise is 'Iraq' and it's being said over and over again and you want to ask Mum: what is that? But you don't because you feel stupid and your arm hurts and that noise – that same loud sad bored droning noise, up and down and on and on – is making her hurt you and making you scared. But scared of what?

The noise stops. The girl sniffs, fishes the noodles back out of her bowl.

'Are you alright?' says the other, not-so-thin owner. There is someone behind him in the mirror, white as a sheet with eyes sunk like dull marbles in a black soup.

•

The building's door is wedged open with a suitcase. It's turned upside down and the wheels point in the air like surrender. The stairwell is filled with the detritus of other peoples' lives, the worthless rubbish that marks their passage from birth to death. At least a dozen boxes with their lids open cascade down the stairs and through the entrance hall, their knick-knacks poking out: a chipped porcelain cookie jar in the shape of a fat pig; a pistachio green mixer, its power cable snaking down the cardboard's side; a family photo with the glass smashed.

That's them now: voices raised like banshees wailing out of sight.

Sufi didn't like the noise when it started. She was already sick then. When their baby cried she used to whimper and curl in a corner, shaking violently. She hated conflict.

Someone steps heavily down the stairs. She lumbers under the weight of yet another box. Despite best efforts, the key isn't yet in the door, so she still has time to say: 'Hi.'

'Hi.'

She's pretty in the stolen glance, skin fine like the porcelain pig. There's no excess to her, and her clothes cling to her slender frame. Her hair is pulled back in a ponytail that swishes left and right with every sideways step down each stair, always just about ready to fall. From above, the disembodied voices grow louder and she pauses, shakes her head. The smile drops and disappears from her face.

'Can you always hear them?' she says.

Her face pops against the dirty grey of the once-white walls. Each delicate feature is perfectly defined: the peak of her ski-slope nose and the strong delicacy of her chin. The roundness of her freckled cheeks, the crevices that house her wide brown eyes.

'Did you hear anything?'

She seems confused. 'You mean them?' she says.

'No.' Stupid. 'Never mind.'

'Oh. OK. Bye then.'

The door is shut before she is finished.

There was no noise. You were imagining it. See? It's your mind, dragging you back to yet another place you don't want to be. That's all your mind is good for: making certain the present *is* the past.

Did you turn on the television? Was it on when you arrived? Rockets hanging, plumes of smoke, people talking, people crying. Nothing's changed in the intermission.

Yet—

Something *has* changed. The scenery is almost imperceptibly different: less brown, more grey, awash in concrete in denser patterns. Not familiar, no, but grasping towards familiarity.

A ticker tape of red and black jogs across the screen from right to left:

ROCKET REACHES RISHON LEZIYON

Rishon, one of Tel-Aviv's ugly suburb cities, south along the coast. Twenty minutes by car. Thirty minutes with traffic.

The phone is ringing. Whoever it is must have called many times because it has moved itself to the edge of the table and it dances as it vibrates and falls to the floor. There it keeps wriggling and writhing. In the dive it's flipped itself and Dad's face stares up at the ceiling, unsmiling. He never smiles.

He never calls either. Only hollers occasionally in the distance as Mum relays some intrigue about Auntie Dina's bad taste or the woman down the road who's after him. No, Dad never calls, he never acts. He never intervenes or interferes or asks, 'how are you?'

'Hi.'

'How are you?'

'I'm OK.'

There's a breathless silence over the line. The conversation's utility is spent, but neither side is quite willing to call time.

'Did you hear about the rocket?' His voice is calm and low. It sounds so soothing, the product of thousands of cigarettes still present on his spicy breath and yellow fingers.

'It was in Rishon, Dad. I'm not in Rishon.'

'I know,' he growls. He chews his words, grinds down the offence. 'They'll send your brother in.'

Somewhere in their home a woman is talking. Her words are in perfect time to the lips of the woman on the TV here. Perfect, but fractionally askance. The world always did move slower in the kibbutz.

'You brother might go in,' he repeats.

'I heard you the first time.'

'Well you didn't answer.'

'It wasn't a question.'

'OK.'

'OK.'

There's a click and the television speaks in silence once more. OK. It'll all be OK. Mum will boil a chicken for soup till the bird is drained of life's colour and they'll sit down for dinner and a rocket won't alter the order of two lives too familiar to be upset.

But here; has it always been this quiet? A heart beating faster than it should – the loudest sound, louder even than that of other people's fights falling through their floor, the accompanying dull thud of something dropped or something thrown.

Fear the silence, for in the silence ghosts shriek. That soul you cut down; Sufi; Rafi's purity hanging on a thread beside another's blade.

Was it better with Sufi? Of course it was: louder, fuller, no time for the trapdoor to open, to be tripped and tumble in. She'd pick up her toy monkey and she'd wait by your feet, offer relief in a concerned lick.

But she's gone now.

Perhaps it is time.

The stool's leg scrapes against the floor tiles as it is dragged into the centre of the room, beneath the light. Some join groans uneasily beneath the weight of thirty-three years of flesh as the ceiling's lampshade unclips. There beside the naked bulb is the hook, the plaster rough where the drill detached chunks and they fell to the floor.

'I'm thinking of getting a boxing bag.' That was the story, but nobody ever asked. No one noticed that this was the apartment's only clothed bulb, not swinging naked, but sheathed in Ikea cotton. The intent, concealment, seemed always so obvious and clear, though probably only to a troubled mind. Damaged; that's how Dr. Katz describes it. Nobody begins this way.

The rope is wound into the carcass of the cabinets in the corner that acts as a kitchen. Seven Tel-Aviv apartments and all had these same units, smooth shiny plastic masquerading as smooth shiny wood. Modular for your convenience, distinct square and rectangular sections rearranged to squeeze into whatever mousetrap was reserved for the purpose. The rope drops heavily, coiling like a disturbed snake as it slams against the grey floor.

Then to work: hands, practised on thread and floss, make short work despite the unfamiliar scale. Over. Under. Loops to stretch and thread and loosen and tighten until a hole is formed in space, supported by one two three four braces. It's simple really, once your fingers are adept. Now it feels like second nature; the body is a great engineer of its own destiny.

And then, there it is, all laid out on the ground. It spans the entire expanse of your place on this earth, one corner to the other, ready to be fed through the hook, fed its flesh.

So close. This is it. You know what to expect. No surprises.

The stool creaks and wobbles again as the weight shifts and the rope is fed through the hook. It flops down, limp and lifeless. There it is: man's final endeavour. A tug to check the strength; hopefully it'll snap your neck as gravity does its thing, otherwise it's a slow, painful asphyxiation. Thirty minutes even – one forty-eighth of a day. Swinging. Thinking. Waiting to die.

But what does it matter? Death is death after all.

Another tug; the ceiling holds.

Should there be a note?

No.

Adjust the stool, make sure it sits directly beneath the noose. Wood cracks – the beam holding the legs must have finally snapped but no time to check or to fix it. Affairs in disarray and all that.

The rope scrapes the skin around the neck as it tightens. Perhaps it has drawn blood, but that's no biggie, it'll soon pass from pink to red to blue. On to tiptoes and the stool shifts left, then right, the rope swings like a pendulum.

Everything's ready.

All it would take is just a tiny flick, a little toe extended just a teeny bit, just enough to shift the weight beyond the margins of equilibrium, to tip it sideways and send the mass plunging to the feet, the body diving down towards the floor, the rope creaking as it grabbed and the neck snapped—

A roar breaks, rumbles through the four walls of the room. It starts low, ends high before doubling back on itself and starting again. It's lazy and its boredom belies its intensity, belies the sudden adrenaline that tenses all the muscles, nearly does what the toe hasn't done yet. But no, the stool remains standing and holding this useless body as something big is happening, something more important than an insignificant premeditated death in a dingy rented apartment in the Kerem.

•

Stupid. Stupid. Stupid.

To be standing here, sheltered in the stairwell as the siren assaults all ears, fearful for a life you were about to take.

Idiot.

No doubt Dr. Katz would pass it off as some entirely predictable human behaviour, fob it off as us being fundamentally contradictory creatures, or the overwhelming instinct to protect and to survive, hard-wired into our DNA.

'Do you think it's safe here?'

The woman from upstairs leans on the bannister and holds her kid to her chest, pressing his head into her breast so that one ear is smothered by the crumpled fabric of her top, the other by her hand. It's not clear to whom the question is directed. It could be any of us five crouched here. Six with the child. Mrs Stern from the penthouse seems to be taking it all in her stride. She must have seen it all: independence, Suez, the Six Day and Yom Kippur wars. All the old wars, the real wars, where leaders heckled and international borders were crossed and people killed other people in uniforms. Where everybody signed up for the same game.

The couple's husband: 'Lia, don't panic.'

'I'm not.'

'Maybe we should take Ben to the public shelter.'

'Where's that?'

The boy is clawing at her clothes, pulling her top down to expose the roundness of a breast. The bra is all red lace in bows, frayed at the edges and turning black. He seems confused: excited by the tumult but concerned by his mother's anguish.

'*Ima*. Down!' he cries.

'I think there's one under Magen David Square,' her husband is saying. 'And another somewhere on Tchernikovski Street.'

His face is all haggard. There is no connection between you and him. Never was. A reluctant nod, maybe a word, then on and away, retreat behind closed doors. Daily, weekly, ever since the lease was signed, and the foul-smelling man with the huge belly and the greasy hair handed over the keys. 'A nice bachelor pad,' he said.

The baby was tiny then, wrapped up warm and still and silent in wool and fleece. Content and protected. How must they feel now, when his safety is not in their hands? The child wriggles and squirms until his mother places him on the stairs. For an instant he beams, but his footing is uncertain and he tumbles down two three four steps, lands in a heap as the siren blares.

'Ben!' Both she and her husband rush to the child. She is crying hysterically. 'Why didn't you fix the door to the *mamad* like you said you would? Then we wouldn't have to leave the apartment.'

'I said that before we knew we were leaving. Why should we spend time and money just to benefit the next people to rent the place? God forbid the landlord will have to pay for something out of his own pocket.'

He pauses, breathes deep, scratches too hard at his dark stubble with a violence at odds with his still voice: 'And how could I have known there'd be a war?'

'There's always a war!'

She's crying; the baby's crying; the siren's crying, and all the noises are battering each other and ricocheting around the stairwell.

'Sis, stop it. It's OK.'

It's the girl from before; the one who didn't hear the harbinger. She places a hand on her sister's arm but it is pushed off as she steps away.

'Leave me alone.'

All at once quiet descends, the siren fading like a voice dropping from a cliff. Sniffing the air, Mrs Stein nods to each person in turn, and then pulls herself up the stairs towards her flat. Yonatan and Lia slope off towards their doorway, suitably apart. Ben is back in her arms.

'Sorry,' says a voice as the key turns in the lock. It is close, right there, breathed over a shoulder to stroke the hairs of the neck. 'Do you mind if I come in?'

'Where to?'

'To your place. I just can't deal with them any more.'

Shoulders brush. She smells like soap and oranges and lavender and teal; clean and fresh as she pushes in through the open doorway.

'I don't think it's a good idea.' It doesn't matter, she's already past.

There are footsteps: she's following the natural flow of all apartments, sucked into the centre, but there the footsteps stall, replaced by quiet that lasts for an eternity. Of course she's seen it. Yours is the archetypal no-hoper Tel-Aviv apartment: two rooms and a narrow, mouldy bath. Everywhere she looks will be rope.

But there's no scream, there's no violent shove to clear the path to the exit and run towards Allenby and the nearest police officer to hospitalise the crazy for his own good.

She calls from out of sight: 'Are you coming?'

Her legs are crossed on the sofa, her arms are outstretched, her nose not more than a few hand-spans from the noose that swings leisurely from the ceiling in some invisible draught. Intermittently, the rope blocks the light and then her face emerges once more. She is beautiful. Small, dainty, delicate, elegant in the shifting glow.

A finger unfurls, follows the noose through its arc.

'Are you going to use that?' she says. Your nose moves a fraction, left then right. 'Good.' Then, after a while, 'You should probably take it down.'

A slow, embarrassed nod. She watches studiously as the

rope is untied, pulled down from the loop and wound into a corner. It will not be deconstructed, and the lightshade can remain on the floor.

Sit down.

'Can I get something to drink?'

'Is water OK?'

She looks disappointed. 'Anything a bit more effective?'

'Sorry, that's all I've got.'

Her face rises, her eyes narrow, about to burn a caustic wound. Don't look away.

'You don't drink?'

'No.'

'Well maybe you should. It's less final.'

'Not really. It just takes longer.'

She shrugs, blinks first. Her weight shifts and she rocks in her spot, shoves her fingers into the pocket of her jeans. They are so tight that she wears them like a blue skin, and the finger is like an animal burrowing away beneath.

She teases out a long thin white tube, crumpled and bent but still intact.

'Do you mind?' The tip fizzles and cracks as she inhales. 'You don't smoke either?'

Not any more.

'Cos it'll kill you?'

Cos the fun has gone.

'Do you know my sister Lia then?'

'The one with the baby?'

A little laugh, a little cough. 'I'll take that as a no.'

'Do you know your neighbours?'

She nods, then thinks a little harder.

'I know their names. Some of them. Anyway, it doesn't matter. My family won't be your neighbours for much longer.' She inhales again and the smoke oozes from her cracked lips, framing her nose, her eyes and the little lines of her forehead. 'They're moving out.'

'Where are they moving to?'

'They're not going anywhere. Not together, anyway. Yonatan told her that he needs to find himself. To be alone. And now he's started talking about some dead-end job in the US.'

'And Lia?'

'She's moving back home.' She draws little quotation marks in the air around the word home. 'With Mum and Dad. Never moving forward. Guess that's our generation, isn't it?'

Her presence is unnerving. Her body, so close on the sofa. The proximity of another human being, a beautiful woman, so unfamiliar that it's setting off a chain of unwelcome reactions. Sweat pricks the brow, heart beats so loud it's deafening to a light head; hands that feel every touch so clearly, that knead the rough dusty blue material beneath clammy palms.

'Why doesn't she move somewhere else?'

Dry throat too.

'Are you kidding? Where have you been living this past decade?'

Nowhere. In the tank. You never left.

'Why did they split?'

A sigh. 'He did something. Bad.'

'And she can't forgive him?'

'No. She was good. Too good. The perfect, understanding, supportive wife. He's just been spiralling. Can't forgive himself.'

Does she glance at you?

'Do they still love each other?'

'Who knows. What does that even mean?' She sighs. 'Love is all bullshit.'

She's acting so cynical, but there's no conviction to her words.

'You can't really believe that.'

Who just spoke? It was your voice, but whose words?

She snorts. A torrent of smoke cascades from her nostrils.

'I didn't exactly take you for a romantic.'

'I'm not. Not really, but...' What comes next? 'But without love, what's the point?'

She points up towards the naked bulb and the metal hook.

'That's not fair. And how do you know I wasn't doing it for love?'

'Like Romeo and Juliet?'

'Exactly.'

'Were you?'

'Well... no. I... just...' Grasping, faltering. 'It's important to believe that there's the possibility. That at some point, at some time, we won't be in this all alone.'

Her hand hovers in the air, the joint perfectly aligned with her lips. They don't touch. But there comes no derisory laugh, no aggression. She touches the spliff to her lips, breathes deeply and leans back in the sofa, uncrossing her legs. She closes her eyes.

'My brother was loved. He loved too, I think.'

'See?'

'It's not enough.'

'Maybe not, but it's a start.'

'He killed himself.' She opens her eyes, glances towards the rope. 'At least I think he did. I'm not sure. Can't be sure.'

'What makes you think that?'

She bats something away through the smoke.

'It doesn't matter. The facts are the facts and there's no way to know. I can interpret them one way and it doesn't mean I'm right. He crashed his car and died. End of.' A muffled shout from upstairs. Her eyes roll upwards towards the ceiling, her head tilts back. 'They're just fucking assholes.'

Her ponytail cascades backwards over the velour of the sofa.

'You know,' she says, 'I don't even know your name.'

'Nadav.'

Nobody's asked for it in a long time, and it sounds wrong.

She offers a manicured hand: 'I'm Sharon.'

Fingers touch and linger. She doesn't immediately disentangle, and with each flowing instant a pulse emanates from the stillness of her palm.

That now familiar sound is returned, the urgently bored rise and fall. It's so loud that it fills the space between you and her, pushes out all the air.

'Another siren,' you are about to say, as panic begins to rise, but Sharon is still holding your hand and instead of standing, of running into the stairwell, she grasps you to her, envelops you in her embrace. All you can see and smell is her, and the wailing is somewhere distant. Her hands close upon your head, soft but firm, pull it down so that it rests upon her chest, and now there is a hissing loud and overhead, and as an explosion shakes the walls and the siren still howls you realise...

It feels... safe.

The conversation begins stilted, but flows easier as Yonatan and Lia make the short walk from the Stephan Braun to Neve Tzedek, spurred on by the relief each feels.

At the Nana Bar, they outline themselves, their lives, smooth the pointed edges from the truth. The whisky flows. With the inebriation, so rises the quick and sincere intimacy between strangers.

Lia enjoys the weight and warmth of Yonatan's arm on her shoulder as they walk through the city's streets, still full of revellers despite the latest round of violence in Gaza. They climb the five flights of stairs to his apartment where everything is neat and organised; prepared for someone else.

'I should go,' Lia says. Yonatan turns on the lights. 'It's getting late.'

'Stay,' he says.

He retrieves a half-drunk bottle of scotch from beneath the sink, pulls down two glasses from over his head. Lia acquiesces. When the bottle is spent he displays it with the other empties above the fridge.

They kiss awkwardly but passionately. The sex is clumsy. Neither climaxes, and finally they both collapse in drunken exhaustion. Yonatan kisses Lia's neck, strokes her body with his fingertips. They pause at the wounds and scars on her thigh.

'The cat,' she says.

'Tell him to stop,' he says.

'He's a she,' she says with a smile.

When he wakes, Yonatan finds Lia dressed and collecting her things.

'You leaving?' he says. She shifts self-consciously, covers her still-bare breasts with her shirt. 'Don't go.' She cannot meet his gaze. 'Please.'

She stops still. Uncertainty lingers.

Yonatan pulls back the covers and she lays her bag on the chair, begins to peel at her clothes once more. When she clambers back in beside him, he kisses her first on the forehead and then on the lips.

'Thank you,' he whispers into her ear.

Sharon

The phone rings: some 90s high-jinks jingle, jolly and bright. It is in her bag which sits on a chair on the other side of the room. Near enough to walk over and flick the switch to silent or reject the call, far enough to not bother.

She wraps her slender fingers around the protruding ledge of the window and squeezes until her nails feel as if they will pop from her fingertips. They have bled all their colour to white.

She breathes in time to the beat, counts down the bars without a word till the chorus is abruptly decapitated and she is back in the silence of her office. No need to check: she knows who the call was from. It must be the tenth time, at least, that he's called. The first arrived just moments after the technological miracle of the Iron Dome batteries saved the city from the rockets rained from the sky. She held Nadav to her as interceptor missiles exploded imminent death above their heads, felt the beat of his heart through his ribs as it slowed, settled, even as the chaos prevailed.

What would Richard think if she answered one of his calls, and without letting him speak said, 'I fucked a boy and he came inside of me and I finally stopped taking the pill and I might be pregnant and it's not yours.'

She smiles.

The knock arrives once the door is already open.

'Sharon, you have a call scheduled with Dr. Goldstein from Assaf Harofeh Hospital. Should I call David?'

Moran, her secretary, stands blocking the doorway. Pretty. Plump. Hair too straight and thin with garish highlights. Her shoes are like a cripple's – high and narrow and uneven and made of leather that looks like plastic. Once Sharon had thought of taking her under her wing, of showing her how to apply her makeup, how to choose her clothes to hide the rolls of meat that ooze from her shoulder above her bra, her lower back above her neon thong. But then she had noticed the girl's unshakeable joviality, her easy good nature, the diamond dust ring on her finger. She had said nothing.

Sharon nods; Moran nods.

'He'll be in in a few minutes.'

Without realising, Sharon has crossed the office. There, below her, is her bag – her tasteful pastel blue Prada, purchased in Rome. Between the packet of Advil and the emergency tampon that she may not need, the small pouch of weed, the Xanax from the Arab pharmacist in the far-flung inner suburb who asks no questions and requires no prescription, the Dior wallet – special edition from the last Galliano collection – the Louis Vuitton makeup holder hoarding collectables from London, from New York, from Paris, is the little sliver of metal and glass. Her phone.

'Shaz. Baby. This is ridiculous. Pick up the phone. For God's sake.' Richard's voice sounds flustered, breathless, as if he's just run a marathon far up a mountain. 'Look, I know you don't want to talk to me, but I'm worried about you. I mean. Fuck. Rockets. Bus bombs. It's fucking crazy. And it's madness for you to be there. To put yourself in danger like that.'

Yes. The rockets. The bus bomb down below, six days after that first rocket strike against Tel-Aviv. Her office, a courtside seat to carnage. It shook with the force of metal being torn, bodies being mutilated, lives being shattered just beyond the glass. Moran came running in without knocking, and they both stood and peered down. She had started to cry, but not Sharon; she had squinted, looked harder, tried to pick out the once-human from the once-bus in the chaos below.

Richard's voice has paused, as if to let her meander and round off the memory. Now he continues:

'I told you before. That. Anyway. What happened between us. The argument. It was stupid, Shaz. You just didn't understand what I was trying to say. I was angry that you lied, but before that. I don't want you to give up everything. I'm sure you can find something to do, to keep you occupied. It's just. Shit. Just talk to me, OK?' He's chewing his words like a piece of husk. 'I bought you a ticket to London. If you log into your BA Executive Club account you'll see it there. It's booked for Thursday.'

Another pause. Another calculation.

'Look, I know you're busy, so...' He's scared of her. 'First Class, of course.' A rough little laugh. 'You can change it. Or cancel. Or. You know. Whatever you want.'

His voice trails off. Outside the door she can hear David and Moran making small talk.

'I love you. Just come home.' Thousands of miles away in a time not now, Richard sighs and says, 'Fuck it,' and is no longer there.

Sharon presses open palms down her trousers, corrects her blouse, is nearly ready for them when her phone rings again. It's still in her hand and she gazes down, confused to see her own face staring up at her.

'Hello?' she says.

'Hi.' The voice is soft and warm like a fluffy blanket on a cold day. 'Am I interrupting?'

'No, go ahead.'

It's Nadav. She forgot he was there, at her home. Or knew without knowing.

'I just wanted to know what time you'll be back tonight. I wanted to cook you dinner.'

'About eight.'

'OK. See you.'

The phone clicks off and the voices are louder just beyond the door. She prepares herself once more. It's only when she checks her expression that she realises she is smiling.

'Interrupting something?'

David watches her as she places the phone back in her bag, makes her way towards the window and sits down at the desk. *Her* desk. In front of *her* window. Her face is placid and superior. He just has a cubicle, nowhere to feel the sun. His animosity is now an open secret. She waits patiently, quietly, as he does a tour behind her, runs his hand across the empty space where the photograph of her and Richard used to be.

Chatichat-chara. Piece of shit.

No doubt Moran has told him about the breakup. Over the Nespresso machine with the choice of coffees. Caffeine or no caffeine? Did you hear? They split up. I bet he dumped her. It's over. He even took his things. I know, right? I think she's already thirty. So alone. It's so sad.

Moran wouldn't have understood how the revelation would enrage him. She's a simple person – Kiryat Gat in the morning and after nightfall. No education past high school; mediocre *bagruyot*. No ambition. Poor thing.

David runs his open palm across the bookcase, filled with dozens of well-thumbed tomes. She spent hours scouring Goodreads and the required reading of ivy-league MBAs to draw up a definitive list of books to intimidate, to impress. Then she went through each one, dutifully breaking spines and folding random dog-ears as Kohav Nolad played on the television, searching for the next superstar, the next Ninet, a glass of wine by her side.

Back then, David was civil. She was just a woman, no competition.

Is that what she's doing now, fighting back? Or is she just continuing, simply churning the wheels because to stop is death? Like those people just beyond the window, their hopes, if not their lives, wiped out by the heat and the air and the nails and the bombs and the gunpowder and explosives in retaliation for retaliation.

David has seated himself on one of the leather chairs across from her.

'Well?' he says. 'You gonna get them on the phone?'

'Moran's putting us through,' she says, and envisions a bomb blast ripping through the office right then and there, through his fleshy belly first and then her own, popping off their heads like champagne corks.

A crackle and Moran's voice creeps out of the little speaker between man and woman.

'Dr. Goldstein, Sharon and David are on the line.'

David leans forward, opens his mouth wide and takes a breath but she cuts him off, begins to speak in a manner both controlled and restrained. The voice is someone else's.

Lia does not return to her parents in Kiryat Ono. She goes to SuperPharm, buys a toothbrush and some basic hygiene products, makes room for them beside Yonatan's sink. She buys a change of clothes and spare underwear at the latest closing clothing store on Shenkin, supplements them as required. As the days pass, her influence on the apartment becomes more pronounced. Already full and bursting at the seams, it clearly now houses them both.

Yonatan proposes a cull, and they cart the purged items down the stairs, leave the good junk on the pavement and toss the bad junk into the skip that resides in the street outside. Next door, a Bauhaus building is being remodelled and refurbished. Two new floors are growing from the roof. The site is a hive of noisy activity, and Arab contractors in thick wool sweaters sweat dust as they walk.

'Maybe we could buy one of the apartments,' Lia suggests, but they have all already been sold to Jews from France, Britain, Switzerland and America.

As they breakfast at a kiosk on Rothschild, Lia overhears talk of a business development position at a start-up on Lillenblum Street. Soon after she begins work the company folds, but within days she has moved to another nascent venture in an adjacent building. So begins a perpetual cycle of fail-quicks in a scene of repeating faces.

Yonatan accepts a teaching position at a photography school on the third floor of a grim monolithic building in the Shoken industrial estate. At first he resents the imposition on his time, but he is a popular and much admired authority, and he finds that his students begin to inform his own work, providing welcome and unexpected sources of inspiration.

Despite their dual income, however, it quickly becomes clear that they cannot afford to buy a decent home in the city. Even finding a rental proves difficult. Eventually, they hire a van and cart their belongings to an apartment on the wrong side of Allenby. Split between two narrow floors, its windows look out over the cramped streets of Kerem Hateymanim, infused with the electric buzz of the Carmel Market a few blocks away. Smoke billows from rusting steel chimneys; the army of stray cats that prowl the streets seem here even more numerous; homeless addicts reside on the benches of microscopic parks. The aged and worn Yemenite men that gaze down through filthy glass make no bones about their hatred for their suspiciously white new neighbours.

The week after they move, Lia invites Yonatan to meet her family. She sits quietly, her leg jumping beneath the table, as her father launches an interrogation.

'I don't understand you kids,' he says. 'You've just moved to a slum. You should be settling down, in a good place. Somewhere suitable for a family. You're just playing house.'

Yonatan smiles passively. He thinks of his father, wonders lightly if it is a generational disruption that has his words emerging from such a different man's mouth. Perhaps age now binds values and beliefs closer than geography, class, ethnicity, industry.

The chirruping of his phone calls Michael away. All eyes follow him as he cups the receiver tightly and the other hand fumbles to lower the volume. He is out of the room before his father calls after him.

'Tell your girlfriend we want to meet her,' he says and laughs raucously. Yonatan does not understand why.

Sharon's apartment is awash with the smell of something savoury burning. It hits her as soon as she opens the door. She's not curious, just slides open all the narrow, head-height windows along the corridor as she makes her way towards the kitchen. She discards her bag, laying it gently on the heavily patterned chair by the entrance. Without Richard, this will soon be gone. Only a few weeks until the next cheque is due, and she must leave.

Nadav stands with his back towards her as she slides open the door. His torso is bare save for the fasteners of her apron, the thin strip of material that crosses the nape of his neck, ties just above his waist. He is so thin. His ribs protrude from the crevices of his skin and no muscles seem to flex with his movements.

Chopped vegetables emerge from one of her olive-wood bowls in a green and white and red mound. She and Richard bought that in St. Tropez, in a little shop that sold lavender and honey and all the things she thinks of when she thinks of the beautiful French Riviera. Beside it, strewn across a cutting board shaped like a pig, are the cinders of what may once have been a sausage – maybe one of the Bratwursts they wrapped with cool-packs and carried back all the way from Sternen Grill in Zurich.

A frying pan smokes on the hob.

He turns towards her. His face is pale and crestfallen, a child who has just tried and failed. A smudge of something black has made its way from a sausage to his left cheek. It looks like a scar.

'I thought I'd surprise you when you got back.' He kicks open the shiny steel bin, scrapes the world's best sausages inside. 'I just. I don't usually cook.'

That night when the rockets flew overhead, they'd lain together, still and silent long after the sirens had stopped. She had asked him to join her home, wanted to provide him with somewhere safe, if only temporarily. Air from large windows. Clean paint. A *mamad* for any new round of rockets.

No worn pet beds occupied by ghosts. No gallows swinging from the ceiling.

He'd slept with his knees tight against his chest and a pillow crushed between his forearms and his chin, soft padding betwixt bone. She'd fallen asleep to the sound of his laboured breath, and then woke in his arms.

She didn't go to work the next day, dozed as he brought one of her books into bed, her head on his bare chest. He told her of his experiences in Jenin, the terrors and guilt implanted that only grew more monstrous with the passing years. How with his dog Sufi's death, he felt the final link to living severed.

Sharon had listened. Then she'd begun to speak. Of her brother, of the sense of betrayal at the secret he didn't confide. Of Richard. Of her disappointment in Israel, the country's duplicity that, once she had seen it, she could not ignore. She'd told him of her dreams of escape; of how, somehow, Tel-Aviv always dragged her back.

To him, and only to him, she'd admitted that the city felt like home.

He'd gazed up at her, met all her silences with a light stroking of her arm. The kindness of his eyes, the lack of judgement in his tone, the softness of his words, it had edged her always further.

'I've never told anybody any of this,' she'd said.

'Why?'

'Because I'm trying to be somebody I'm not. Do things I don't want to do. Don't care about.'

She'd felt his head move on her stomach, sensed his jaw move as he spoke. 'We all have to live with who we are. That seems to be the most difficult thing.'

She'd kissed him then, because nobody knew her better.

Now, in the kitchen, she plants her lips upon the bald spot between his oily hair at the crown, takes a deep breath. He smells so insubstantial. Somewhere beneath, she smells herself, only discernible now that it is shaken up, mixed with something else.

'There's schnitzel in the freezer,' she whispers. 'Try again.'

She enters the study from the kitchen. As she slides the door closed, she hears the soft sucking of the freezer door opening, a ruffle as his hand rifles through its contents. Ice cream. Vegetables. Meat. Healthy, balanced.

Her computer is already on, the screen bright and open at *Ynet*. The website's innocuousness is suspicious. Perhaps he left it open as an oversight. Or maybe he left a trace so as not to leave a trace.

Or maybe he was just checking the news.

The freezer door closes far far away.

Sharon logs out of the guest account, inputs her username and password. Uppercase, lowercase, uncommon characters. Hebrew too. Everything done secure, done right. The rainbow beach ball whirs into life and then a photo of her and Richard appears against a sapphire sea, the Maldivian sunset a riot of yellows, pinks and purples. Their faces are dark, underexposed against the view, but they were never as important as where they had been. The image unsettles her, but then the browser window smothers it all in white and she waits for the site to load.

There it is in black and white and blue and red: Richard's promise. First Class, Ben Gurion to London Heathrow

Terminal 5. She knows the flight number, could recite the take-off and landing times in her sleep. She closes her eyes, traces the route from Paddington to his duplex apartment in Maida Vale.

It all tugs at her like gravity from a far-away moon.

But. But. But.

She opens a new tab in the browser, types a search into the menu bar and hits the enter key. The microwave pings beyond the divider and she hears its door squeak open, crash shut.

On the screen now: the scene of the bus bomb, that small patch of earth that she's studied a thousand times. The whole night after the explosion, she just sat right here, watching videos, news reports, scouring Facebook, Twitter, Instagram and all the newspapers and agencies for the decimated bus. Yes, she saw the carnage, the aftermath, with her own eyes, but her own experience lost its immediacy and reality under the bombardment of alternative viewpoints. Her single memory has drowned in the collective.

She clicks through more images. The clock on the wall behind her ticks away as she moves quickly and methodically, uses the residual vestiges of her army training to collate, evaluate, discard. She is looking for something specific, but everything she pulls up is too limited, too narrowly attached to a single pair of eyes. So she keeps going, sifting through the sites and pages and pictures and viewpoints until finally a photograph grabs and stills her hand just as it is about to discard and continue, the action habitual already. At its centre stands a man – ultra orthodox as they always are – his black beard bushy over his chin and his white shirt straining over the tyres of fat that sits where his waist should be, stained with sweat. Over his body is a neon orange vest, the type that the Arabs and Sudanese wear as they work the roads, but this one has the word *ZAKA* emblazoned upon it. The same letters grace the plastic bag gripped in his left hand. *Zihuy Korbanot Ason*, Disaster Victim Identification. 'True kindness' they call it, collecting the most insignificant of human remains after a *pigua*, though she's not certain where the kindness lies.

He is bending down, his feet hidden by twisted metal and bits of the post-explosion detritus in lurid colours, stripped of their source. His hand is gloved in the same misty rubber of a surgeon, and it holds something with a delicacy and deference so incongruous to the scene of such vicious annihilation.

Sharon leans forward, squints at the screen. That thing he holds is too small to make out. Too small within the confines of the monitor, within the limitations of the photographer's perspective, within the camera's reduction of reality, within the pixel density and definition, to make out. She begins searching once more, though this time refining with the word *ZAKA*.

Plates clank in the kitchen. A drawer opens, cutlery protests, the drawer closes again. She works faster now – opening pages, scanning images, closing windows, all in a demented frenzy as she feels time, like water from a widening leak, dripping against the nape of her neck.

There he is again, hidden beneath a hashtag search deep within Twitter. She does a cursory investigation of the handle, tracks the account to a middle-age mother and housewife in Ramat Gan: sixty-seven Facebook friends, fifty-six Twitter followers, thirty-five of them bots. The vantage point is closer now. The man may be a smidgen straighter, his head higher, looking further ahead; an instant before or an instant after the last pic.

There, gripped lightly between his forefinger and thumb, is a finger. Or rather, part of it, severed obliquely below the second knuckle. Only the de-saturated stub of a fingertip and nail, a nail still gleaming with the unearthly blue of what may be Dior Vernis or a cheap knockoff from the stoned sixteen-year-olds in Dizengoff Center.

She stares at it, transfixed by the vibrancy of the blue against the bloodless stump of lifeless flesh and bone, the dead pink of a too-often washed cleaning rag. There is a chip in the varnish up by the cuticles. Is that the fault of the explosion or did she – the person who chose this colour, applied this lacquer – swear as the colour flaked off? Did she keep her hand in her pocket, wonder whether others would notice and judge her, think less of her for such a visible flaw?

Sharon's attention falls upon the *ZAKA* bag. It's still mostly empty, but with a silky blackness like a water level stretched out against the bottom. If she squints she can make out the wispy shadow of hair, the heaviness of flesh dragging the bag down, the sharp pressing of a bone threatening a tear through the plastic.

A voice from the kitchen, 'Dinner's ready. Are you coming?'

The boy's head pokes around the partition. She didn't hear it being slid back. The silence of his actions is unnerving, as if he has practised not making ripples in the universe. She clicks upon the trackpad, destroys the window, but there instead is the British Airways page. It's now faded to transparency, the details of her ticket barely visible. Atop it, vivid against the electronic fog, the words:

SESSION TIMED OUT. LOGIN TO RECONNECT?

The kitchen is a mess worthy of preparation for a state dinner, not salad and frozen schnitzel for two. She can barely believe the lonely breaded cutlets on their sorry plates, the salad bowl flanked by her prize-winning Extra Virgin Olive Oil and the flaky English sea salt in its dedicated ceramic dish. So much effort for something so modest.

It all fills her stomach with an explosive, deadly dread. He must pick up on this, for his face falls.

'Is it alright?' he says.

'Yes, of course,' she says, but she is already through the kitchen and into the hall. She searches for the car keys first in her Prada bag and then in her Burberry Kensington trench. 'It's just I forgot. I have to go out. I have to go and do… something. It's really important.'

The slamming door muffles whatever he may reply, if he replies at all.

In November 2010, when they've been a couple for nearly a year, Lia and Yonatan take their first holiday abroad. They book onto the inaugural Tel-Aviv-London EasyJet flight, eager to be part of the low-cost revolution that is dragging Israel free of its geographical isolation. It is Yonatan's first time in Britain, and the short days and close greyness that hovers over London evoke in him a deep malaise. They check into a dour hotel by Victoria station. Only the narrow reception hall is in any reasonable state of repair.

Although Sharon is in Tel-Aviv, Richard extends an invitation to join him at a famous Japanese restaurant in Mayfair. The vestiges of the building's former life as a strip club are still readily displayed. Overdressed for a Tel-Aviv wedding, Yonatan and Lia are bedraggled by the standards of London's moneyed postcodes.

Richard has brought Natascha, his PA. Blonde and of immaculate complexion, the sexual charge between them is palpable. Richard's ceaseless monologue, the list of his own achievements in life, sounds vaguely sinister to their ears. Yonatan quietly eats his toro tartare, plans the rest of their trip in his head.

The next day they visit the British Museum, share pride that Israel and the Jews threw off the monarchy and the

Commonwealth, struck out on their own. As they leave, Yonatan guides Lia into the network of small streets behind Oxford Street to a cluster of photographic stores. He browses the cabinets excitedly, pulls a tatty old camera down from a shelf. It is small and delicate and worn, its black paint pitted and rubbed around the edges so that the dials, the film lever, the top plate, all reveal the warm gold of brass beneath.

'It's a Leica,' he says. 'I'm going to buy it.'

A tag dangles from the strap lugs. The row of numbers makes Lia wince.

'You can't,' she says. The words surprise her. She wished to make him think twice, to pause, to consider, but instead her tone is insistent, domineering.

Yonatan's whole body stiffens. He replaces the camera on the shelf.

'This is not your decision,' he spits.

'I'm sorry, I didn't mean it like that,' Lia says. She grabs his hand but feels him slip from her. 'Please,' she calls as he leaves her alone in the shop. The salesman eyes her suspiciously.

She gets lost on her way back to the hotel, wanders through Hyde Park as far as Bayswater before finding a local and doubling back. As she retraces her steps, she worries that he will have packed his things, abandoned her in this unfamiliar city. Her breath catches as she pushes open the door of their room; when she sees Yonatan sitting on the bed, she begins to cry and collapses to her knees in relief.

He wraps her in his arms, parts her hair with his fingers.

'What happened to you?' he says. 'I went back to the shop after five minutes and you'd gone. I couldn't find you anywhere.'

'I thought you'd left me,' she says. She shudders.

'Quiet,' Yonatan whispers. 'It's OK. It was stupid. I reacted like an idiot.'

'I never wanted to stop you buying it. It's just... I got a shock when I saw the price, converted the pounds into *shkalim*. It was like two months' rent.'

'That was without a lens,' he says and she laughs lightly

through her heavy breaths.

'You can buy it if you want,' she says.

'I know.'

It is the first time they've fought, the first time they've been apart in anger. As he walked back to the hotel, waited for Lia in their dank room with its insistent scent of cabbage, Yonatan had wanted to search for her, but what if she'd come back and he'd been gone? So instead he'd just sat there.

They make love in the narrow shaft of jaundiced light that falls through the window from an opposing room. As Yonatan rolls onto his back, he reaches over for the pack of duty-free Marlboro Lights on the bedside table.

'You should stop,' she says.

'I know,' he replies. 'I will.'

The photograph of the severed finger haunts Sharon the forty familiar minutes through Tel-Aviv, the Ayalon Highway, the southern suburbs. The heaters beneath the supple black leather of her new car's seats warm her in the damp chill. She follows the route like a pre-programmed robot. The four-ringed steering wheel rocks and writhes in her hands. The world passes by as if through a screen, one dimension removed. All she can concentrate on is the man and the finger. That bright blue rebuke.

She gazes down at her own manicured hand. 'It wasn't your nail,' she says out loud and finds herself alone in her car, driving far too fast.

She slows down. The car slurs into a lower gear and the cabin fills with an obnoxious boom. Richard always said that faster cars had engines that licked your ears as you drove, kissed your neck and played with your hair. But this Audi's engine is just noisy and abrasive, an unpleasant cacophony with two settings – quiet or loud.

She had felt the need to do *something*, after Richard's departure and Mickey's death. She'd tried to get a mortgage, to buy their apartment – her apartment – but after the third refusal she set her sights on something smaller, more attainable. A new car to overcome the loss.

She picked it up and drove it slowly past the office entrance, made sure that David could admire its sleek black paint and massive wheels. Audi. S3. German. They killed the Jews but they sure can make a car. The *S* is the important bit, what makes it special. Leather. Something called a *double-clutch*. More than a car, it's an aspiration, a dream.

So why does it make her miss her old Mazda?

She ducks down as she rings the doorbell, pokes open the letter box and peers through. It's a routine she has followed since she was a child, since the bending wasn't required. The latch snaps shut just as footsteps, muffled by the slippers of encroaching old age, are audible from within.

'*Ahuva*. My love,' says her mother as the door swings open. Then: 'Ah-ah,' motioning down to her shoes and the neat pile on a mat beside the door. She waits patiently for Sharon to slip off her sandals and then outstretches her arms, embraces her daughter. She smells of mothballs and Chanel and Sharon feels herself pulling away even as she is rooted to the spot. The withdrawal is a reflex action.

'Fine,' says her mother, pushing her slightly away. 'Don't hug your mother.' She looks gaunt, tired. Mickey's loss has aged her terribly in such a short time. 'Your sister's upstairs. But please say hello to your father or he'll get upset.'

She does as she's told; ducks her head into the kitchen to see his wiry frame, shirtless with sagging, hairy breasts. He is listening to someone shouting on the radio. There's no mention of the bomb at the heart of Tel-Aviv, below her window. Maybe because nobody died there – were only wounded and maimed – it served as an equitable conclusion: just enough pain on the mutual balance sheets for both sides to call time on the war. For now.

'Hi,' she says.

He smiles without happiness.

'Your sister's upstairs,' he says.

Lia's door is open. She sits amongst the tower of brown boxes that haven't moved, haven't emptied, since they dumped them there together nearly two weeks ago. They soar above Lia's head, cover every wall, jut out into the middle of the room like a spit of land into the sea. Lia has a box tucked between her legs and is sorting without sorting – pulling out an object and studying it before returning it to its original place and moving on. Sharon just watches, unnoticed in the doorway. Only when Ben comes bounding unsteadily towards her does Lia look up.

'Auntie Sharon!' he cries, latching himself to her leg and spraying her knee with thick globules of spit. She strokes his soft blonde hair, has to bend her knees slightly, curl her body down. He is nearly two. He hugs her tighter.

'It's amazing how much shit you can accumulate,' says Lia. It doesn't sound as if she is talking to Sharon. She sighs, throws half a dish, unevenly smashed, onto the bed.

'Where does he sleep?' says Sharon, curving a finger down towards Ben.

'Your room. Hope you don't mind.'

She doesn't.

'Mum wants him to sleep in Michael's room,' Lia continues.

'Well that's creepy.'

'I think she just wants us to clear it out for her. She hasn't been in there since he died.'

'How's she doing?'

From Lia's look, Sharon knows not to push.

Ben has found a partially inflated beach ball and is hugging it to his chest. Sharon sits down, pulls her feet in towards her and crosses her legs.

'How are you dealing with it?' she says.

'With what?' Lia says. 'Michael's death? Or being separated, with a kid, and living in the same bedroom I grew up in?'

'Yeah, that.'

Her eyes glint. 'Pretty well I'd say.'

Lia's hair is scraggly and unwashed. Her skin is oily with a series of pussy spots around her nostrils. Her eyes are large and red.

She jumps up, yells 'Ben', as he stretches himself across the bed and picks up the shard of plate. He pauses for an instant before grunting and hurling it across the room. It crashes to the floor, splinters into more pieces. 'Ben, for fuck's sake. Stop it. Just leave it, will you? Just behave.' And then, to Sharon, 'Don't you dare say anything about me swearing.'

Lia's up on her feet, towering over them both and pulling Ben skyward. 'Why can't you just sit still? Just be calm, for a few minutes, OK?'

He starts to wail – an ear-splitting shriek that drills itself deep into Sharon's head and presses up against her eyeballs. His legs are kicking furiously and he looks as if he is struggling for his life.

Lia's yelling even louder now, 'For fuck's sake – Ben! Just stop it. Just calm down. Just fucking STOP!'

Each word seems to draw on some long-depleted inner strength. Tears are forming in her eyes as she wrestles with her son.

Sharon places a hand on Lia's shoulder, feels it rise and fall with every one of Ben's furious kicks.

'Calm down. You're the adult. Remember that. Just put him down.' She turns to Ben: 'Ben, please listen to me,' she says with a smile so broad that cracks the corners of her lips. 'Why don't we go and see what *Safta*'s doing?'

The kicks cease and he gazes at her from where he half lies, half crouches, head against the floor. Lia's hands still grip his shoulders, and his muscles are tense, prepared, uncertain whether the offer is a trick. Sharon takes his hand, helps him to his feet and down the stairs, watches him rush into the kitchen.

On her return, Lia's head is clutched tight in her hands. Her fingers muffle her sobs.

'I just can't do this,' she says. 'I'm even taking it out on Ben. I hardly make enough at work to pay for his *metapelet*, some stranger I don't even know, and when I come home I shout at him.'

'Hey,' Sharon says. Her hand hovers over the hulking mess, unsure of what to do. 'It's OK. Really.'

Lia lifts her head and sniffles back the tears.

'How did I get... back here?'

'Did you talk to Yonatan?'

She nods, sniffs, rubs her nose. Snot is shiny on the skin of her hands.

'I tried. Of course I did. But we'd start and then...' She reaches across the room, grabs a tissue, dabs her eyes. 'He just keeps coming back to that night. To that girl, that Milli from the protest. Says that he could have helped but didn't, and then it's all over. My husband's gone. All that's left is this empty man I don't recognise. This stranger, so consumed by self-loathing, that can't see he is loved.'

Sobs.

'And now he wants to go to America, to start again. Like that'll save him. The promised land.' She breathes deep, squeezes her eyes closed. 'He tells us to come too. And when I say no, he loses it, says I'm blackmailing him with our son. It's like he doesn't get it. Doesn't he realise it was him who left me?' Sharon places a hand on Lia's leg. 'I'm fine,' she says. Her voice cracks. 'Really, fine. Just leave it. Just – let's talk about you, OK? I don't want to – just you now, OK? How are you?'

She's smiling a smile that holds an infinite heaviness. What to say? How to start?

'I signed a big deal with a hospital today. Largest order of the year so far. Should help my bonus,' she says, and the inconsequentiality of it burns her tongue. 'And I bought a new pair of shoes. Louboutins. From that store on *Kikar Hamedina* owned by Nicole from *Meusharot.*'

'And how's your car?'

Lia's voice quivers between words.

'Oh, it's great,' Sharon says. 'Such an improvement. It's so true what they say about Audis. There's nothing like them.'

Lia is crying before Sharon finishes her sentence, and her final words peter out. Lia's breathing is heavy and irregular. Her face is a bright raspberry red.

'Lovely,' she gasps. 'Lovely. It's all so lovely. It must just be so lovely to be you.'

'What's that supposed to mean?'

Lia gulps great breaths.

'I ask you how you are and you tell me about shoes? Who do you think I am, Sharon? One of your business associates with their platinum cards and frequent flyer miles?'

Her spit rains down over Sharon.

'You got dumped. Your brother died. Fucking died Sharon. Like, laid out on a cold slab. Your life's fucked too but all you can talk about is your things and your job.'

Sharon tries to interrupt. 'I,' she begins, but the torrent beats away.

'Are you really that shallow? Have you ever felt anything? Ever?'

Snot creeps down from Lia's left nostril. Her lips are pulled back and her teeth and gums flash in the light.

'You're just trying to hurt me,' says Sharon quietly. Her arms have crossed themselves. She will not look her sister in the eye.

'Damn right I am.'

The sound of silence is so abrupt that it fills the room. Lia is panting with exhaustion, but her body is still on edge, braced for another round. Somewhere downstairs something brittle is broken, and a child gives off a laugh that may be a cry. The quiet burrows into Sharon and amplifies the beating of her heart. She rubs her fingers together.

'You don't really see me that way,' she says. 'Do you?' Are they at war? Is that it?

'What do you want to know?' Sharon says after a long pause. She must force the words through.

'How are you?' says Lia slowly. Her features are scrunched up, guarded.

'Not great,' Sharon says.

Lia shifts her weight. She is settling in. She rocks her head, cricks her neck, but her eyes never move from her sister for an instant. She is no longer crying.

'I've been sleeping with this new guy,' Sharon says, looking at the ground. She thinks of the boy, of the dinner left untouched upon the table. So alone, so vulnerable. 'Nadav.'

'Do I know him?'

'You might. He lives in your building.' She takes a breath, pauses, waits. 'You know. Your old building.'

Lia rolls her eyes upwards and Sharon can count through the process of elimination until:

'That guy from downstairs?' She doesn't wait for confirmation. 'The one who looks like he just got out of Auschwitz? With the dog?'

'The dog's dead.'

'How?'

Sharon says she doesn't know.

'Not the dog. I don't give a fuck about the dog. You. How did you meet him?'

'When I was helping you pack your things. At the beginning of the war. That day with the first rockets.'

And the day after. And the day after that.

And today.

'He's not OK, Sharon. Really. I don't…' A pause. 'Is he OK?'

'Of course he is,' Sharon says, but she is thinking of the noose and the pills and the razor blades though he never shaves. Sometimes he cries in his sleep.

'Is it serious?'

'I don't know.'

'Do you like him?'

Yes. 'I think so.' So much. His kindness, his crushing sensitivity, his sense of right.

'I don't even know what that means,' says Lia.

'Does it matter?' Sharon finds her hand raised to her mouth. A long slender finger is pushed up against her face and she is nibbling at the nail, gripping the wounded flesh, prying it free. The Chanel nail varnish is cracked, clear calcium keratin visible beneath. She wants to change the subject.

'I got a phone call from Richard,' she says. She tells Lia about the ticket, about the choice to go or to stay. 'First I've heard from him since we split.'

'Didn't he call you when Michael died?'

'Sort of, I guess. But it was one of those obligation phone calls. It was pretty obvious he didn't want to talk to me. Doing a mitzvah or however they sell it at his synagogue.'

'And? Are you going to go?'

Sharon spits a piece of nail, a piece of flesh, onto the worn-out carpet.

'What did you think of him?'

'Richard? You know what I thought of him.'

'No, actually I don't. I know what Yonatan thought of him.' Lia shivers at the sound of her husband's name. 'Did I tell you why we split up?'

Lia shakes her head.

'You never tell me anything.'

'It was about a week before Mickey died. We were organising the wedding – finally setting a date, deciding on a place. And we started talking about kids. You know he always wanted kids, well a while ago we agreed to stop, you know... stopping it. Only when I say we, I mean him. I never said no, but I never said yes.' Sharon has never said this out loud. Her voice is halting. Her eyes are closed.

'I don't know if I didn't want kids, don't want kids, or whether I just didn't want them with him. But he just kept forcing the issue, and I couldn't talk to him. We couldn't discuss it. I certainly couldn't say no. So I kept taking the pill.'

Lia's eyes are narrowed. Sharon does not look at her.

'And he found out?'

'I told him.'

They'd been having dinner. Sustainable local fish from the Jaffa fishmonger, poached organic vegetables from the moshav near Rishon. He'd talked; she'd been miles away. Then he was talking about their children, about all the time she'd have after they were born, became a mother, gave up her job, changed her life. So she told him. And then he left. And she was relieved.

Lia stares at her. She pinches the fleshy part of her thigh.

'It's not me, is it? Is that why you don't want kids?'

'God no!' Sharon almost yells. 'This had nothing to do with you.'

'Because I wouldn't blame you. I'm a mess.' She sniffs.

'Look at us,' says Sharon. 'Come here.' She hugs her sister. 'It'll be OK.'

'D'you think so?'

It doesn't matter whether she does or doesn't.

Lia wipes a smear of snot onto the forearm of her shirt.

The rhythmic creaking of a child's footsteps, unsteady up a stair, fills the space between them. Concern drives Lia to her feet and out of the room. She returns with Ben. In his hand is a large teddy bear, its ears and nose frayed with time and a thousand hugs.

'Ben,' says Lia, 'who gave you that?'

'*Safta*,' he says, and he yanks the bear away as his mother tries to pry it from his fingers.

'Baby, please give that here. That was our uncle Michael's. I don't want it damaged. Please.'

The last word's pained sincerity is lost on the child. Lia gives up, watches him carry the bear into the corner, roll it under the bed.

'I don't feel comfortable with him touching Michael's things.' She laughs. 'Who am I kidding? I don't feel comfortable touching Michael's things. I don't feel comfortable with his stuff at all, no matter who's touching it.' She rubs her eyes. 'I called Dani you know.'

'The Arab kid? Why?'

'Why do you have such a problem with him?'

'I don't. It's just – maybe if he was someone different...'

Maybe Michael would still be alive.

'We're not having this conversation, OK?' says Lia with a sigh. 'He loved our brother – probably more and better than either of us – and he's the closest thing left to him. I told him he could come and take whatever he wants from Michael's room, as long as he throws out everything else. I don't want to do it, and it's obvious that Mum and Dad can't.'

'And how do you expect to pull that one off? "Hi Mum, hi Dad, there's a little Arab urchin downstairs and he wants to trawl through all your dead son's things. Oh, and did I mention, they were doing it. You know, like you see on TV."'

'Stop it.'

'Why?'

'Just stop it.'

Sharon drums her fingers against the floor. It is Lia's turn to stare at the carpet.

'They're going to Rome next week,' she says. 'He's coming then.' She pauses. 'I can't help thinking. What do you think they'd do?'

'Do if what?'

'If we told them the truth. Do you think they'd love him less?'

A long quiet.

'Probably not.'

Inspired by their trip to London, Yonatan begins a new project soon after their return. He travels the city with a borrowed field camera, documents the ghosts of the British Mandate that dot Tel-Aviv: the post boxes, the abandoned customs house on the old railway line, the cluster of administrators' houses behind Carmel Market with their decorative battlements and truncated towers. Soon he is criss-crossing the country to crumbling outposts down untended roads. He turns the *mamad* into a darkroom, pipes in water from the bathroom through a hose. He hangs the developed photos from a wire strung across the room to dry.

'They're haunting,' Lia says as she helps him select the strongest images for the upcoming show.

On the day of the opening, Lia is collecting the last of the prints from a framer in Noga when she is interrupted by the insistent bleating of her phone.

'Can you come to Mum and Dad's house tonight?' says Michael.

'I have the opening,' she says. 'You know that.'

'Please.'

There is a desperation to his insistence that makes Lia nervous. 'I have something I need to tell you all. Sharon's already said yes.'

Lia runs it past Yonatan. His disappointment is clear though he urges her to go.

'It must be something important,' he says. 'I'll meet you at home afterwards.'

He kisses her softly on the forehead.

Sharon collects her from the Kiryat Ono bus stop in her Mazda.

'What's this all about?' she says.

'No idea.'

Michael is sitting on the stairs waiting for them as they enter the house. Their parents are already in the living room.

'What do you want?' Their father's tone is crisp, somewhere between concern and irritation. There is clearly somewhere he would rather be.

'Thank you all for coming,' says Michael. 'I know this is unexpected, but...' He takes a deep breath. 'There's something I wanted to tell you.' Lia notices that his hands are shaking.

'*Nu?*' their father says. 'Come on. We haven't got all day.'

Sweat breaks across Michael's face.

'I'm—' he stammers. 'I – I just...'

'Spit it out!' There is joviality there, but their father is already up, heading for the door.

Michael's forehead creases. Sweat bubbles on his brow.

'I just wanted... to... tell you that...'

'Come back,' their mother calls after their father.

'I just wanted...' Michael's gaze flits among his family. His eyes are wide in abject terror. 'To tell you...' His voice cracks. 'That. I've decided to try... for Sayeret Matkal.'

He smiles weakly.

'Oh that's wonderful,' says their mother. She beams as she stands, takes his hands and presses them together, pulls them towards her chest.

Their father is returned. He grins as he zips his light jacket.

'Special Forces, huh?' He pulls Michael to him in a bear hug, squeezes him tight. His son's face is a ghostly white. 'You'll do great,' he says. 'And make your country and your family proud.'

Lia ignores the contemptuous look he shoots her over Michael's shoulder.

'That's great,' says Lia. She does not let her irritation show. 'I just don't know why you couldn't tell me on the phone.'

'What do you think that was about?' Sharon says on the way back to Tel-Aviv.

'Who knows.'

At home, Lia washes, douses herself in perfume, plucks and moisturises and applies mascara and makeup, does her hair. She drapes herself in lace and silk and hops and twists in front of the mirror before stripping off once more. She fills a hip flask with arak, downs one swig and then another before slipping it into a pocket as she closes the front door to their apartment and takes a seat upon the step in the dark.

Her body is naked beneath the long coat.

When Yonatan arrives, she places his hand upon her breast and his fingers between her legs. She leads him in silence through the empty market down to the beach, climbs atop him and guides him inside her. They groan and grind in unison until he grunts and shivers to a stop.

'I love you,' he says and caresses her face as they lie together, close.

'I love you too,' she says.

Life seems so perfect in each other's arms, and the waves lap against the sand.

Thirty-eight weeks and three days later, Ben will be born.

The front door squeaks on its hinges. In the kitchen, the dinner remains untouched. Cold, no less ridiculous. Sharon wonders where the boy is, whether he's left. Whether he's dead.

She finds him sitting at the computer. His eyes peer out at her from above the screen and he clicks a few times on the trackpad, hiding, or housekeeping.

'You didn't eat,' she says, towering over him.

'I wasn't hungry.'

She expects a challenge, a note of abrasion in his voice, but it's so open and unprotected that something in her slackens. She crosses behind him, places an open palm atop his head. It feels warm and slightly damp, as if he has recently taken a shower; recently enough that the traces remain. He tilts his head back and looks at her. She slides her hand off, and her fingers stroke the wiry bristles on the side of his face, on its way down to his shoulder.

'Are you hungry now?' she says.

'Are you?'

She feels his bones, so close beneath the cloth.

'Starving. Let me just take a shower and I'll join you, OK?'

He nods.

In the bathroom she locks the door, pauses, checks it again, and then once more. He has left the toilet seat up so she lowers it, sits down and reaches across the bath to turn on the shower. She's not fast enough to remove her hand and a sheet of scalding-hot spray dapples her skin.

'Shit,' she whispers, shaking the droplets off onto her leggings. And then again, lower, 'Shit.'

She holds her breath, listens, waits till satisfied by the silence beyond the door. She draws her Prada bag towards her, rifles around inside and pulls out the white and blue *SuperPharm* bag. The three identical boxes tumble onto the shower mat with a muffled thud, and she picks one up, rolls it around in her fingers to read the Hebrew and then the English.

'You don't really need three,' the Arab woman said as she put them through the till. 'It's just a myth.'

It's been less than ten days since they first had sex. They won't work anyway. Not yet.

But maybe it'll give some indication. Some pattern. Best of three.

The white plastic cylinder – friendly, clinical, mundane – slides from the box and sits in the palm of her hand.

There is no need for this.

She's pregnant. She knows it, can sense it already, some changes occurring: the cells doubling and doubling and doubling again.

Yet she is not unhappy. Richard so desperately wanted children – conditioned their life together upon it – and yet she gets knocked up by a terrified, troubled child no more a father than she is a mother. She could take that free flight to London, fall into Richard's arms, into his bed. He only cared for money, for things. Something as mundane as ovulation calendars never interested him. The biology, the timetable, she could fudge, keep to herself. She'd be able to pass this child off as his own.

Or she could make an appointment at the clinic and be done with it. Surely it is not just to bring a new life into this world.

She runs the test through her fingers: so light.

Rising from the seat she pulls the lid upwards with one hand while the other pulls down her leggings, the test gripped between her teeth. She begins to pee but her muscles are too tense and it's only a sporadic, pressured dribble. The sound of droplets slows and then finally stops, but the test remains in her teeth.

Defeated, she collapses back down.

Why the hurry to know? Why the pressure? The baby either is or isn't. This will not change that.

She shoves the open test in with the others, ties the bag and opens the toilet's cistern, dumps it inside. Then she strips and climbs into the shower. The steam rises around her and she lets the water wash away her thoughts.

•

Nadav is waiting for her. His hands are in a v, leaning off the end of the table. She pulls out her chair, surveys his ridiculous handiwork once more, begins to eat the ice-cold meal. He waits for her to place the first forkful in her mouth and then he starts too, picking away at his plate, at the shared salad, like a bird. He is moving more than he is eating.

Not a word is spoken, and although Sharon is prepared for probing questions, has readied a stacked tower of half-truths and lies, nothing comes.

The boy seems entirely consumed by the act of not really eating, and after a while she just watches him work: the slight movement of his hand left to right, the way he delicately dangles his fork and pokes and prods. He has no need for a knife.

The fear and defensiveness, the uncertainty and trepidation, it all dissipates. All that remains is a quiet confidence fortified by the fragile soul across. She knows instinctively that she could tell him anything. He would not judge.

He would understand.

The boy's chair screeches back across the terracotta floor. He removes a bottle from the wine rack, hands it to her to inspect.

'I went to Derech Hayayin,' he says. 'They said it was good.'

The label is suspiciously pretty – all flourishes and flowers and a dubious coat of arms – but she goes through her checklist of place, grape, year. Yes. A good bottle. Not great, but, good. She nods, smiles even, watches him struggle with the bottle opener until there is a sucking pop and the cork breaks free.

'Let it breathe,' she says.

'I think I love you,' he replies.

Her smile sticks. A warm tingling sensation spreads outwards from the base of her skull.

'I have to tell you something,' she says. He hovers over her, holding the bottle. 'I got a message from my ex—'

'Richard.'

'Right. He wants me to come to London. To just pick up where we left off.'

He looks crestfallen.

'Why are you telling me this?'

'Because I wanted you to know.'

'Are you going to go?'

She stares into his eyes, winces as she sees the pain they hold, that she has caused.

'No,' she says.

He stands still for a moment, then returns his attention to the bottle. She spreads her fingers over the top of the glass as he offers to pour.

'You don't want any?' he says.

'Aren't you going to ask why I'm not going?' she says.

'Why?'

'Because I love you.' It is a relief to say something so true. She rises, crosses to him and wraps a hand around his waist. Her chin rests in the crevice between his shoulder and neck. 'I really do.'

She feels him give as she kisses his skin, turns him around and rubs her face against the hair of his cheek. She sucks in the soft humid warmth of his breath.

She takes his hand, leads him through the apartment.

'Is everything alright?' he whispers.

'Yes,' she says, as she pushes open the door to the bedroom. A tear drops from her eye. It is. It really is.

For there is only them, only now.

And now is good.